Deranged VOWS

USA TODAY BESTSELLING AUTHOR
T.L. SMITH
KIA CARRINGTON-RUSSELL

I'd tell him I'm sorry, but I'm really not. Because we both know when he's fucking you, you're thinking of me.

Sincerely,

Your Book Boyfriend

COPYRIGHT @ T.L. SMITH & KIA CARRINGTON-RUSSELL 2024

All Rights Reserved
This book is a work of fiction. Any references to real events, real people, and real places are used fictitiously. Other names, characters, places, and incidents are products of the Author's imagination and any resemblance to persons, living or dead, actual events, organizations or places is entirely coincidental.
All rights are reserved. This book is intended for the purchaser of this book ONLY. No part of this book may be reproduced or transmitted in any form or by any means, graphic, electronic, or mechanical, including photocopying, recording, taping, or by any information storage retrieval system, without the express written permission of the Author. All songs, song titles and lyrics contained in this book are the property of the respective songwriters and copyright holders.

Warning

This book contains sexually explicit scenes and adult language and may be considered offensive to some readers. This book is intended for adults ONLY. Please store your books wisely, where they cannot be accessed by under-aged readers.

Blurb

Lena

Our worlds shouldn't cross. I'm a performer in the spotlight, and he's the monster people in the underworld fear most.

He's someone who doesn't feel, let alone touch another person. The thought revolts him, so much so that he always wears gloves.

So why can't I seem to stay away from him? And why is he able to touch only me?

Aleksandr

I will stop at nothing in my pursuit to free the dancer, but the moment I lay eyes on the singer, Lena, my world changes.

She's a bright ray of sunshine, lighting up the shadows I walk in.

I won't leave her alone. In fact, I force her into a contract to sing only for me.

But it's not her voice I'm after.

CHAPTER 1
Aleksandr

Three months ago...

Her hand slips from my gloved ones as she looks at me. I've been chasing her for what seems like years when, in reality, it's only been six months. My pretty ballerina. My little Russian beauty. I first met her when I was five, then reunited with her just over two years ago. She always smiled. I hated her smile as much as I loved it. But just like me, she had her own demons. And she wasn't willing to chase them away, whereas I became the demon.

The buildup of my feelings for her was gradual. Some would say I loved her, but I think I was fascinated with her. I have only ever truly loved one person, and that's my sister.

So why did I chase her?

Why do I feel the need to protect her? She clearly never asked for it or wanted it.

But chase her I did.

And I would do it again in this life and the next, without a doubt.

"Alek," she whispers my name, and I have a feeling it will be the last time I see her. Just when I finally found her.

Don't ask me how I know. I just do.

"You need to stop. Just stop. Promise me you'll stop," she begs. Cinita has a thing for dangerous men. I should have known better the first time she danced for me.

I didn't.

I was sucked in by her, by all that she was. It's how she got around in life. Her attraction to dangerous men led her to a precarious lifestyle, constantly chasing a high.

"I don't need you to protect me. I don't need protecting from them." The lie falls from her lips so easily.

And that's exactly what it is—a lie.

Cinita dances for all types of men. Being a ballet

dancer has sent her all over the world and introduced her to all the wrong people—by her choice. I tried to pull her out of that scene, to right her path in a way that wouldn't lead to her demise.

"You want me to leave?" I ask, and she nods. Her hands clasp my gloved ones again.

"I don't need you to protect me anymore. You found me, and you did good. Thank you for protecting me. I'm not really sure where I would be without you, but I'm good now. The Bratva don't want you around, and I work for them. This is my life, Alek, and while I wish you were going to be in it, you can't be."

"They'll kill you," I inform her matter-of-factly.

She flicks her pin-straight black hair over her shoulder.

"No, they just wanted to watch me dance." They do, I have no doubt. But it's everything else they offer her that's worse for her. She was in a bed somewhere in Russia with a needle in her arm and on the verge of death.

As I said, she likes to mix with the wrong people.

Why the fuck did I chase her in the first place?

Cinita is a dangerous beauty with her long, raven-colored hair and perfect dancer's body. The way she smiles as if she's doing it for just you. And the way she moves? Fuck, can she move. It's a mesmerizing combination, a carefully woven spell as she comes to life on stage. But she's nothing more than a broken doll.

When I reunited with her two years ago, she was at one of our auctions, accompanying someone else. I remembered her from our orphanage when we were five years old. And as an adult, I was stunned by her beauty. I didn't speak to her. I'm not one for talking. I simply watched her from a distance until she approached me. I flinched when her hand landed on my shoulder because I hate being touched. It makes me feel like I'm drowning in a grotesque pool. I can't breathe, and so many voices come to the surface. *Filth. Disgust. Pain.* It's easier to avoid contact. I also hate doing the touching. I've hated it all my life. But then she touched me again. I didn't move away, and she smiled that big, beautiful smile at me.

I've only ever made a few exceptions as to those who can touch me. A handful of people who I try to fight against the feeling and voices for. She had been one of them.

We stayed in contact. Well, she stayed in contact. Somehow, she'd gotten my number and would send me flirty messages when she was here.

I never replied.

Until a few months later, when she came back to

another one of our auctions. The man who accompanied her had a hold on her arm so tight I could see the bruising. She was smaller than the last time I saw her—and she was already a tiny little thing, all legs and arms, and I guess that's how she moved so effortlessly around the stage.

"She will dance," I'd said.

"What?" Anya, my sister, had asked, confused.

"For payment, she will dance. For her to dance, she charges upward of a hundred thousand. She will dance for your men tonight."

Cinita's silver eyes found mine as if knowing I was speaking about her. And right then and there was the moment I knew I would kill for her.

The look in her eyes was so sad, and I fundamentally understood sad. I thrived in its misery. But fuck. They were empty too. Soulless. Devoid of any other emotion. All her messages over the past few months were cute and bubbly, and it's why I never replied.

And there she stood, being controlled by another man.

"Do you own her?" Anya had asked.

"She is owned by many, slutty ballerina that she is." And Cinita's silver gaze dropped away from mine.

"Fine, take her to the stage." Anya waved off the current performer. I'm sure not even my sister took much note of the ballerina. Of what kind of hold she already had over me.

I stepped toward Cinita and held out my elbow to her. The man she'd come with wouldn't dare argue with me taking her, considering it was my auction and event. With a smile, she threaded her arm through mine and accepted my offer, and a silent agreement passed between us. I would protect her.

I took her to the stage, played the music, and she danced. To say I couldn't take my eyes off her was an understatement.

It was impossible not to watch her.

Later that night, she was gone. Leaving one simple message.

Find me.

And I did. I found her. But as she stands in front of me now, telling me to leave, I wonder why I did.

Was it those silver eyes and that raven-black hair that did me in? Or was it the loss of her touch?

"Don't find me this time. Promise me?" She steps up to me, her hands going to my shoulders. Her lips are inches from mine.

"You asked me to find you," I remind her.

"And I may ask you again, but don't, okay?"

I should be angry. She wasted my time, but I can't be angry with her. I would do it all again.

"Why?" I ask.

She takes another step closer.

"I'll probably end up in the same situation, no denying that." She pauses, and I can feel her breath on my face. "But I need to get myself out of it. Otherwise…"

"You want me to let you die?" I ask incredulously.

She leans forward now, her lips touching mine in a whisper of a kiss.

"I think, if we'd met again under different circumstances…"

"You'd still be the same," I say, and she shrugs.

"You're probably right." She once told me it was the high she was chasing; the dance, the feeling of having all those powerful men watching her, wanting her. And once she was in, she couldn't escape.

She was stuck.

I tried to save her. But she wouldn't allow me to.

"Kiss me, Alek." I don't move a muscle. She's asking for a goodbye kiss, but it's not something I'm willing to give.

"I could kill them all," I tell her. She lifts her hand and rubs it over my shaved head. It's spiky now, longer than usual.

"I have no doubt that you are the most dangerous of them all, Alek." She leans in again and gives me another kiss. She tastes like cherries, and it takes everything in me not to pull her into me and take her.

I won't do that, though. I will not use her as others have used her her entire life.

She drops her hands and steps back.

"Don't find me," she orders softly.

I clench my jaw but say nothing as I turn and walk away.

I'd flown from New York to Russia to find her. I left my sister in a lurch, leaving her to run our business and auctions alone, all for a woman.

Yet I'll return empty-handed.

CHAPTER 2
Lena

Present Day

A man stands before me. I don't know who he is, but he's staring at me. He has gloves on his hands and watches me intently.

"Do you know him?" Julie asks as she sits next to me on the floor. My chocolate-colored hair falls in my face, and I push it back, mimicking her stretches as we cool down. I don't necessarily need to do them, but I enjoy it, and it helps me unwind after a show.

"No, do you?" I ask, not looking away from his intense green-eyed stare.

"It's not me he's staring at," she points out. It

doesn't escape me that she didn't deny or confirm she might know who he is. "He's kind of hot in a he-might-kill-you-and-dismember-you way." She laughs, but I get that exact feeling. "Anyway, I have to go check on the other dancers. Don't get murdered in the time I'm gone."

She stands and does one more quick stretch before she turns and walks off, leaving me sitting on the floor. As I continue my own stretching, I consider the intensity with which he's studying me, and think that's a lot easier said than done.

I just did a set, and Julie was one of my dancers. I'm a singer, and I love it. I went to school for singing, and manage to make a living from it. While I haven't hit it big, I earn more than most within the industry, especially living in New York.

Glancing back up at the guy with the shaved head, I see he hasn't moved an inch. He's still watching me. Intently, I might add.

"Lena, you sang beautifully." I'm grateful for the distraction as the head of the off-Broadway theater, Matthew, approaches me. He stops, and when I look up, all I can see is his large belly hanging over his pants. He adjusts his belt, and as he does, his belly moves. Yes, I'm grateful to see him, but perhaps not from this angle.

"Thank you. I was a little nervous but loved every moment," I say, surprised by his generosity. Tonight was my third night performing on stage in front of an audience. My gaze darts back to where the gloved man stood only a moment ago. He's gone now. How did he even get backstage? Only those who work here or are a part of the show have access. Unless maybe he's an employee and I haven't seen him before?

He definitely didn't look like someone who works here, though. I go to ask, but Matthew cuts me off.

"You did splendid. If you wouldn't mind, I have a few big paying clients here looking forward to meeting you."

"Oh." I look down at my bare feet and then my heels lying in front of me. I wasn't expecting to meet anyone, and I've already changed into basic long, loose pants and a yellow crop top with a smiley face on it. "I may need to change."

He waves me off. "No, you look perfect. They may want to invest more."

I stand at his urging and grab my shoes. Fuck, I knew I shouldn't have worn the smiley crop top today. But I didn't have many other options because I haven't done my washing in over a week.

"Just remember to smile, no matter how tired you are, and give them what they pay for. It's clients like them who pay our bills here." I nod, still not feeling a professional vibe from my crop top, but I do as he says anyway.

We aren't a large theater troupe like those on Broadway, but this place has people from all over the world. Dancers and singers try their hardest to get in here. It took me a good two years of auditioning twice a year after graduating and receiving my bachelor's degree to get in. And I managed to snag a lead role.

I've been here now for six months, rehearsing and working my ass off, but tonight is only my third time on stage. We've gone through so many dancers and singers that I wasn't sure I would get a solo shot at first. But now that I have it, I want to keep it. It's my best-paying job so far. I'll be able to give up the bar job in a few months and start living off what I make here, which has always been the plan.

"This way," he says, and I follow him past the line of dancers heading back out to entertain those still mingling and drinking.

We stop at a private room, where several wealthy-looking people are seated and talking. I feel under-dressed for this, but considering I was literally about two minutes from heading home, I must make the most of the opportunity. *Why the fuck would Matthew let me come here dressed like this?*

"Lena Love," my boss says, introducing me to the roomful of people. Heads turn toward me, and a bunch of flowers are given to me by an older lady. It feels more intense than the night of my debut.

"Your voice was truly magical," the lady gushes, and my cheeks redden at her praise as I step forward to the next person who tells me he hasn't heard a voice like mine for quite some time. It's always flattering to hear these things. But I have years of rejections, of "not yet good enough," "we have someone better," and "you're just not ready yet" to negate all of the compliments I receive. But I suppose it's the highs and lows of being an artist of any kind.

After I speak to a few others, I feel the sensation of someone staring at me again. Glancing to the corner of the room, I see the man from earlier sitting on a sofa, watching me.

I suppose it now makes sense as to why he might've been backstage, but even then, clients such as these aren't usually allowed back there. They're in a room such as this, where they can mingle, and they usually choose to focus more on each other than the cast and performance itself.

How long has he been watching me? Do I even want to know? I place my flowers on the bar and take a bottle of water. Turning and looking around, I find everyone chatting. They all appear to be rich, older people. Except for him. He's younger than the others and keeps himself apart from the group. He's still sitting on the sofa, staring at me, almost expectantly.

Taking a sip of my water, I contemplate why he's here. He has to be a sponsor of some sort, but he's made no move to come near me. And I can't really see him all that clearly without staring at him the way he's staring at me. He certainly doesn't look like the other sponsors. Well-dressed. Yes. Wealthy. Undeniably. But there's an air to him that he's not to be fucked with, and even others in the room avoid him and his stare.

I should take that as a warning, but instead, I find myself walking toward him, leaving the flowers on the bar.

Fuck this. I'm not going to feel intimidated by a stranger in my own workplace.

He doesn't introduce himself. He just remains seated, with his gaze locked on me.

"I'm Lena Love," I tell him. He continues to stare me, and now I can really see what he looks like. His red hair is shaved close to his scalp'. His jawline is sharp, his lips full, and I wonder how his voice sounds when he speaks. His eyes are forest green and pop against his all-black suit. It looks like it probably cost a lot of money. Black boots encase his feet and black gloves cover his hands. He looks like a hitman in a horror film. But people like that don't really come to places like this, do they?

"Alek, always a pleasure to see you here," Matthew says, interrupting. And I'm kind of annoyed that the guy still hasn't introduced himself personally, but I'm relieved that someone is here to break the tension. "Alek here, is our major sponsor. He pays your wages."

I look down at the man, not at all wanting to be entirely polite considering his intensity and the fact that he still hasn't spoken to me, but since I like this job, I offer him the same smile I give everyone.

"Thank you. I hope you enjoyed the show," I say.

"Oh, that's Tanya. I have to speak with her before she leaves for the night. Thank you for your continued support, Alek." Matthew smiles before he walks off, leaving me alone with Alek again.

Every one of my instincts tells me to leave, yet I find myself saying, "Do you mind if I sit?" I wave to the seat next to him, but he doesn't answer or look at it. He just keeps those vivid green eyes locked on me. He's a major sponsor so it's natural he'd be in this room. Which means I need to make a good impression.

I also know that if I sit beside someone quiet like him, I might actually be able to decompress after tonight's performance instead of remaining switched on for all these members, most of whom I'm already associated with.

"Thanks," I say, sitting next to him even though he didn't agree or offer. "I haven't seen you here before. Do you not come often?" I ask him casually as I pick at my nails. His gaze flicks to my hands, watching the movement. I stop immediately, and brush my hands down my pants. This is too awkward, even for me, and all my bravery is quickly swallowed. I have the sense that this man has that effect on quite a lot of people. I stand up. "Well, it was nice chatting with you."

"You should sit." He speaks with a very slight, almost unnoticeable Russian accent.

A shiver breaks over my body. It was not a suggestion; it was a command hidden under a beautiful and rough tone.

So now he wants me to sit beside him even when he was ignoring me.

This guy is either socially awkward or an outright asshole.

I don't do well with being told what to do. My parents and teachers called it having an "attitude."

"I have to mingle," I tell him, now defiant and wanting to leave.

"Sit," he says again. If he were anyone else, someone

who wasn't paying for me to sing, I would have told him to get fucked and walk away. But I notice Matthew briefly glancing in our direction, and I internally sigh in defeat.

So here I am, sitting at his command. His gloved hands rub together as he looks at me. I wait for him to speak, but he just stares at me. *What is this guy's problem?*

"Do you like to keep secrets?" he finally asks in a monotone. It's strange in the way he seems to lack emotion, and that's also a fucking weird question. My nose immediately scrunches up in confusion, and I'm not sure what to say.

He continues. "I'm going to ask you a question, and I expect the truth. I'll know if you're lying."

"Okay..." I manage to say. He sits back, eyes locked on me. The longer I'm with him, the more I feel like I'm potentially sitting with a sociopath.

"Where is Cinita?" he asks. My eyebrows furrow. *Cinita? How would he know anything about her?* "She's your roommate, is she not?" Then he adds, "Remember, I expect the truth."

"How do you know Cinita?" I ask. I haven't actually seen her for months. And she owes me rent.

An exasperated sigh escapes him. "You have no idea where she is either," he says. Damn, how did he do that? Was my facial expression that obvious? "When was the last time you saw her?"

"Months ago," I answer. "Remind me how you two are acquainted again?" I press. He stands as if to leave, but I do the same and face him. "So you're only good at asking questions, not answering them?"

His expression doesn't change as his gaze roams me from head to toe. "I don't have to answer any questions from someone who still dresses like a teenager."

My jaw drops. Did he seriously just say that? "Is it the smiley face that pisses you off? You don't exactly seem like a happy chap."

His jaw tics, almost as if surprised that I bit back.

"If she contacts you, I suggest you call me." He pulls a business card out of his jacket pocket and hands it to me.

I stare at it. Why the fuck would I want anything from this man?

"I suggest you take it if you want your next paycheck," he says.

My jaw drops again. "Are you threatening me?"

With a lack of expression, he says, "You would know if I was. Take the card."

This asshole.

When I reach for it, he makes sure our hands don't touch. As soon as I grasp it, his hand disappears. I look at it in confusion until I see his name and number on the card.

"Is she in trouble?" I ask quietly. I don't like this guy, but if he knows anything about her disappearance, then I want to know as well.

"Yes. A fucking lot, so call me if you want her to live." His words hit me: *if I want her to live*. Shit, is she involved in some dangerous shit? Surely, she couldn't be that stupid. But then again, I think she may be. I don't really know her all that well. She kept a lot hidden. But we both started here around the same time, and both were looking for somewhere to live. It worked out well for maybe a month or so, until she disappeared, and I had to call my parents for money to help me cover the rent. That was *not* fun.

They always thought my singing was a waste of time and that I should have gone to college for something more stable, but I love to sing. I will sing until I can no longer breathe. It's a part of me, and no one can take that away, no matter what.

Rent be short or not.

He doesn't wait for me to respond, moving past me and through the crowd, making sure not to brush anyone as he leaves.

Who the hell is Alek? And how much trouble is Cinita in?

CHAPTER 3
Aleksandr

"Will you stop?" Anya snaps as I take a seat in my office. It's in one of the many mansions we own—each of which has a particular purpose and auction associated with it. Tonight's auction is to sell the guns that her husband, River, provides. The moment she raises her tone, he walks out of the room, knowing better than to get between us when she's in one of her moods.

"Stop what?" I ask, going through the paperwork on my desk.

"You know what. She doesn't want to be found, Alek. She's running for a reason. And you will look at me when we're speaking," she defiantly bites out.

I sigh. I'd much rather handle my paperwork than have this discussion with Anya. Again.

I promised Cinita I wouldn't chase her again, but I can't turn a blind eye to the fact that she's back on my turf either.

"I found her once before, and I can find her again," I point out.

"Yeah, and last time, you fucking left me high and dry to manage all of this, and you ended up coming back empty-handed."

A muscle tics in my jaw because Anya isn't the type to let go of a grudge. Neither am I. We've always been inseparable, and although I know she has my back no matter what, I don't want her getting involved with the Bratva, which is where I know Cinita was last.

"You came out of it with a husband, didn't you?" I ask pointedly, already tired of how long this discussion has lasted. Anya is one of the few who can pull a conversation from me, but I would rather keep it short and simple. And when she's in a rage like this, I let her do all the talking because there's no reasoning with her.

"Don't pretend I benefited in some way from your vanishing act. You still have a lot to make up for, Alek!"

I pointedly look at my paperwork, insinuating that's exactly what I was trying to do before she interrupted me. She and River weren't even supposed to be here tonight.

"Do you even love her?" Anya asks.

I clench my teeth at her question. We're so fucked-up that neither of us really knows what love means. Let's just say I've seen and done a lot of shit. Fuck me, Anya getting married is the biggest abnormality I've witnessed in my life. And I wasn't even there for the ceremony.

"Do you, though?" she pushes. Anya will always be a pusher, especially with me. She's a spitfire and fiercely independent. It's what I admire about her the most. But like any sister, she can get on my last fucking nerve.

Like right now.

"What the fuck is love? I care for her, I know that."

Anya lifts her hand toward my shoulder, but I pull away before she can touch me.

I love my sister. But I won't even let *her* touch me. It's difficult to push through the insufferable sense of drowning and being repulsed by the contact. It's certainly something I've never attempted to explain to her either. I'd simply rather avoid the physical contact.

She let's out an exasperate sigh, clearly frustrated that I pulled away. "We are both so fucked-up, Alek. So fucked-up. But if I can love River and feel like I can breathe with or without him, then you can too."

"I breathe just fine," I point out.

"Do you, though? You sound like you're struggling. You're still asking around about her. Let the fixation go."

I stand and readjust my suit. Cinita is not a fixation. At least I don't think she is. Either way, I'm done with this discussion. "Excuse me while I make the rounds during the auction. You can join me or take over on the paperwork."

"Don't you dare try to distract me from this conversation," Anya hisses behind me, but I'm already at the door and opening it, making my point very clear.

River's waiting patiently in the hallway, leaning against the wall, and looks up with a hooded gaze. "River, if you wouldn't mind joining me?" I ask. It's expected, really. I'd rather him deal with the spitfire of a sister behind me, but since he's supplying the guns, I need to solidify my front with him. Not just his and my sister's marital one.

Anya went quiet the moment I stepped into the hallway because she knows better than anyone that we always present a united front. Even if she's so obviously ready to rip my throat out.

She remains in my office, most likely processing the

paperwork on my behalf because she can't help herself. That's why I suggested it in the first place.

River and I walk out into the main bidding room. The auction has already begun. The auctioneer showcases the first gun and runs through the details. I look over the numerous bidders sitting at their tables, watching intently.

"The three in the back corner have just come in from Germany," River says as he leans into me slightly. I avoid anyone stepping into my personal space at the risk of them touching me. The mere thought runs an icy chill of revulsion through me.

I know they're eager buyers. River wouldn't have invited them otherwise. I trust my sister to make decisions on who we should partner with, considering we keep the number fairly limited. And although I'd been dealing with River for years before they met, it was the first time I'd considered partnering with him aside from simply purchasing and marking up his stock.

"It goes without saying, but you need to make it up to Anya as soon as you can, because I'm the one who has to listen to it when we get home," River says, and I'm surprised by the balls on him, but then again, anyone who deals with my sister certainly isn't easily intimidated. He and I both have our reputations. And although I don't necessarily like him, I'll tolerate him.

"You're the one who chose to marry my sister. I was simply forced into the same womb as her. I had no choice. You do." Not that he would ever make it out alive if he ever tried to leave her.

I step away from him, tired of this conversation. I love my sister. Will kill for her. Have done so hundreds of times. But the matter of Cinita is off-limits.

Tonight, all I'm focusing on is the money to be made.

CHAPTER 4
Lena

The following week is weird. I see him several times, and not once does he approach me. Nor do I want him to after his insulting comment about my outfit from the other night. What a total ass. Yet he shows up at every rehearsal when I'm practicing, and Matthew sucks up to him like he's hit the jackpot.

Plus, he's not doing anything wrong so far.

Just watching me. Like a total stalker. A *hot* stalker. Which is a fucked-up thing to think. I wonder how many other women he casually insults, as if he's God's gift to women.

Like usual, by the time I finish my last set, he's gone. When I look up at where he was sitting, his seat is empty. I'm not even sure what he wants. I told him

DERANGED VOWS

everything I know. I haven't seen Cinita, nor has she bothered to contact me. She hasn't been on set for months and she lost her position as one of the lead dancers. So why is he coming here like some kind of lovestruck puppy? Or is *he* the danger he alluded to last time?

Even if she does contact me, the first thing I'll be asking is where her rent money is since I still owe my parents, and it's been hard getting extra shifts at my bar job since I work evenings here four times a week.

"It seems Mr. Ivanov has taken a liking to you," my boss says, shifting his shirt over his well-fed belly. He points at where Alek was sitting.

"Yeah. So what's his story?" I ask, trying to sound genuinely intrigued. "I haven't heard of him before."

"He's a very wealthy young man," Matthew begins, sounding like a fanatical teenage girl himself. "He's an investor with an appreciation for the arts such as music and dance, I believe. I've heard unfavorable rumors about him, but we all know to never trust rumors," he says with a wave of his hand. And I have a distinct feeling he should very much listen to those rumors because that man is involved with something illegal in one way or another. It just oozes off him. "Cinita took a liking to him as well. Speaking of, you're my shining star at the moment, so don't do what she did to me and just up and leave."

"I love it here, Matthew. I doubt I'll be going anywhere anytime soon. Unless Broadway calls me directly from Manhattan, I'm here to stay." He seems pleased with the response, waving goodbye to me and walking away.

Everyone seems to think Cinita and I were good friends because we got an apartment together, but she was actually closer with Julie. So I decide to find her to see if she knows anything about Cinita's disappearance.

I head backstage, and find her in the dressing room, taking off her makeup as she talks to another dancer about how awful the pay is. She notices me right away and gasps in exasperation. "Lena. Tell me you get paid better than what we do."

I slide the chair out next to her and sit down. My contract states I'm not to discuss my pay with other employees, so I avoid specific figures because I don't want to lose this job. "The pay could always be better," I say vaguely.

"Damn right. We hustle on that stage. And look, I have to run to my other job just to pay the bills." She shakes her head.

"Other job?" I didn't know she, like me, was working two jobs.

"I dance, of course," she says, as if it's obvious. "It's hard, though. I don't have time for dating or anything. But I'd be stupid to pass up the money. It's decent pay," she explains as she swipes on some eyeshadow.

I sigh, feeling her pain. Not so much about the dating because I couldn't be bothered with that right now, but the two jobs are hard to maintain, and I feel like I'm getting nowhere.

"You know how to dance, right?" she asks me as she applies eyeliner.

"I do." While I was also trained in dancing, I am nowhere near as good as half of these girls. They can fucking dance. Singing is where my talent lies.

"Want some extra cash?" she asks, and I'm thrown off by her question. "Not singing. I know you probably have a clause in your contract about singing anywhere else, but dancing..."

"I can't dance like you," I'm quick to say.

"It's not that type of dancing. It's sexy and sensual. I've seen you move your hips on stage. You can do it."

"I'm not sure..." I hedge, biting my lip. Sure, I have curves and know how to use them, but that and dancing professionally are two different things.

"It's two thousand cash for four hours to dance, and you have to sign an NDA beforehand."

"Two thousand for only four hours of work?" My jaw drops at that.

Holy shit.

She nods as if she's just given me a cheat code to adulting.

I could pay my parents back and still have money left over.

I might not be able to depend on Cinita to pay me back, but if I can get a one-off gig like this, then I won't owe them anything.

"I'm in," I tell her.

She smiles and puckers her lips as she checks her lipstick. Then she looks at me. "Okay, let's tweak your makeup a little, and they'll give us dresses when we arrive. Let's go make that money, honey!"

That is a lot of money for only a few hours of work. And I plan to shake my ass for every dollar. Fuck, I should ask her if I have to get naked.

But does that really matter?

I'll do whatever I have to for that money, because it's not every day you're offered a two-thousand-dollar job.

CHAPTER 5

Lena

"Sign," the woman who stands in front of me says with a hint of a Russian accent. She is stunning, like supermodel gorgeous. She's wearing a pencil skirt with a slit up the side, has porcelain skin that would give those vampire movies a run for their money, and has silky red hair that is pulled back in a perfect bun.

"I won't have to be naked, will I?" I ask her. She eyes me, and her emerald eyes look familiar. I just can't put my finger on where I've seen them before.

"No. Though, if you want to, feel free," she replies, handing me the pen.

"I'm good, thank you." I take the pen and sign the NDA she handed me.

A dark-haired man walks up behind her and wraps

his arms around her waist, then kisses her neck. I avert my gaze but quickly sneak another peek, unable to look away from the duo. They're menacing and powerful in a beautiful but scary way. The man has tattoos all up his arms, and his eyes, which are an interesting mix of blue and hazel, clearly burn only for her. And he looks like no more than an accessory to her right now as she focuses on getting all the dancers situated.

Julie has already gone off and started to change, obviously having done this before. The red-headed Russian in front of me told me my outfit is in the back, but I couldn't go farther until I signed the NDA.

"Go." She waves me off as if I'm no more than a fly being swatted away. However, I can feel her gaze on my back as I leave. When I push open the door, I peek over my shoulder. Since I'm the last of the dancers, the couple are left alone in the room. Her head is tilted to the side, giving the man better access to her neck, but her eyes remain on me.

Because that's not intimidating as shit.

Taking a deep breath, I make my way to the dressing room, where I find ten other women, all wearing leather dresses. Very showy leather, I might add.

"Here," Julie says, grabbing my dress from a rack

and handing it to me. "Get dressed. We have to be out there before the guests arrive." I take it from her and look down at it. It's obviously going to expose my ass, and considering I'm thicker than all of these women, it's going to be a whole lot of ass. It's not nudity... but sort of?

"How often do you do this?" I ask, curiously, because I'm still not entirely sure if what we're getting ourselves into is legal. But if there are contracts in place, surely it is, right?

"Cinita got me the job here about a month before she ran off." She shrugs. "She knew a lot of shady people, but I appreciate it. You know, doing this every now and then helps pay for all of this." She waves a hand over her body.

Not legal, then.

"A man was asking about her," I say, seizing my opportunity since she brought Cinita up.

"Yeah, she was popular with the men," she adds, like it means nothing.

I study her as she puts on a black wig. Then I tie my hair back and do the same. My blue eyes are a stark contrast to the black in the mirror.

"Have you heard from her at all?" I ask Julie as I pin the wig into place.

"Nope, she ran off. But Cinita does that. Runs off

with men." She laughs as if it's so normal and not at all a scream for help. Perhaps their friendship wasn't as deep as I thought it was.

"You don't worry about her?"

"You lived with her. Were you not worried?" Julie asks, confused.

"I didn't really know her well enough. She wasn't home half the time either."

"No one really knew her. Cinita came to rehearsal and stuff but very rarely hung around. She always had somewhere to be or would have various guys picking her up."

Well, shit. I thought she was a lot more personable than that. Everyone seemed to love her whenever we practiced, so I thought her friendships were deeper than they actually were.

Julie glances at the dress I still haven't put on. Everyone but me is dressed and ready to head out. Standing, I quickly tear off my clothes and let them fall to the floor. Grabbing the leather underwear, I decide to keep my G-string on underneath it, as I don't know who might have worn it before me, but I do remove my bra.

It's hard not to notice how much smaller the other women are than me. It's always the same in my industry, but I love my curves. I haven't had to pay for my ass or tits either. Not that I mind those who do; mine just come naturally.

Standing there in only my G-string, I hear a man's voice bark over the chattering of the women. It's not unusual for men to enter the dressing rooms—some are hairstylists and others even do makeup, but this voice sounds awfully familiar.

Looking up, I see him. His gloved hands are on the doorframe as he tells the women to move, but his narrowed green gaze is locked on me.

"Everyone out. Now," he says, and the women quickly file out. "Except for you," he adds, still staring at me.

"Uh, I'll see you out there, Lena." Julie skirts around me.

Why is this fucker here?

I turn so he can't see any more of me as I pull up the leather underwear that my ass hangs out of, then put on the dress that cuts low, emphasizing my cleavage. When I'm dressed, I turn toward Alek just as the door clicks shut. We're now alone in here.

"Well, if it isn't Mr. Happy," I say sarcastically.

"Leave," he says.

"Sorry, what? You can't tell me what to do," I scoff.

"You're fired. Leave."

"But I need..." He turns, opens the door, and

strides out as if whatever I have to say isn't important enough for him to hear. That his word is law. My blood boils. Fuck this guy and him thinking he can tell me what to do in any type of way.

He doesn't own me, and he sure as fuck isn't telling me where I can and can't earn my money.

Nope, no way. I want this money. As soon as he's gone, I take a deep breath and try to contain my emotions. Brushing my wig back out of my face, I slip on the boots that were left for me and then peek out the door. Two security guards stand there but say nothing.

"Do you know where the other girls went?" I ask politely.

One of them arches an eyebrow, and I wonder if he heard what Alek said, but he seems slightly amused as he points down the hallway.

"Thank you," I say as I follow his direction and head down the hall. I'm quick to find Julie, who seems to be walking up a short set of stairs that most likely lead to a stage. She waves me over before grabbing my hand and pulling me onto the stage with her.

It's not like our stage at the show. No, this one is circular, and two dancers fit on a podium together. I find myself sharing one with Julie. *Fuck, what have I gotten myself into?* But it's only a performance. Four hours and two thousand dollars. I can shake my ass for that. I've done it for less, picking up an asshole from a club once or twice.

"Want a hit?" Julie asks me. I'm confused at first until I see her pull a tablet from her bra and put it under her tongue.

"No, thank you." Each to their own, but it isn't my vibe.

Music begins to play, and Julie rubs her body against me as the curtains raise. I realize we're in human-sized birdcages. The main part of the room is dim, and I can't really see the faces of those in the crowd who sit at the tables.

I notice a large stage at the front with what looks like an auction podium, if the hammer is any indication. I wonder what they're selling. I'm shocked as a woman walks out naked onto the stage, and I turn my focus back on Julie.

Okay. Sex. They're selling sex here.

Fuck, I hope I haven't put myself on the market.

Oh shit. What if I've signed up to be trafficked?

Fuck. I knew this type of money was too good to be true.

I need to calm the fuck down, because it doesn't mean I'm here to be sold.

The sound of voices increases as I grab Julie by the

hips and roll down her front, then I mimic licking up her leg as I roll back up.

Just think about the nights out with the girls in your college days, I tell myself. If I start freaking out now, I'm going to cause more issues for myself.

Turning ever so slightly, I spot Alek. *Fuck.* But with this lighting, he doesn't seem to recognize me. He stands near the door, watching as others walk in. I quickly look away and face Julie as I continue to move my hips to the music.

I'll have to be careful not to draw his attention.

"Damn, girl, you were being modest when you said you can't dance like us," Julie whispers as she bends over in front of me. I glide my hand up the back of her leg as she flicks her hair over her shoulder and slowly straightens back up.

"*You*," I hear someone growl, and I know whose voice it is. Swaying to the music, I don't look down to where I know he's standing, instead pretending I don't hear him or notice his presence. Which is very fucking hard to miss.

"Umm, Lena." Julie is frozen and tapping me on the shoulder.

"Dance," I tell her through gritted teeth.

"He's the boss, Lena," she tells me quietly. Of

DERANGED VOWS

course he is. I offer another forced smile as I turn around.

"I told you already, you're fired," he grits out.

I put my hand to my ear. "Sorry, can't hear you," I say over the auctioneer's voice as bids increase for the naked woman on stage.

With the music still going, other dancers in highlighted cages seem to notice the commotion, as their gazes turn in our direction. Some look curious, while others are sneering as if I'm receiving special treatment.

"Oh, you can't hear me?" he says, lifting his phone and pressing a few buttons before the room falls silent. The music is cut off, and the girls are no longer dancing. The female auctioneer seems to stumble only momentarily but then continues.

"We're currently at ten million. Do I hear eleven?"

Ten million for what? I want to look in the direction of the main stage but can't tear my gaze from the piercing green eyes that are seriously pissed with me right now.

"Can you hear me now, sunshine?" he asks.

My teeth hurt as they grind at him calling me 'sunshine'. So it's not that he didn't hear my Mr. Happy insult before. He just didn't address it.

"I can," I say, swallowing, and hating that he can

probably hear that as well. Because this guy is intimidating.

"Get down," he growls.

I lean down, purposely giving him a cleavage shot. "I need the money," I tell him desperately.

"I'll pay you double. Now, get the fuck down." I look at the stairs that lead up to the cage. They seem slightly scarier than when I came up them. I also consider it's easier just to jump. But I have these boots on, and I may hurt myself. The music starts again, and before I know what's happening, Alek reaches for me and pulls me down.

I'm startled by his featherlight touch and want to cling to the bars, suddenly feeling like this man is a far worse danger than dancing in the cage. He holds me effortlessly, but I notice his uncomfortable expression, his jaw tight, his lips pressed into a straight line.

The moment my feet touch the floor, he immediately steps away from me, then turns and storms off. Without a word, I know I'm supposed to go with him, and I don't defy him this time.

I follow him out, trying to ignore the few people staring, until we step out of the auction room and into the main hall, where it's significantly quieter. I thought it was strange when we came to a mansion to dance. I thought it was a rich person's party. But this shit is next-level wild. He stops, turns to me, and his jaw loosens just a little.

"How much?" he asks.

"Sorry, what?"

"How much are they paying you?"

"Two thousand," I tell him just as the doors open and the redheaded woman walks out. Her eyes narrow as she looks at me before she looks at Alek.

"Tell me why you stopped my music. This is my auction," she demands.

"She's not supposed to be here, Anya," he tells her, referring to me. Her gaze narrows on me.

"Why? Is she with the police?"

I snort a laugh. "Me?" Then I realize she's deadly serious.

"No, she's just a ray of fucking sunshine," Alek mumbles under his breath.

"Who are you?" she asks, glancing between Alek and me as if there's some burning secret she must uncover.

"Lena," I tell her. "Lena Love."

"Well, Lena Love, my brother here says you aren't supposed to be here, and I would like to know why."

"I just needed the extra money. My friends worked here, and I don't know why I'm not allowed to. Maybe because I sing for an off-Broadway show?" Even I'm confused by that since my contract doesn't say I can't dance anywhere else.

"Who are your friends?" she asks.

"Julie and Cinita."

Her eyes widen, and she looks back at Alek, who is staring at me. His jaw tics as his sister gapes at him, almost in disbelief.

"You can leave," he says as he hands me four thousand dollars in cash from his pocket as if it's loose change. I take it. The tension between these two could be cut with a knife, and I don't know why he's so fucking mad about me being here. We don't even know each other. But I'm certainly not going to say no to four thousand dollars for less than an hours worth of work.

I think about Julie, but she says she's done this before, so she'll be okay, right?

"I need my stuff," I say. When neither of them makes a move to stop me, I walk past them to grab my belongings.

She starts talking to him in a hushed tone, and I try not to listen, but I hear Cinita's name.

How could I not?

This guy is fucking obsessed.

CHAPTER 6

Aleksandr

"Is this going to be the same problem as Cinita?" Anya asks.

"No," I tell her as I watch Lena walk off. She's beautiful. Too fucking beautiful to be up there dancing in a cage. Her ass peeks out perfectly beneath the dress.

All those luscious round curves, not like Cinita, who was all skin and bones. She worked herself until she was sick. How opposite they are.

I turn my gaze to Anya, who studies me intently. She never misses a thing.

"Do not let her work here again," I grit out, unimpressed by the entire situation.

"Why?" she asks, not backing down. Anya is persistent.

"Is my word not enough?"

"No, it's not. Now tell me why." I shake my head and walk past her. We might be close. We might have each other's back no matter what. But there are some things even I have the right to keep to myself.

"Alek, tell me why," she yells out from behind me, but I don't answer. Once upon a time, I would have told her everything, but ever since the fiasco with Cinita, things have changed.

A lot.

For one, where the fuck is Cinita?

I found her once and can do it again.

How does she manage to keep slipping through the cracks?

Pushing open the door to the dressing room, I find Lena swearing at herself as she strips the clothes from her body.

"Stupid fucking men. Who does he think he is?" she says, and I want to smile. If I were capable of such a thing. "Thinks he can tell me what to do, like I don't have enough men in my life thinking the same thing." She swears at the end.

"I wasn't telling you what to do, and I'm still paying you." I make a point to look at the four thousand dollars on the side table. "Do not come back." Her blue eyes are almost like crystals as they shine back at me. She's furious. "*That* is me telling you what to do, in case you were confused." She glances at the cash, then back at me.

"Don't worry, I'm sure my teenager brain can process that much, old man," she bites back.

My eyebrows shoot up involuntarily. Does she have any idea who she's speaking with? Obviously not. "Old man... that's one I haven't heard."

"I just assumed because you have no hair."

"It's shaved."

She casually shrugs. "I have yet to see otherwise."

I step into her space now because this woman clearly doesn't realize the danger she's in when speaking to me.

She stumbles back, her ass hitting the table behind her. Her tits are on full display, and they're more than a handful. When she rights herself and turns her back to me, I get a view of her hourglass figure from behind.

"You seem not to understand danger when it's facing you," I say, cautious to keep my distance but remain close enough to intimidate her.

She spins back around to face me. "Sounds exactly like something an old man would say," she retorts, but her chest heaves. Those breasts rising and falling.

"I'll have you know I'm not even thirty yet," I

reply, and it boggles me why I'm still even talking with her.

"Already halfway in the grave if you ask me."

This abnormality of a woman. She's nothing more than someone to give me information on Cinita, yet... here I am... dare I say, arguing with her?

I take a step back and lean against one of the pink chairs as I shove my hands in my pockets and watch her. Her gaze flicks between me and her clothes that are in her bag on the floor.

"Are you so young you still need help getting dressed?" I challenge.

"I'm not sure if your shaky old man hands are up to the challenge of clipping a bra." She leans over for her bag, and a smile tugs at the corner of my mouth. I'm bemused and bewildered by this little singer.

"Maybe she ran from you," she says.

Ignoring her bra, she pulls her dress out of the bag and puts it on over her head. Although she probably intended for me to, I don't look at her breasts, even though her perfect nipples are noticeable through the material. I won't pretend to be some gentleman, because clearly, I'm not.

"Maybe," I agree as I pace back to the center of the room. She watches me cautiously from her periphery.

"Thanks for my money, asshole."

She grabs the money, opening her bag and pushing it in, then steps toward me.

"Move," she says as I block her path. "You told me to leave, yet your assholeness is blocking my way. Or have you lost your sense of direction as well, sir?"

She's fiery. And has an attitude that will certainly get her in trouble. I'm surprised she hasn't found it sooner.

"Why were you friends with her?" I ask. The two are nothing alike. Despite her not-so-good qualities, Cinita was a people pleaser. While I get vibes that Lena is only that way if it benefits her, she's showing me a different side right now.

"Is that any of your concern?" She pushes past me then, her shoulder hitting mine. I go to move, but she barges straight into me. I tense at the contact. "Good night, Alek."

She flips her chocolate-colored hair over her shoulder and glances back at me as if expecting that I might say good evening in response.

"Whatever." She huffs and then walks out.

CHAPTER 7
Aleksandr

This thing with Lena isn't like the situation with Cinita. She and Lena are entirely different sides of a coin. I justify the reason I'm watching her walk into her bar job is because I'm not letting anything slide when it comes to Cinita. Although she might not know where Cinita is now, I'm certain Lena will be her first point of contact.

My jaw tics at the tight jeans Lena's wearing and that stupid fucking crop top that leaves very little to the imagination. This one doesn't have a smiley face on it, but it's still more revealing than I'd like it to be the moment she removes her black leather jacket. I have no idea why that actually bothers me. I usually don't even notice what a woman's wearing. So why has she gotten under my skin? Is it because she called me old? My nostrils flare.

My phone buzzes, and I check the screen. Anya.

"Where the fuck are you?" she asks the moment I answer on the third ring.

My grip tightens on the steering wheel as I prepare myself for the onslaught I'm about to receive.

"Out," I grit as I keep an eye on Lena, who is casually talking to someone at the front of the bar, her hands in her back pockets. Is she not receiving enough income from her singing job? Or does she enjoy smelling like smoke and entertaining seedy riffraff men for an evening?

"Out? You were supposed to be over here for dinner that I made," she snaps.

"You actually made the meal? Physically cooked it yourself?" I query, disbelieving.

"Of course I didn't cook it myself, but I specifically told the chef what we felt like eating tonight. And your sorry ass was meant to be here three minutes ago."

"Something came up." The truth is, I intended to go to Anya's house. But then I went through Lena's contract and found her address, and drove over there. Just out of curiosity, of course. Then Lena walked out from the apartment building, shifting that ass this way and that beneath her jeans. And then I somehow ended up here.

Lena touches the woman's shoulder with a bright smile as she indicates she has to go inside. Or what if she's here for a date? I was tipped off that she had a second job in a passing comment by Matthew, but what if this isn't the bar she works at? What if...?

"Aleksandr, are you even listening to me? You better not be chasing that ballet dancer, or I swear to God I will bury you ten feet under myself."

I expel an exasperated breath. "Please. You wouldn't get your hands so dirty."

I can imagine her popping a hand on her hip. "Well, maybe not, but that's why I have River now. To dig holes for all my bodies." I hear him laughing in the background. "You owe me a fucking dinner once a month. That was our agreement when you came back from Russia."

No, that was her demand, but I don't disagree with her. I know it's because she feels "disconnected" from me. That's River's word of choice, not mine or Anya's because we don't really understand this emotional connection bullshit. But what we do know is it's her and me until the day we die. Always has been and always will be.

Lena walks inside, waving to the lady smoking at the front and looking pleased by their discussion.

I glance in my rearview mirror and glimpse my shaved head. I don't often look at myself, but I know I'm considered attractive to most women. But most have the sense to stay away.

"Do you think I look older than what I am?" I ask Anya.

There's a pause on the other end of the line.

"What?" Anya asks, as if she didn't hear me right.

"Never mind." I start the engine, reminding myself that I only came here to stake out Lena's living situation. I haven't been able to get her out of my mind since the auction four nights ago. "I'm on my way."

"Good. Then after that, we have to deal with that asshole who tried to slander our name and take some of our business."

"How thoughtful of you to make sure we have dinner first before murder," I say before pulling out onto the main road.

"Don't pretend the dinner isn't just an appetizer to you on nights like these."

I'd smile if it were something I was capable of.

CHAPTER 8
Aleksandr

Alek Ivanov is a dick. No, worse. He's a *lovestruck* dick who's involved me in his fixation. But he's also a wealthy asshole who made my life a hell of a lot easier.

I paid my parents back the moment I received the money two weeks ago. I couldn't have been happier to have that weight lifted off my shoulders. It felt so good, even if I didn't actually work for the money. They asked me a lot of questions about the money, all which I deflected. They wouldn't believe I got it from my singing. With my brother being a doctor, you can say their disappointment in my chosen occupation is very real.

But I never let it stop me from doing what I want. Even if it means hurting the feelings of those I love.

Singing is what I was put on this planet for, so stopping it would be like denying my next breath.

I haven't seen Alek since that night two weeks ago, and to say I'm relieved is an understatement. I was nervous the first few nights coming in for rehearsals, almost expecting his uptight assholeness to be sitting in his usual chair. Maybe what I said offended him. Good.

We're finishing our rehearsal as my boss approaches me before anyone leaves the stage.

"Fantastic. Everyone, go have some refreshments in the back." He applauds and looks up at me on the stage. "Lena, please follow me to my office. There's something we have to discuss," Matthew says, and he isn't his usual happy self this time as he walks away.

Fuck, have I done something seriously wrong? Matthew is never mad. Stressed sometimes but never angry.

"What did you do to get his panties in a twist?" Julie leans over and whispers.

I shrug, not entirely sure. Although the extra cash helped, I still haven't quit my job at the bar—it's good to be cautious—but there's no way I can lose this job. I'm not really sure what I would do, and the bar work isn't enough income for me to live on. It's also not what I love.

I jump from the stage and walk in the direction of his office. Matthew is already waiting inside, sitting at his desk. It's a small office, crowded by framed photos on the walls of previous casts and shows. His desk is flooded with scribblings of what might be another script, and the room is far too dusty for my liking.

He indicates that I should close the door, but a cold dread washes over me. Fuck, am I going to be dumped from the show? What did I do?

"Tell me honestly, have you done something to our investor?" I look at him, confused, unsure as to who he's even talking about. "Alek Ivanov. Did you do something?"

Goose bumps erupt over my skin.

Shit, maybe I shouldn't have sworn at him. No, he deserved it. The asshole.

But would he really stoop so low as to cost me my job?

"No. Why, what's wrong?" I ask. I can't lose this job, and the desperation quivers in my voice.

He sighs and reaches for a piece of paper on top of the crumpled-up scripts. He pushes it toward me. I lean over the desk, too scared to be close in case the chaotic mess swallows me whole.

The piece of paper is a new contract. My eyebrows furrow in confusion as I skim over it. It has my name on it and a wage that is double what I receive now. *What the hell?*

"I have a contract," I say, unsure as to what the fuck is happening. Usually, when someone sees their wage has doubled, they're excited, but this feels far more ominous than that.

"This is another contract requiring that you sing outside of work once every two weeks at his choosing." I look down at it again. "It's an unusual request, and Alek didn't seem entirely pleased when making it. We don't usually accept such requests, but we don't want to upset him since he has been a major sponsor for a long time."

"He wants me to sing for him?" I ask, confused. I assumed he hated me. Maybe I was wrong. No, he does hate me. He must be trying to use me for information. Information I don't have.

"He does. There is an additional clause in there, however."

"An additional clause?" I pick up the contract to read the entire thing thoroughly.

"Yes. You have to quit your job at the bar," he says so quietly I'm almost certain I didn't hear him right.

When he doesn't correct himself, my jaw drops. "What?"

"He said he doesn't want you overworking yourself, so you're consistently in top shape to perform for him."

I scoff. "Oh, I bet he does." I bite my lip, suddenly remembering who I'm talking to. This is way more than I'd earn at my bar job in two weeks anyway, but still, that's not for him to decide.

I don't think my boss is upset with me at all, rather we both realize how odd the request is.

I feel like I'm making a deal with the devil.

"Once you've signed the contract, he's waiting outside with a car for you."

"He wants me to sing *now*?" I ask, shocked. I haven't had time to get dressed, and I'm wearing a throw-over loose dress because I had adjustments made to my costume.

"Yes. He wants you to sign and go with him now."

I look at the contract and take the pen Matthew holds out to me. I offer a curt smile as I hesitate to sign.

The money is double, so can I really complain? No. I'll sing in his bathroom if that's what he requires. But the clause of having to quit my other job? That's just some controlling assholeness right there.

"I'm just going to read over it quickly," I say with a sweet smile. "Actually, do you mind if I speak with him about the contract?"

Matthew seems reluctant but agrees. "I need the

contract on my desk next time you're here. Remember, though, Lena, we need his sponsorship, so don't do anything that jeopardizes that."

"Of course," I wholeheartedly agree. I do want that money. It will help me pay my student loans off so much faster, and maybe I can move to a nicer part of town. But I don't want to depend solely on the man who threw me out of my last gig.

Walking past the dressing room, I head out the back door to find Alek waiting for me, leaning against his expensive-looking car. His gaze lands on me the moment I walk out of the door. It's almost dark, and seeing this man parked in an already empty parking lot looks strange. He adjusts his gloves expectantly.

"A new contract?" I say with a hand on my hip, the contract pinched between my fingers.

He takes in my bright-purple dress, but surprisingly, he makes no comment about it. But neither does he comment on the contract.

I walk closer, and he goes to open the door, but I wave my finger back and forth. "Hell to the no, old man. You and I are going to negotiate on this contract."

There's a slight shift in his expression. I'd even say he might be surprised if he weren't so robot-like.

We have an awkward standoff. This guy might as

well be mute in the way it seems as if speaking inconveniences him so.

"Okay, then have a good day," I say as I flip my hair over my shoulder and turn back toward the door.

"I don't negotiate," he grits out.

"Oh, he does speak," I say audaciously. "And I'm not someone who is told what to do," I add.

He appraises me, almost curiously, as he pushes off the car and comes toward me. Not so he's close enough to touch, but enough to try to intimidate me. "What is it you wish to... negotiate?" His jaw clenches. "Is the money not generous enough?"

I scoff in disbelief. "Generous?" It's fucking incredible money, but I don't give that away. "I mean, it's okay. I won't be quitting my job, though."

"You don't have to leave here."

"I'm talking about the bar job, and you know it," I say with my hand on my hip again. "You don't get to dictate what I do and don't do in my spare time."

"On the contrary, you signed that you won't sing elsewhere professionally in your current contract. This is no different. A sacrifice."

"Not the same thing, old man." I sneer. His eyes flare hot at the use of "'old man,'" and I realize I'm getting under his skin. For better or for worse. I must be an idiot for sassing someone who is clearly as dangerous as this guy is. "Why do you even want me to sing for you? You clearly don't even like me."

He seems to struggle with his words until he plucks the contract and pen out of my hand, making sure not to touch me. He presses it against the car window and begins to write. Once done, he steps to the side, as if summoning me without words. I move into his space, which he's clearly uncomfortable with, and see that he's scratched out and signed the clause about me leaving my bar job. Instead, it says:

Thou shalt not call Aleksandr Ivanov "old man" or imply in any comment, jokingly or not, that he is older than he appears.

I bite my bottom lip to keep from smiling, and raise my eyebrows. "You're serious about this." I point at the contract, trying not to laugh. He doesn't seem amused. Who even writes "thou" these days?

I pluck the pen from his hand and sign on the dotted line. I'll take that as a win today. Once it's signed, I tuck the contract in the pocket of my loose dress because... hello, pockets in a dress.

He steps around the car and opens the passenger door for me. He waves for me to enter, but I stay where I am.

"Where are we going?"

His gaze pins on me, but again, he says nothing. I

think he's hit his threshold for speaking for the day. This guy is all sorts of unusual, and it's a crime to package someone with such a terrible personality with the looks of model. He's polished in a terrifying way, but I have the impression those muscles under his shirt aren't for visual purposes only.

"I won't allow you to kill me," I tell him, crossing my arms over my chest as I round the hood and make my way to him.

"Get in the car," he finally says. I huff and step up closer to him, and instantly, I can smell him. He smells like a fresh breeze on the ocean. Light but memorable. I regret that I got this close to him, because he reminds me that despite his personality, he is hot as fuck. Not only do his shaved head and gloved hands intimidate me, they also make me think I've been chasing the wrong kind of men most of my life.

Even then, I distinctly know this is a man no woman should chase or try to attract.

"Where am I singing?" I ask as I slide into the car. He shuts the door behind me and walks around to the driver's side.

Give me strength if I have to deal with this man once every two weeks. But at least it'll fast-track my goals.

When he opens the door and sits next to me, it's

only seconds until he revs the engine, works the stick on his manual car, and takes off. *Shit*. I reach for my seat belt and quickly put it on.

This guy is a maniac.

"Where am I singing?" I repeat.

He reaches for the volume dial on the radio and turns it up, effectively shutting me up.

This guy can't be serious.

What the fuck have I signed myself up for?

CHAPTER 9
Lena

After ten minutes of listening to classical music, I mute the radio.

"Where are we going?" I ask him again, folding my arms over my chest.

He looks over at me, his brows knitting together as he keeps driving. I glance at the road—the one he is not paying attention to—before I look back at him.

I'm uncomfortable with the way he looks at me and terrified with the way he doesn't look at the road.

"Why were you friends?" he asks, then focuses back on the road.

I throw my arms up in the air in disbelief, not that I should be entirely shocked. "Cinita again? Come on, dude. You obsessed with her?" He slams on the brakes, and thank fuck I put my seat belt on. I gasp and look at him as my hand clutches the belt around me. "Are you crazy? That could have killed me."

"You're fine," he says before he takes off again. He drives to an underpass and stops under it. Okay.

The noises from the cars above are deafening as they pass over us, yet under here it's oddly lonely. He gets out of the car and slams the door, leaving me alone. I watch as he walks in front of the car toward the river and stops in a particular spot, assessing it. No fucking way am I getting out. This looks exactly like a place he would kill me. No, thank you very much.

"Lena." He calls my name. I hear it. Even over the noise, I hear his summons. But when I don't move, he explains as if I don't understand. "Get out of my car."

"Why?" I yell, knowing he can hear me if I can hear him.

He nods his head to the spot next to him, clearly exasperated, though he doesn't make a show of it. I've come to learn the subtleties in his body language. It's the only thing that gives him away... slightly.

"Do not make me get you out," he warns, and I notice his slight Russian accent comes out with his impatience.

"I'll stay here, thank you very much," I tell him, slinking into the seat and holding my seat belt as tightly as I can. He cracks his neck from side to side, cursing under his breath before stepping in my direction. He grabs the door handle and pulls the door open. I clutch the seat belt as I stare up at him.

"Out," he says again.

"No."

"This is a part of your job."

"No, I get paid to sing."

"You get paid because I allow it, but your ass is mine while I have you. Now, get out of the car." He motions for me to get out, but I shake my head.

Nope, no fucking way.

Does he not think I'm smart?

I know better than to get out of a car with a strange man in the middle of nowhere, where he could kill me, and my screams would be muffled by the noises above.

Nope.

He reaches into his pocket, and when he pulls out a knife, I gasp.

He's going to kill me. I'm going to die here.

How the hell did I end up in this situation?

As he leans in, I try to move away, but the seat belt —the one thing I thought would protect me—is now holding me down.

"Get away from me, you crazy ass." I try to kick at him, but my legs aren't getting me very far. I try to hit him, but he blocks my hands with his gloved one as he reaches in and puts the knife closer to my face. I scream loudly as he lowers the knife, and I watch in horror as it gets closer. He slices the seat belt above my shoulder and then steps back.

"Get out, now," he growls. My heart pounds as my scream dwindles. The knife is still in his gloved hand. The seat belt is loose around me as I step out of the car obediently, my hands shaking. "Follow me."

"Why?" I gasp. *What does he want from me?*

"Fuck, you're annoying. Follow, woman." His piercing green glare is back on me. I huff out a shaky breath and follow him but keep my distance. I search the ground for something, anything I might be able to use to defend myself. I spy a good-sized rock, lean down, and pick it up, clutching it close to my chest. We reach the same spot where he was standing before.

There's a small pool of dried blood.

"Whose blood is that?" I ask cautiously, making sure not to get too close.

"Cinita's." He pauses. "I think."

"You killed her?" I ask in disbelief.

"While I take great pleasure in killing those who annoy me"—he pins me with his icy gaze—"I did no such thing."

"So why am I here?" I ask. He then looks at the rock in my hand.

"Do you plan to hit me with that?"

"Do you plan to stab me?" Alek glances down at his hand, like he didn't realize he's still holding the knife.

"I thought about it," he muses, then looks back at me. "We shall see." His words offer me no amount of comfort. Asshole.

"Where is she?" I want to know where she is and make sure she's okay, but I also despise her for somehow dragging me into her mess.

"She called me from this spot while I was preoccupied with other commitments."

"So how do you know she called from here?"

"I had tracking on her," he says easily.

Oh my gosh. This guy really is out of his mind. Do all the wealthy think they can own women like branded cattle?

"Why?"

"That's none of your concern. Her last known location before the tracker was destroyed was in the apartment you two share. So tell me, do you know where she is?"

I shake my head in disbelief. Did Cinita get involved with a gang or something?

"No, I told you. She didn't get her shit or tell me she was leaving. She was just gone and left me with the bills. Now, I need to go. I'm cold, and you are scary," I tell him, stepping away.

"Are you not worried about her?" he asks, motioning to the blood.

"No. Right now, I'm more concerned that I may end up like her," I answer truthfully. "Whatever that is"—I wave to the blood—"has nothing to do with me."

"Get in the car," he says with a sigh, and I turn, almost running back to the safety of the car. When I shut the door, I notice the keys are in it. And he's still standing near the spot of dried blood. *How long has it been there?*

Climbing over the middle console and into the driver's seat, I start the car. His head swings my way, and I press the gas as hard as I can and take the fuck off.

Out of here and away from him.

I will not die today, and I will not put myself in this position ever again.

Contract or not.

CHAPTER 10
Aleksandr

She tried to steal my car.

Fucking tried to steal it and then spun out, making the back end hit the concrete column and crash.

Fucking hell.

Walking over to where my car is wrecked, I see that the back end has all the damage. Sliding my hand along the black paint, I wonder if I should just let it be and set it alight. As I move around to the driver's side, I see her with her head resting on the steering wheel.

"Didn't get very far, now, did you?"

"My head hurts," she whispers, and when she sits up, blood drips down her forehead. I'm guessing that's where she hit her head on the steering wheel. Who the fuck presses the gas all the way down on a V8? She does, that's who. Lord have mercy, this woman is a liability.

I lean into the car to move her over. She's hardly able to help herself but manages to get back into the passenger seat as she groans. I slide into the driver's side and start the car again. I slowly pull it away from the column, and thank God it still moves. Calling my sister to get one of her men to come out and remove the car is not what I am after. The questions that would follow would fucking annoy the shit out of me, and I'd just rather torch it.

It's just another reminder that I really should hire my own men, but personal protection has never been a necessity since I'm deadlier than most. For clean-up duties like this it comes in handy, though, which is why I usually call Anya's men in.

Her hand touches her forehead in disbelief as I drive. She tries to wipe away the blood, but I see her tense as she looks at it in the visor mirror.

"It's still bleeding," she says, and tries to wipe at it again.

Leaning forward, I unbutton my shirt and slide it off. I can feel her eyes on me as I hand it to her.

"Hold it to your head." She doesn't take it at first. Why is she so defiant even in a situation like this? "You already wrecked my car. Now you want to get your blood all over it? Hold it to your head." She takes it silently and lifts it to her head, wincing when she presses against the wound. "Fucking stupid, really."

She doesn't reply. In fact, she's very quiet on the drive. I'd usually enjoy the peace, but coming from her, it's uncharacteristic. I type in the code to my security gate, waiting patiently for it to open as I assess her and make sure she's still awake.

"Where are we?" she asks.

I drive down my driveway as she looks at the yard in amazement, and I'm certain that's because of her daze.

"I'm not going to kill you. I'll fix you up and have someone drive you home."

When I pull up to the house and get out of the car, I walk around and open her door for her. My jaw clenches as I get another look at the destruction she managed on the tail end of my car. I'm not overly attached to materialistic things, but it's more the inconvenience of having to go out and buy another one that irks me. I wave for her to get out. "Get the fuck out of my car."

She obeys, holding my shirt to her head as she slowly climbs out. The moment she does, her eyes roam down my chest and torso but then quickly look away.

She pretends she wasn't looking by asking, "Why do you wear gloves?"

"Why the fuck do you crash a sixty-thousand-dollar car?"

She gasps. "I can't pay you back."

"Ohh, you'll pay me back. Just not with cash," I tell her and then head toward the front door. I keep an eye on her to make sure she can walk unassisted at the very least.

I've owned this home for five years. It's close enough to Anya to appease her but enough out of the hustle of the city to offer me silence.

When I returned from Russia after looking for Cinita, I'd noticed my sister had hired more house staff, all of which I had to fire because I don't like people in my home.

"I don't want to go in there," she whispers from behind me. She looks up at my two-story mansion as if it's straight out of some horror film.

The twenty million dollars I spent, on the other hand, suggests it's far from some run-down ruins.

"You will. Now, fucking move it," I tell her, scrolling through the few contacts I have on my phone. I'll just have Clay, one of my sister's men, drop her off at home.

Holding open the large wooden door, I motion for

her to walk in ahead of me as I flick the lights on. "To the left and into the kitchen," I instruct. "And don't get blood on my furniture." She starts walking, and I look at her from behind. Her maxi dress covers her legs, which I have seen and, might I add, are fucking perfect. And her round ass, which is way more than a good fucking handful. The dress doesn't give any of that away, but I've memorized it from the night at our auction two weeks ago.

"Umm, I don't think there's much furniture to get blood on even if I tried. Where are all your things?" she asks, looking around.

"What things?" I ask, pulling open the drawer that I know has a first aid kit in it. Beside it is a gun, and she doesn't seem to miss it because she takes a heavy gulp as she walks in.

"Like personal things. This house feels so generic and cold. Is this actually your house?" She squints at me accusingly, as if I'd just broken into someone's home.

"I have no need for personal things. It's only a place to sleep," I say matter-of-factly.

She stares at me in disbelief.

"Do you have a charging station or something?" she asks incredulously. I don't understand, so I ignore her, but she adds, "Since you're clearly a robot or something."

"Don't make me add another clause to the contract that says you can't call me a robot."

She still hasn't come any closer to me. I point at the island barstool and wait for her to come willingly. She stares at me but eventually gives in and sits down awkwardly.

"Stay still, and do not touch me," I warn her, stepping up closer.

"Why would I touch— Motherfucker!" she screams as I clean the area with disinfectant. She lays her hands on my chest, and her nails start digging in. My jaw clenches as hard as hers, conscious of her pressing against me.

Filth. Beneath me. Forbidden. Infectious.

"I told you not to touch me," I growl as I try to pull away, but she clings to me, nails sunk deep. I want to clean myself. The sensation comes over me every time someone touches me. It's too much. A reminder of the reason I first put gloves on at six and have avoided physical contact since.

She doesn't pull away as I grab the glue and apply it to the cut, then I pinch the skin together and hold it closed while I look down at her hands, trying to push down the screaming thoughts in my head.

I have blood and glue on my gloves, but I can't seem to look away from her hands resting on my chest. I go to pull away again, to wrench myself from her, but then I realize she's going a shade too pale.

"I'm a little tired." Her eyes start to close, and before either of us says anything else, she falls straight into my arms.

My entire body locks up as her full body weight presses against me. She's not heavy, the furthest thing from it, but I try to blink away all the screaming words that churn in my head.

Filth. Touching. Human.

They eat at me alive.

Fucking hell.

I told her not to touch me. I should have let her fall.

CHAPTER 11
Lena

My head is hurting, and people are talking around me.

"Welcome back," an unfamiliar man says.

I'm lying on the cold floor. I notice Alek right away as he points for the man to leave. The older man looks down at me, and I attempt to sit up.

"Stay fucking still; you may have a concussion," Alek grumbles as the old man takes his leave.

"Who was that?"

"The doctor," he says, as if it's obvious.

"Oh. Why was there a doctor here?"

"Well, I figured you didn't want to go to the hospital and get hit with a bill. So I called him over."

"That's awfully nice..." I stop myself and look up

at him. More likely, he doesn't want questions about his shady business.

"Wait, why am I on the floor?"

"You fainted, and I didn't want to touch you."

"Okay, that makes sense," I say sarcastically.

I try to sit up again when he walks off.

"Do not faint again. I need rest and can't get it if you won't leave." He reaches for a single glass on his counter and fills it with water, then hands it to me. It's then I realize he still hasn't put a shirt on. His toned abs are hard not to look at, and he has ink snaking up one arm.

"It's still really weird you own this house; it feels like a display home," I tell him, glancing around at the almost empty rooms and trying to avoid his bare chest.

"You just say the first thing that comes to your mind, don't you?" he asks, not at all impressed.

"It comes naturally. In the way that you snap your fingers and expect people to jump for your attention and at your next command because you have the money," I reply.

"Do you hold bias against those who have money? If I pay for a service, I expect it to be fulfilled, no questions asked," he states. "I came from nothing, and built up everything I have." He pulls the glass from my hand, careful not to touch my fingers as he does so. He puts it in the sink and looks down at me. "Stand. Slowly."

"I don't come from money. My parents are middle class. Same house, same cars, same jobs all my life. They worked hard and never really went any further than where they started," I tell him, and brace myself as I push myself up. "So I suppose I just don't like you, personally, because of your shitty attitude. Money aside." I get a little dizzy, but I manage to stand.

"Must be nice to have parents. Shitty attitude aside." His words hit me, and I pull back as I look at him.

For the first time, I don't have a snide comeback because I never even thought of this man as human, let alone... lonely. Then again, Alek seems like the type to isolate himself. He hates talking to people. Was Cinita the only person he confided in?

"Why are you searching so hard for Cinita?" I ask. "She never committed to any man, that much I know. So why her?"

I think he's about to stop talking entirely, like during all of our other encounters, but instead, he simply says, "Because she needs to be protected. She gets lost in the danger."

"And you're not dangerous?" I ask rhetorically. It leaves my mouth before I can think better of it.

"Yes, but I am the lesser of the evils. I saved her once in a brothel; she had a needle in her fucking arm and was half dead. And she ran off to them again." My jaw drops. I had no idea Cinita was in that deep with this type of shit. "I need to find her."

"I don't understand why she's your responsibility. She's made it clear she doesn't want help, hasn't she? Not once did she mention your name." Clearly, she doesn't want to be found by Alek.

He steps up to me, getting close but not close enough to be touching. "What do you know?"

"I know nothing. I was making an observation on what you told me."

"I found her once. I can do it again."

"Are you in love with her? Is that why you're trying so hard to find her?" I ask, but he doesn't answer or move. "Have you even slept with her?"

His gaze dips to my lips as I lick them. Being around this man is scary, and adrenaline is pumping through me in the way you know you're too close to playing with fire.

"No." I don't know which question he's answering, but I don't push because I sense his uneasiness. And Alek Ivanov seems unpredictable.

He continues to stare at my lips, and I clear my throat, reminding myself that it's not okay to objectify this man in a sexual way. Even though without his shirt it's really hard not to consider what might be past his defined V-line.

"Okay, can you call me a cab or something?" I ask, my voice cracking. Stupid horny thoughts.

"Who will watch you when you get home?"

"Watch me?"

"Yes, your head. If you sleep, you need someone to wake you every few hours to check on you."

"I..." Well, it's only been me since Cinita bailed.

"You live alone," he states. I hate how he already knows that, but he acts like he knows everything about me. I look him dead in the eye, still trying to avoid his gaze, and nod. He curses under his breath. "I'm going to take a shower. You can get into my bed in the meantime."

"What?" I snap to attention. "I'm not—"

"Now, Lena." He starts to walk away, and when I don't follow, he calls out, "I'm not being liable for your death only hours after you signed a new contract to privately perform for me."

Oh, so he's saving his own ass. It makes sense. but still... He looks over his shoulder, that no-nonsense gaze landing on me. My feet start moving at this silent command that seems more potent than the first. I follow him down the hallway, a massive space without a single painting or picture on the walls. He's waiting at the end of the hall, holding open a door.

I peer inside, and it's just like the rest of his home—practically bare. A large bed is centered against the far wall, two side tables, a mirror on his cupboard and no other furniture. But I do see a TV across from the bed. But when I take two more steps in, I notice a large painting of a ballet dancer. It's unsettling since he most likely associates it with Cinita.

"I can go home," I say. "Call a friend."

"It's late; get in bed. I don't sleep anyway, so I can check on you."

"How do you not sleep?" I ask, my brows pulling together.

"Just get in the bed, sunshine. I want to shower." I bite my lip to hold in the old man joke that comes to mind about it being past his bedtime.

Am I out of my fucking mind? Well, yeah, but I also have a concussion and passed out on the floor minutes ago, so what's the worst that could happen?

"Shoes off before you get on my bed," he orders. I walk past a large mirror on his cupboard and look at myself. My head has dried blood on it, and the bandage covers my forehead near my hairline. I look like a hot mess; my hair is everywhere, and most of it has fallen out of the tie I had it pulled back in.

"Do you at least watch TV?" I ask as he pulls the covers back. I just can't imagine him watching... well, anything.

He grabs the remote without answering. "Here, get in bed and put some shit on. Don't die while I shower." He throws the remote back on the bed, then stalks past me and straight into the bathroom.

Not long after, I hear the shower turn on as I look around. It's so bare. Apart from the bed, you wouldn't even think someone lives here. Sitting on the mattress, I kick my shoes off and cross my legs as I look for something that might tell me this man won't kill me while I sleep. I know I should run, but I'm so fucking tired that I can't fight it or him. And if he wanted to kill me, surely he would have done it by now, right? I mean, I passed out, and he called a doctor. Clearly, that's a good sign. Isn't it?

Fuck, I don't even know. I hear the shower cut off, and I quickly turn the TV on. The volume is up high and assaults my ears. When I look up, I see a naked woman on the screen, and a man lies on the bed stroking his hard cock as he beckons her to come closer.

Shit, is this porn?
How do I turn this off?
"Tell me, baby, front or back," she whispers and

turns around to give him her ass. He slaps it as he gets up and spits on his fingers before he shoves them up her ass.

"I'll take this later," he says, then slides his very hard cock into her pussy. I'm trying to switch the channel and failing miserably, but I'm also stuck in a trance, watching it. So much so that I scream when Alek speaks.

"Do you like it?" he asks, standing in the bathroom doorway, wearing long, black cotton pants. He casually walks around to the other side of the bed and then climbs in. He looks way too good, lounging beside me in nothing but those pants. How could he look better than the man on screen? I wonder if his cock is just as big.

Fuck. Clearly, I need to get laid. It's been too long —a year, to be exact.

I've been focusing so much on my career that I haven't really had time to date anyone. Or wanted to either.

Maybe I should invest in some toys.

I snap back to my current reality with a half-naked man beside me, dazed that I lost focus so quickly.

"It was already on," I tell him, handing him the remote as if it were poisonous. He takes it and switches the channel. "Does porn help you sleep?"

"Why? You want to watch some to help you sleep?"

The only light in the room comes from the glow of the TV, so I look at the screen to see he put on the news. I scowl. I hate the news. "You prefer the porn?" he asks, noticing my reaction.

"I prefer neither."

"Has it been so long since you've seen a cock that you can't help but blush?" he asks. I turn to look at him, shocked that he has the audacity to ask me something so personal. Well, at least that confirms he's not a robot. He does understand the motions between being a woman and a man.

I then notice he's not wearing his leather gloves.

"Why do you wear gloves?" He clearly hates physical contact, and I wonder how someone can cringe away from a touch.

"Why don't you like porn?" he throws back.

I turn onto my side, giving him my back.

This man is insufferable.

Maybe not a robot, though.

But possibly a vault. Unmovable and most likely empty.

"Put on a movie," I tell him. He switches the channel to a horror movie about a nun. *Fuck*. I close my eyes and try to think of something else.

"Scared of nuns too? Fuck. Cock and nuns; weird combination." He changes the channel again, landing on a comedy. How did he know that? He wouldn't have been able to see my face. The bed shuffles slightly, and curiosity gets the better of me. I peek over my shoulder and see a book in his hands.

Hmm… didn't take him for the reading type at all.

"Go to sleep, sunshine," he growls out.

"Make sure I wake up, okay?" I say. "I'm too young to die." Before he can say anything, I add, "And no, that wasn't an old man joke."

"You're a strange one."

I don't know why, but a smile tugs at the corner of my mouth, because he is the last person who should be calling anyone weird.

CHAPTER 12
Aleksandr

She's a quiet sleeper but also a mover. Or maybe I'm overly conscious because I haven't had anyone sleep in my bed since Anya and I were children and she was scared of our foster father in the second home we were in before Meredith, our final foster mother, took us in. Meredith is the very same old bitch who Anya put a bullet in months ago when she uncovered she'd been the one to kill our parents when we were four.

That doesn't disturb me in the slightest, but the fact that Lena has shifted numerous times beside me does. It's been two hours since she fell asleep, and she's mumbled a few things, but I can't decipher what she's saying. Perhaps she's having nightmares?

Putting on my gloves, I lean over and brace myself

as I give her shoulder a nudge. Her shoulder is softer than I imagined it to be, even through the glove, and I try to focus on that instead of the uproar of immediate disgusted oppression. She grumbles something but falls soundly back to sleep. I curse under my breath, tempted to hit her with a pillow. I nudge her again, a little harder this time. Her eyes fly open, and she looks at me with startled blue eyes.

"What's my name?" I ask.

"Asshole," she mutters, turning back over. I guess that's a good enough answer. She falls asleep again pretty quickly, and over the following six hours, I wake her two more times before I get out of bed. I didn't sleep, but then again, I've hardly been sleeping much at all lately.

Not that I was a big sleeper to begin with. But my mind is getting tired now. And I can't afford not to be sharp. Climbing out of bed, I walk into my en suite bathroom. I slide off my black sleeping pants and am grabbing for my change of clothing when she walks in.

"Shit, I need to pee," she says groggily. I straighten and look at her in the mirror. Her attention is focused on my ass.

"Pee." I wave to the toilet. She gives a little hop on each leg before deciding to push past me as I put on my pants. I reach for my black dress shirt but notice her staring at me through the mirror, hopping from side to side in her flowing dress.

"Can you leave?"

"You're asking me to leave my own bathroom?" I ask incredulously.

"Well, don't make it fucking weird. I'll sing for you, but I'm not going to piss in front of you. That's weird."

"What if you piss *on* me?"

She stares at me, taken aback.

"It was a joke," I add.

"No reason to gain a personality now, Mr. Happy. Now, get out. You don't pay enough to see the show." She shoos me out.

I shake my head as I take my shirt and close the door behind me. Kicked out of my own bathroom.

I swear she's just as pushy as Anya, if not worse.

I hook the dress shirt over my shoulders and leave it unbuttoned as I go through my drawer of gloves. I grab a pile of cash and place it on the bedside table for her. I have numerous stashes of money throughout the house. When I begin to button up my shirt, she comes out of the bathroom, seeming unsure as she looks between me and the door.

"Okay, so this was great and all." Her cheeks flush

as she adds, "I only vaguely remember last night, but we didn't...?"

I wait for her to finish the sentence.

"Never mind. I need to go home. Can we not tell my boss about this?"

When I don't reply, she takes that as confirmation enough. I nod toward the side of the bed she slept on. There's a little bit of dried blood on the pillow.

"I paid you," I tell her, and she scrunches her brows up.

"For what?"

"For your time, which I took away. Well, considering you smashed your own head and my car in the process, you would consider it generous, yes?"

She seems shocked. "And you're also still paying my wage with the new contract?" she asks, confused and still not moving toward the money.

"Yes. Now, take your money. I have a driver waiting for you."

She seems hesitant to take the money but does so anyway. "I'm sorry I can't help you with Cinita. But everything going forward will be strictly business, right? Just singing?"

I don't reply because she won't like the answer.

"Okay," she says, putting her hands in the air. "I have shit to do. So thanks, I guess."

She walks past me, and I adjust my collar.

She says my name over her shoulder, and I turn toward her. "Thanks for not touching me while I slept."

"Why the fuck would I do that?" Not that I didn't think about it. Her skin is stunning, and a part of me wanted to touch, taste even. But I know how loud the voices will become, revolted by the idea. I wonder, though, if, in time, they would lessen with her.

I squash that thought.

She throws me a smile over her shoulder on the way out. "Goodbye. Thanks for the injury."

I shake my head and go to the window to watch as she leaves out the front door, where Clay, one of Anya's men, waits for her. I can imagine the questions Anya will have about her, but I don't trust anyone more to drop her off other than myself.

I'm due to receive a shipment of guns with River this morning, and I doubt Little Miss Sunshine would be able to swallow that harsh reality.

I thought I was done with Cinita six months ago, but she somehow keeps pulling me back in. On the other hand, this woman couldn't get rid of me soon enough.

But I have other things in mind for her.

CHAPTER 13
Lena

Another four thousand dollars in cash. Shit, maybe I should get my head injured more often. But right now, all I can think is the money cannot possibly be worth this shit. I'm furiously wiping down the bar from spills, trying my hardest to ignore a set of blazing green eyes aimed in my direction. The whisky he ordered over an hour ago has barely been touched. He looks out of place here. He's in his usual all black and looks way too expensive to be in this run-down bar.

"Lena, who's the tall, broody, handsome hunk looking your way?" Kara, one of the women I work with, asks.

At this point, it's too hard and awkward to deny we don't know each other, because I'm pretty certain if I get Mal, the bouncer, to ask him to leave, he'll be the one who leaves on a stretcher. And Mal is as big as they come and twice the width of Alek, yet I'm certain Alek would definitely come out on top.

"He's one of the sponsors of the theater company I sing for," I say dismissively. I catch a glimpse of myself in the mirror behind the bar, admiring the red headband I had to wear today to hide the bandage on my forehead.

"Is he stalking you?" Kara asks. "If stalkers look like that, then sign me up."

"It's not all it's cracked up to be," I say under my breath, not loud enough for her to hear. And I'm sure as hell not announcing that I was in his bed this morning. Or that I crashed his very expensive car the evening before.

Besides, it's not me he's obsessed with. It's Cinita. So why the fuck is he here?

"Hey, bartender, another one." One of the patrons snaps his fingers at me.

I tuck the bar towel into the back of my tight jeans and snap my fingers in front of his face. "Do this again, and I'll cut you off."

He seems taken aback but doesn't say anything as I grab his empty glass and pour another beer for him. I can't help but look up as I wait for the pint to pour. Alek's green eyes are locked on me.

I huff out a breath of irritation. *Why is he here?*

Is it because I refuse to quit? Not that he has any say in what I do and don't do. Sure, it doesn't pay much, but it never hurts to have a fallback plan in case something happens.

"Like the new belly ring, girl," Kara says as she comes up beside me to pour a beer for another customer.

I look down past my crop top and to my stomach, almost forgetting that I'd changed it a few days ago. It has a cute little emerald in it. My only splurge for the month.

"Thank you," I say, finding something small to appreciate for the day.

"Matches your new boyfriend's eyes, doesn't it?"

I turn the tap off and grit out, "He's not my boyfriend."

I turn back to the customer and hand him his pint. He puts down cash and includes a generous tip. Good.

I put the money for the drink in the till and the tip in the tip jar. Popping my hand on my hip, I face Alek, who's still staring.

"Kara, I'll be two secs," I tell her. It's a quiet night,

so I can slip out for a moment. I approach Alek and glare at him.

"Most people don't flirt with their whiskey and actually drink it." I mean, he did purchase the most expensive whisky in here and gave me a two-hundred-dollar tip. The least he can do is actually drink it.

"You should stop wearing things like that." He motions to my shirt.

My eyebrows shoot up, and I stare at him in disbelief. "Like a crop top?" *Are you fucking kidding me?* "Please don't tell me you came all this way to tell me how to dress."

He says nothing.

Oh my god, this asshole.

"Cinita isn't coming here. She never has and never will. She doesn't even know I work this job because she didn't exactly stay around long enough to find out."

"I'm not here for Cinita."

"Then what are you here for, Alek?"

His jaw clenches, and he focuses on his glass as he swivels it in one spot.

I throw my hands in the air. I'm done with this conversation. When I turn to walk away, he speaks again.

"I wanted to make sure you hadn't died. That's all."

My eyebrows shoot up in surprise, and I swing my dark-brown hair over my shoulder to stare him down. "Most people would send a 'hope you get better soon' card."

His brow furrows in confusion, and it's strange to see this man offer any type of expression. "You could be dead in the time I mail a card."

"I'm not dead, Alek. Clearly."

"No. But *he* will be if he keeps staring at your ass." His jaw tightens again as he flicks his gaze to the patron who snapped his finger at me earlier. "And that crop top," he adds with a hint of sass. I almost want to laugh at how strange it is to see him be anything but serious.

"Why does that even matter to you? If he's tipping well, I don't care."

"Were you not satisfied by the funds you received this morning?" he says, and it looks like he's about to shatter the glass.

Kara walks past as he says it, and her eyebrows shoot up.

I step forward, closing my fingers like a beak in front of him, miming that he should shut his mouth. "Can you not say things like that?" I lean over and quietly whisper, "You make it sound like I'm some kind of hooker."

"There are plenty who make good money from such services. I don't know why you're looking down on it."

"I'm not looking down—" I stop myself. "You're awfully chatty tonight, and you can direct that to some other woman to fixate on. I am not Cinita. I don't know where she is and want nothing else to do with this absurdity. If you keep showing up to my workplaces, then I'm tearing up that contract," I say and walk away before he can reply.

Did the motherfucker really comment on how I look? As far as I'm concerned, he's the only one who can't stop staring.

When I return to the bar, I notice the patron who'd snapped his fingers at me has left. I notice him in the back of the bar, past the pool tables, stumbling to the door that leads to the back alley.

"Sir, no, that's not the exit!" I shout, then curse under my breath. Why do they always go that way? It's a closed-off alley that leads to nowhere, yet even when there's a sign that clearly says "'NOT AN EXIT,'" a drunk fucker does it every time and sets the fire alarm off.

Annnd... off goes the alarm. Yep, just like said. I roll my eyes, and Kara is quick to bite out a curse. A lot of our regulars don't even flinch as I go to find the man while Kara deals with the alarm. I look around, but Mal, the security guard, must be on his break.

I open the back door and find the man vomiting into the trash can. I sigh. Maybe quitting this job isn't such a bad idea.

"Come on, sir, you can't be back here. Come back inside," I say with arms crossed over my chest.

He wipes away the vomit, and I notice then that tears are in his eyes. "She left me for him!" he sobs.

He steps toward me, arms stretched as if to hug me, but I put my hands up. "I'm sorry to hear that, but you need to come back inside."

"You wouldn't leave me, would you? You seem nice," he says. A cold chill runs down my spine, and I put my hand on the pepper spray in my back pocket. It's always there because a girl can never be too safe.

"You need to come inside," I repeat, opening the door. Alek steps out as the man reaches for me. It all happens so fast that I can't even scream.

Alek grabs his outstretched hand and breaks it, then slams his head against the dumpster. My hands cover my mouth, shocked by his violent outburst. Any fear I might've had from the drunk man is quickly replaced by this monster. When he looks back at me, those piercing green eyes stare at me as if from the darkest corner of hell.

A dog barks in the distance as the door slams shut behind me. I realize I'm aiming the pepper spray at Alek now.

"You intend to spray me with that?" he asks, brow raised.

"He didn't deserve that," I say, but my words sound distant.

"He also doesn't deserve to put his hands on you."

He goes to step toward me, but I raise the spray higher. "I will, Alek. I don't care if you're a sponsor."

He steps forward, and I press down on the button. He's so fast. His gloved hand covers the spray and my hand. His other lands on my hip as he slams me against the brick wall.

My heart races as I stare into those forest green eyes, my breath coming in hot and fast, my chest rising and falling as he consumes me.

His jaw clenches, and I know it's because he's touching me. It physically pains him to do so, but then, unexpectedly, his gaze drops to my lips, and the atmosphere changes. Fear begins to mingle with... a warmth spreading down to my core.

No.

I can't be turned on by this, can I?

"I'll send a card next time, sunshine," he says as he pushes away from me and the back door opens.

Kara and Mal take in the drunk who's sobbing and holding his hand with blood oozing from his forehead.

"Oh my gosh, Lena, what happened?" Kara asks as Mal looks between Alek and the drunk man.

"He tried..." I clear my throat as I try to bring my thoughts into focus. "He tried to grab me." I might be scared of Alek, but when I recall the events, the man had tried to grab me. And that is far more terrifying.

When I look around, I see Alek has already slipped back inside.

Mal is quick to deal with the sobbing man as Kara rubs up and down my arms. I don't hear what she's saying as I walk back inside and notice his expensive whiskey still untouched. And Alek is gone.

What the fuck just happened?

CHAPTER 14
Lena

My boss at the bar lets me go home early. My head is reeling, replaying what happened tonight. It isn't the first time a guy has tried to get grabby with me. But I've never had a deranged psychopath to stop him before. Just good old Mal. It's a nudge that maybe I should leave the bar job, but it raises so many other questions about why Alek was even there.

I don't understand him and don't think I really want to. But every time I see him, it's like I discover a new layer of him. That maybe he's not entirely a robot. Nope. I'm going to upgrade him to a psychopath.

I walk up the five flights of stairs to my apartment. I pull out my keys and open the door, switching on the light as I step inside. I immediately notice something isn't right.

Cinita's stuff that I had piled near the door looks like someone went through it and forgot to put it back together.

Someone's been in here.

Cinita maybe? She's the only one with a key, right?

Opening my bedroom door, I find all my things ruined. My mattress is cut open, my blankets thrown everywhere, and the room is just a mess of chaotic destruction.

What the actual fuck?

A chill runs down my spine at the thought of someone being in my space. What if it wasn't Cinita? What if someone else was in here?

I look around, but it's a small apartment, and I know whoever was here has already left.

My heart hammers in my chest. This past twenty-four hours have been intense, and the one common factor is a man with green eyes.

Finding the card Alek gave me, I dial his number and press call. I run my hand through my long hair in disbelief. Oh my god, how am I going to replace all of this? He answers on the first ring, and I'm shocked at his efficiency.

"Lena."

"Someone was here and went through Cinita's things and destroyed my apartment," I say. I don't know if he's the right person to call, but he's the only one I have.

"Go outside and wait until I get there," he instructs and hangs up.

"Okay," I reply anyway.

I do as he says, leaving the apartment and not even bothering to lock it on my way out. It's not like they could destroy or take anything else that belonged to me. It's not until I'm already outside that I realize I never gave him my address.

I take a deep breath. Okay, weird shit is definitely happening because of my association with Cinita, no matter how superficial it is. I don't know Alek, and he's intimidating as shit, but instinctually, I think I can trust him.

I mean, he was the first person I called. If I called my parents or brother, they'd force me to leave my job and New York immediately. It would only encourage my mother's reasoning as to why I shouldn't have followed this career path into the city.

I bite the edge of my nail, more furious than anything. How the fuck am I going to replace all of my furniture? I pace the front of my building until I see a car I don't recognize. It makes sense that he'd have a different car now since I wrecked the other one. I watch as he pulls up to the curb and gets out of the car. He walks around to me, adjusting his gloves as he does. I have the urge to run up to him because, fuck, sometimes you just need a hug, but I sure as shit won't get one from this man.

"Did you see anyone?" he asks.

"No, I just got home. And all my shit is ruined," I say, trying not to cry. *Fuck*. I mean, I have that four thousand dollars he gave me, which I was hoping to save. Now I guess I'll have to use it to replace everything.

"Get in the car and lock the doors." He pulls open the passenger door and I climb in, then he shuts it and stalks off. Who would have thought the very man I was running from would be the one I called to come check for any other bad men in my apartment?

I wish Cinita would pop up just so I could strangle her myself for getting me involved in whatever bullshit this is.

I wait for him, bouncing my knees for a good ten minutes. Yet, surprisingly, I feel safe. I look around the interior of the car. I don't know cars, but it's expensive and has that new-car smell. I'd be tempted to snoop out of curiosity but know I'll find nothing. If he doesn't have furniture to make his house look lived in, then his car sure as shit isn't going to have anything personal in it. When he finally comes back out, I open the car door, step out, and look up at him.

"Anything?" I ask.

"Yeah, a mess. How do you live like that?" I scoff at his joke, realizing Alek does have a sense of humor, but it's very dry and only rarely makes an appearance.

"They destroyed everything," I say, biting my lip. "Is it safe, do you think? I need to clean up the mess."

"It's not you who they were after. By the looks of it, nothing was taken. Just destroyed. So yes, it's safe," he says as he scrolls through his phone. I don't know who he could be trying to call at this time.

I cross my arms over my chest, realizing how cold it's starting to get. "They were after her, right? Like you are?"

His finger hovers over the call button on his phone and he looks me over. I imagine someone like Alek is constantly moving. But he pauses as if to accommodate my shock. He nods his head.

"I'll have someone else clean it up for you. Get in the car. You're not staying here tonight."

I let out a laugh. I suppose this is what I get for thinking money could come to me so easily. "And where am I going to stay tonight, Alek? Your house again? No, thank you."

His eyes seem to darken, but he says, "No, I have a meeting I'm currently late for. I plan to drop you off at a hotel for the evening until your apartment is cleaned up."

"Oh. That's nice, I suppose. Wait. Who the fuck has a meeting at two in the morning?" I ask.

He gives me a pointed look as he opens the passenger door, insinuating I shouldn't ask questions I don't want answers to.

A part of me wants to stay in my apartment and start cleaning up, but another part of me just can't be bothered with dealing with this tonight, not with everything else that's been happening.

I get into the car and sit back down. All of this shit sounds like a tomorrow problem.

Alek makes a phone call outside. I don't know who he's talking to, but I overhear him mentioning a cleanup and addressing it immediately.

He slides into the driver's seat and starts the engine. Then he looks at me. "Are you..." He seems at a loss for words. "Okay?"

"*Okay*? Alek, someone destroyed my apartment tonight. I hit my head on a steering wheel like twenty-four hours ago and had a man try to assault me at the bar tonight. So no, I'm not okay."

He nods and pulls away from the curb, and I sigh,

frustrated, almost feeling a little better for being about to scream and shout. I doubt Alek's ever asked anyone in his life if they're okay, but that doesn't make me feel any better.

"Does she have a golden pussy, or are you men just dumb as fuck?" I ask boldly.

"Excuse me?" His eyebrows perk in surprise at my question.

"You men... You aren't the first one to ask about her. But I must say, you're the only one who's gone to such extremes to find her."

"Who else came looking for her?" he asks, and there's a lethal edge to his tone.

"I don't know. I didn't care to ask. Someone stopped by the bar and asked if she still lived with me, and I told them she moved out."

"How long ago?" he barks, and I notice his grip tighten on the steering wheel.

"Fuck, maybe a month ago. Before I met your crazy ass," I tack on. "So, tell me, does she have a golden pussy?"

His head swings to me then. "You want to know if I fucked her?"

He's doing that thing again where he intently stares at me while not looking at the road. It increases my heart rate, and a small thrill rushes through me.

"Yes, I do. Did you fuck her?"

"I don't know if she has a golden pussy because I didn't fuck her." He looks back at the road.

Then why go this far for her?

"Okay, so either you have a savior complex or are just outright stupid."

"I've been called many things, but stupid isn't one of them."

"To your face anyway," I mumble under my breath, and notice the hint of a smile on his lips. It does something to me, easing the tension. It's like I've hit the jackpot by being able to get this man to even give a hint of a smirk.

He pulls over, and I look out the window, my jaw dropping. The hotel is something I know I definitely can't afford.

A well-dressed man in a suit opens my door expectantly and leans down to speak to Alek.

"Mr. Ivanov, your sister phoned, and your suite has already been organized," he says with a charming smile.

Alek nods. "It will be for my guest this evening. Make sure she gets anything she wants, and charge it to my card."

The gentleman nods and steps back.

I feel like I'm in some kind of weird fairy tale.

"You're not coming in with me?" I ask in disbelief.

It feels strange that he wouldn't at least have to go in to the registration desk to sign for it or something. Or is this how all the wealthy people do it?

"No, I'm late for a meeting, remember?"

"Oh. Right," I'm quick to say, and a hot flush rolls over me. "Why would you go this far for me?"

He doesn't answer, and the silence is a tangible weight in the car.

"How old are you?" he asks.

"Twenty-four."

"I'm old enough to know better," he says.

My eyebrows furrow in confusion, and I realize he's not going to elaborate. Because why would he? It's Alek. For some reason, I have the impression it has something to do with our age difference. Does he think I'm too young? I internally chastise myself. *No. I cannot think of him in a romantic light whatsoever.*

"Miss?" prompts the gentleman waiting outside the door.

I step out of the car and look back at Alek.

"Everything will be sorted for you by tomorrow. Go inside and get some sleep," he commands.

The car door is closed for me, and Alek drives away. I'm left to stare up at the hotel, wondering what the fuck just happened.

CHAPTER 15
Aleksandr

I clean up my knives, feeling rather disappointed. Harold Spencer, who is tied to the chair and gagged, gave up his information way too freely. Unfortunately, it checks out with everything I already know about Cinita's last moves.

I'm not in the habit of leaving loose ends—the dead can't talk, after all—but considering he's also a client of our auctions, it's good business to keep him around to continue filling our pockets. At least that's what I'll have him believe for now.

I remove his gag, doing my best not to touch his face.

"You know I hired her for only one night to dance. That's it," he says. I know this because he's already told me as much. Cinita had performed for him two weeks ago, which means she's most likely still in New York. "She can't love anyone. That woman is empty. You believe me, right, Alek?" he says, breathlessly.

The sound of clicking heels makes its way toward me, and I turn to see Anya and River walking in. Her bodyguards, Clay and Vance, are only a few steps behind.

"Couldn't choose a reasonable hour of the morning to conduct business?" she asks indignantly. But I know she has issues sleeping, just as I do. Or maybe that's changed since River.

"Miss Ivanov?" Harold pales at the sight of her. "I think there's been a misunderstanding with all of this."

"Are there misunderstandings when it comes to late payments?" She raises a brow at him.

No, because we only understand money, blood, and business.

"Did you get all the information you needed from him?" she asks me, looking at her manicured nails.

I didn't tell her what I really wanted to discuss with him, using the fact that he can't make his payment because he's drained his newfound fortune that he received from his father's inheritance as an excuse to question him about Cinita.

He's bleeding from a few gashes I've made, but

they're nothing life threatening. Yet. "Yes, I did. He doesn't have the money."

"Wait. What?" Harold says, hopping in his chair. "I can get it. I can get it."

"You've had two weeks, Harold," Anya says sweetly. "Also, it appears my husband has an issue with you personally."

Harold turns a shade paler. River gets a crazed look in his eyes as he steps forward. "Did you try to sell photos of my wife? You see, she can be careless at times with her nudity."

Anya rolls her eyes because, to her, it's nothing. But River will kill tonight for her.

Things have changed since I've returned from Russia. Whereas it was once my role to kill for her, she now has a husband who is just as crazy as us.

I turn to take my leave, and my sister follows me. Harold's screaming begins behind us. I know it'll be quick, though. Unlike Anya and me, who have taken pleasure in torture, River just likes to get the job done.

"Do you want to tell me why you're breaking a random man's hand at a bar and calling me for cleanup duty in some shitty apartment block?" Anya asks as she walks beside me.

I'd rather not.

She steps in front of me, and I feel my jaw clench.

"Alek, you don't even go to bars. What the fuck is happening? Does this involve Cinita? Because I swear to God, I will hunt her down myself and slit her throat to end this shit."

I clench my gloved fists. I love my sister. But her threats are as valid as mine. She will do it. "It's not Cinita. I owe..." I don't know how to finish that sentence.

"Owe? We don't owe anyone shit," she defiantly says.

"I misspoke."

She pops her hip with her hand on it. "Oh no, you're very intentional with your words, Alek. Who do you owe?"

I shake my head. "It's not like that. But I do need you to do something for me."

Her eyebrows raise in surprise.

I rarely ask my sister for anything, but even I know when I'm out of my depth.

CHAPTER 16
Lena

I honestly thought I wouldn't be able to sleep, but as soon as I stepped into the oversized hotel suite that's two times the size of my apartment and found the bed, I passed out. The sheets and blankets are divine and probably cost the same amount as all the furniture destroyed in my apartment.

I ordered room service twice. Because why the fuck not. This shit didn't start happening until Alek rocked up in my life, so why not take advantage of this moment? I'm searching through the multiple outfits that were delivered. Apparently, I can choose any of them I want, as they're mine now.

Whatever the fuck that means.

My mouth gaped at the expensive price tags, but the one I was most inclined toward was a loose yellow dress. I'm under no illusion that Alek picked these out himself, because if he had, they'd all only come in one color. Black.

Whoever chose them has some serious style.

Looking at all this nice stuff, I contemplate setting my apartment on fire.

But then I remember I don't have insurance.

This is the lifestyle I've dreamed of. Well, sort of.

I want to see how far I can make it with my singing. I want to make it to Broadway and thrive there until I settle down and have a family.

A knock on the door rattles me, and I whip my head in its direction.

My heart is pounding. I know it's probably Alek, but I can't help the paranoia that causes me to hesitate. I know it's Cinita they're all after. Whoever "they" are.

If it was someone else, surely they wouldn't knock, right? I grab a glass vase just in case, and pull the door open. Standing there is the redheaded lady from the auction. What was her name again? Anya? I think so. She has on a tight black dress, with red heels to match her fiery red hair that's pulled back in a ponytail. Her emerald-green eyes look me up and down.

"Why is my brother wanting to help you?" Those are the first words to leave her mouth.

"Umm."

"Umm is not a word," she snaps. Fuck, she's brutal.

"Your brother, Alek?" She looks at me like I've grown a second head. "He didn't help me. In fact, he kidnapped me, tried to make me get out of the car under a scary bridge, then made me stay at his house," I tell her. Her gaze falls to the vase in my hand.

"Do you plan to hit me with it?" she asks.

"Do you plan to hit me?" I ask back. "Because if so, then, yes, I will hit you with it."

"And are you on drugs or potentially have a complex where you have to please men?"

"A complex?" I ask, then it dawns on me. "Oh, you mean like Cinita." That makes sense. She does have that.

"Do you know Cinita well?" she questions as her gaze narrows, and I can tell she is not very well-liked.

"Not well enough for our association to be the reason my apartment looks like a bomb hit it," I mumble, feeling deflated. "Maybe I should've just accepted a loan from my parents to get my own place in the first place," I say as I place the vase back on the stand near the door. She makes no move to step inside.

She eyes my jeans and crop top once again. "Get changed. I'll wait downstairs in the car." She turns to leave.

"Get changed for what?" I shout. "You and your brother are so bossy." When I add the last part, she spins back around and raises a perfect brow.

"You clearly need assistance in"—she waves a hand at me—"life. I offered to help since Alek has to work."

Most people would probably be offended by that remark, but I've come to discover it's the Ivanov siblings' specialty.

"Help with what?" I ask.

"Furniture."

I pale. I can just imagine what type of furniture they have in mind, and it's not the cheap kind that comes in a box that I build myself.

"Oh no, I don't want him paying for anything," I say, shaking my head.

"He isn't. I am." She turns, and her ponytail whips out behind her. "And I hate to be kept waiting," she adds. As the elevator doors open, I recognize Clay, the guy who drove me home from Alek's two nights ago.

She studies me, as if I'm a tiny bug on the wall, as the elevator doors close.

I shut the door in a panic because I definitely think pissing someone like Anya off would be a mistake.

I feel almost overdressed as I grab the loose yellow dress I was admiring only minutes before. I look at the wide selection of heels and then the boots I wore with my jeans last night. They work, so I opt to wear them instead.

Checking myself in the mirror, I run my hands through my hair. The red headband from last night doesn't match my dress, so I quickly change the bandage to a smaller Band-Aid and then all but run out the door with my things.

When I make it downstairs, Clay is holding the passenger door open for me. Anya has her glasses on, her nose pointed high, as she looks down at her phone.

"Thank you," I say to Clay as I climb in. He nods curtly. I notice another man sitting in the driver's seat, and realize these two were the ones standing outside of the dressing room at the auction I was hired to dance at.

I wonder, if I hadn't gone to that, would any of this escalated to where it is now?

"Did you even shower?" Anya asks.

"No, you told me to hurry," I remind her.

"At least tell me you'll shower when you get back."

"Of course I will," I scoff.

"That head gash looks nasty," she comments. "So does Alek's car, by the way."

I cringe at that.

She gestures for the driver to start the car. It's intimidating as shit to sit in the back of the car with such a powerful woman. These men are clearly at her beck and call. My parents might claim I have an attitude, but mine is a candle flame compared to the inferno of Anya Ivanov.

"So what is his name? Is it just Alek?" I ask, wanting to fill the silence.

"Aleksandr," she says with a slight Russian accent. I like the way it leaves her mouth. It suits him more than Alek.

Anya makes a call and almost immediately begins negotiating a price for, from what I can tell, is a rare jewel. It makes sense, I guess, since she's sporting some pretty expensive jewelry. Compared to her, I almost feel like the teenager Alek once described me as. I'm only two years out of college and truly starting my career now, whereas this woman has built an empire and she doesn't look old enough for it.

My phone buzzes, and I look at the text message that comes through.

> Mr. Happy: You can stay in the hotel for as long as required until your apartment is ready.

I squint at the message. I mean, it's as direct as any message could be. I reply.

> Me: Thank you, but you've both already done so much for me. If I can at least have a new mattress by today, I'll go back home.

No reply. Until my message receives a thumbs-up emoji. *Thumbs-up? Seriously?* I stare at it in disbelief, reminding myself that Alek probably has no idea about the silent social killer of the thumbs-up emoji.

The car comes to a stop at a store I know I should never walk into because it's one for the rich. Anya gets out. Someone opens my door, and she doesn't wait for me. She walks in as if she owns the place, and starts bossing people around. They all jump at her command. A glass of champagne is handed to me, which she immediately takes from my hand.

"Water for her," she says, then looks at me. "Did you forget about your head?" She taps her head and looks around. "Okay, your current style is more dumpster chic. Let's change that up a little."

My jaw drops. Did she just say my style was dumpster chic?

"I'm sorry, but at least my home has any type of style. Have you seen your brother's attempt at home decor?"

A vein in her temple pulses, and she smooths a hand over her dress. "He won't allow me to decorate for him. He's told me multiple times no."

A mischievous thought comes to mind. Maybe it's the bump to the head. Or a small part of me who wants to get back at Alek a little for all the confusing hell he's put me through these past weeks.

"Okay, but he hasn't said no to me." I smile at her.

That's when I see her smile for the first time.

"No, I guess he hasn't."

CHAPTER 17
Aleksandr

When I walk into my house, I see it's full of furniture—a lot of it. And a brunette is sitting on a couch in my living room with her feet tucked under her ass as she laughs at something on the TV. The TV I didn't have before.

The color scheme has changed, and I squint into the corner where there's a vase full of fresh flowers. Daisies, to be precise.

"You break into everyone's house and fill it with furniture?" I ask, scanning the space. I should've known better than to leave my sister and Lena alone together, but Anya doesn't take a liking to anyone. But she'll also find a loophole in any situation.

I told her she couldn't change anything in my

house. So she used this ray of sunshine to do it. Then again, I don't think Lena would let anyone use her.

She flicks her hair over her shoulder and looks up at me as she chews on some popcorn, then holds out the bowl to me in offering.

"Want some?" My stomach growls, but I pin her with a stare until she answers my previous question. "And no, *you* technically bought it. I just used your card, the one you told your sister to use." She winks as she holds up the popcorn, somewhat smug with herself. I reach in and grab a handful. "Your sister's a vault. She wouldn't give me much in the way of details about you. But she loves you, that's for sure."

"We're twins," I tell her, and her eyes go wide.

"Oh, I see. That's why."

"Why what?"

"You both seem to hate the world." She smiles and pops another piece of popcorn into her mouth as she turns her attention back to the TV.

It's peculiar that she's made herself right at home, considering how much she fears me. But right now, I don't notice a hint of that previous trepidation. Maybe that bump to the head really got to her.

"Aren't you getting a little too cozy here?" I ask.

She shrugs, her gaze not shifting from the television. "Hanging around your sister makes you less scary.

Besides, when was the last time you actually had a guest over?"

"Guest's are those who are invited," I remind her.

"'You're only a guest if it's a home. Now, because of your sister and me, this place is a home. And, honestly, I wanted to see your face when you walked in," she says with a smile, then crunches down on another piece of popcorn.

The nerve of this woman. I can only imagine it was spending time with my sister today that encouraged this type of confidence in her. And, for some reason, I haven't thrown her out yet.

I look back to the television.

"What are you watching?" I scrunch my nose up as a screeching woman yells at another, her hands waving around and tears streaming down her face.

"Oh, *The Real Housewives*. I'm obsessed," she says giddily.

I let out a sigh and undo the top three buttons on my shirt. "Can you be obsessed somewhere that's not my house?"

"No. I ordered dinner, and it should be here soon. Shopping all day makes me hungry." She turns the TV up louder as the doorbell rings. "Wow. What timing. You can get that since you're standing, and make sure you tip," she yells, not looking back over her shoulder.

I glance around, almost expecting to be recorded so this can somehow be used against me for blackmail or used against me by Anya.

When I realize it's just us, I'm baffled that she's telling me what to do. Yet I find myself walking to the door and opening it to find a teenager holding a bag of food.

"That will be fifty-five dollars, please." He holds out his hand expectantly. When he looks up at me, he turns pale. I have that effect on people.

"She didn't pay?" I ask.

He's nervous as he shakes his head. "No, sir. She called to place the order. Payment is due on delivery."

Reaching into my pocket, I pull out a hundred dollars and drop it into his hand.

"I don't have change for that," he's quick to say.

"Keep the change," I tell him, closing the door once I grab the bag of food.

I walk over to the couch and hold the bag out to her. "Take your food and go."

She looks up at me. "No, you're going to eat with me. I ordered enough for both of us."

My jaw tightens. Definitely a bad idea to let her and Anya spend any time with each other because now she's starting to boss me around just like my sister does.

"I'm not hungry." But just as I say it, my stomach betrays me and rumbles loudly. She tries to hide the smug smile and taps the spot next to her.

"Sit. I'll get some plates and silverware." Lena stands and heads to the kitchen.

I hear cupboards open and close, and I look back in confusion.

Anyone would think this is her home.

"Your sister told me you most likely haven't eaten since yesterday," she shouts from the kitchen.

I don't say anything, just find myself reluctantly watching the drama unfold on the television. *Do people really act like that?*

Lena comes back, holding two plates and two forks. I eye her from head to toe in the long, flowy, yellow dress. It reminds me of sunshine. Her gaze drops to the couch.

"Sit, I'm hungry," she says.

She waits until I sit, then she follows me down and opens the food. It's Thai food. "Pad Thai is amazing. I went to Thailand once when I turned eighteen. Best food ever," she tells me as she dishes out some food and then hands me the plate. "Yours."

She makes a pointed look at my gloves but says nothing as I take it.

I stare at it. "Don't you like Thai food?" she asks, concerned.

"I don't dislike it," I say. I just haven't had it since... well, I don't know if I've ever tried it. Most of my meals are prepared for me. I don't care much for taste besides in my whisky. As long as it's nutritional.

"Oh my god, are you carb counting or something?"

"No," I say, dipping my eyebrows. "Is that usually what men do who you share pad Thai with?"

She tucks her feet under her ass again, and a wicked smile appears on her lips. "You curious about my type, Aleksandr?"

The way my name falls from her lips does something to me. I like it. A lot. Too much.

"What?" she says around a mouthful of food as she tries to look between me and the TV.

"Did you and my sister furnish your apartment, or did you get distracted by changing mine without my consent?"

She's half distracted by the television. It's a scene where two women are now discussing the drama that unfolded in the previous scene.

"They're unpacking it all now. We prioritized here first," she admits with a sheepish smile.

I take a bite of the food and am surprised by it's

flavor and that I like it. Lena laughs from beside me at the woman on the TV, and I realize it might be because of her company that it tastes more delicious.

I slowly eat the meal while watching Lena as she watches the TV. She has so many expressions, so much joy and freedom about her. It's so different to the first time I saw her sing.

On stage, she's focused and the center of attention, and she sucks everything and everyone around her in with her talent and poise. Here, she's herself. Just Lena. I think this is the first time I've seen the real her, with her defenses down, around me, and that's a dangerous thing.

She looks at me now and then drops her gaze to my empty plate. "Wow, you ate that fast," she comments as she goes to take my plate, but I grab hers instead.

She looks confused as I take them. Hell, even I'm confused. "You're a guest, are you not?"

"I don't know, am I?"

I don't know what I'm doing. I don't have guests. I don't offer to take dishes, because I don't eat with others. Besides my sister, of course.

I set the plates on the side table and look at the small bandage on her forehead. "Show me your wound."

"Oh," she says as she reaches up and fingers it.

"I can have a look," I say, and brace myself as I get closer to her. I know the voices will start to scream if I touch her. But for some reason, I need to make sure the injury is okay.

It's only a feather-light touch as I pinch the edge of the Band-Aid.

Filthy. Isolating. Pain.

I push away the ambush of mixed emotions and words that flood me, and focus only on the task at hand. The wound is clean and looks like it's healing nicely. Good.

I continue pushing down the nauseating swirl of commotion that tries to tear me apart.

"Alek," she says, and that's when I realize how close I'm leaning in. Her voice is like a white flag for me in the war raging inside me. I can smell her floral-scented perfume. This close, I notice the finer details of her features, like the smile creases at her eyes. I raise my thumb, tracing them, focusing on only her, as it seems to keep the rowdiness away. It's still there but only a niggle compared to how loudly it usually screams.

I trail my thumb down to her lips, and she sucks in her breath. My gaze flicks back to hers. Fucking stunning.

A wild bird inside, soaring. Singing. An inferno and phoenix all in one.

My cock twitches as my gaze dips down to her breasts. This fucking woman has no idea how perfect her body is built, and I can't stand it when she wears those crop tops. Can't stand the way men look at her when she passes by.

Mine.

I want—no, *need*—to at least taste her.

I dip my head to hers, licking her upper lip. She tastes like cherries, and I force my tongue into her mouth. A small moan escapes her, and I press into her. Deeper, harder, and demanding, all the ways my body needs her.

Her hands feather around my neck as she pulls me in. I tense, pushing away the nauseating swirl in my gut, overridden by the need for more of her.

Disgusting. Beautiful. Chilling. Warmth.
Her.

I use her as my anchor as I maneuver her onto my lap and let her straddle me. My cock firmly presses against my pants, screaming to be deep inside her.

Fucking perfect.

She's starving. Ravishing me, and I'll give her all that I have to offer.

Her body grinds against me, every touch a warm embrace colliding with the screaming, revolting ugliness that surfaces within me. But I push through it because I want her more. I slide my hand under her dress and over her outer thigh. And, fuck me, if that ass is not my undoing.

I fucking need her like my next breath.

I grab her throat, and her eyelids burst open in surprise as she pulls away slightly.

We share a breath as she goes to lean in, but I pin her where she is, control slithering back in.

Too young. Too good. Too real.

Disgusting. Alone. Blood.

"I'm sorry," I croak. She's confused as she awkwardly gets off me.

"I don't mind the throat grabbing," she's quick to say. "You just surprised me is all."

She's not the only one who's surprised.

I wipe at my mouth. *What the fuck just happened?*

I've fucked plenty of women, but none where the voices stopped. This fucking beacon of light of a woman was the only time I'd felt a sense of serenity.

And it's fucking terrifying.

I know how to fight my demons. I *become* the demon.

But not Lena. She's too good for this part of my world.

"I'll call for Clay to take you home," I say as I stand.

"Wait? What?" She sits upright.

I step out of the room. Because if I make her mine, I won't let her go.

I'll break her into a million pieces, killing that light inside her.

Whereas I might take satisfaction from it elsewhere, I just can't do it to her.

She screams out my name, but I'm already gone.

CHAPTER 18

Lena

The following week at rehearsals is hectic, the busiest we've been since I started here. It's probably because it's the holidays, but it's been good to be busy and then go home and crash—on my bed with my new mattress. I also got new locks installed thanks to Anya.

She's a very prickly person, but, somehow, I still quite enjoyed her company. Weird.

It's nice to have something to focus on, and because of our extra show times, I haven't worked at the bar since the incident in the alley with the drunk guy. I still haven't decided whether I want to go back.

I haven't heard or seen Alek since that night we had Thai food at his place. Not that I expected to see him or hoped to. I just kind of thought I would. I still can't make any sense of that night. He's hot as fuck. Clearly deranged. Yet I was straddling him like my life fucking depended on it. The man can fucking kiss. And then he snapped shut. Switched off completely and was out the door. I don't know if it has to do with his dislike of touching people or if it's just me, but either way, the guy can go fuck himself.

I take a deep breath as I stand just offstage, waiting for my cue to re-enter and sing. Performing pulls me away from all the bullshit and crazy thoughts. When it's time, I take my place at center stage. The lights dim, and I embrace this part of me. My warmth, my soul, my inner being. The part of me that must be shared with the world that I couldn't even stop when I was forced to try.

I'm free.

I'm myself.

It flows out of me, this emotion and power of the song I've made my own. It's about a woman who has lost her lover and is bidding him goodbye. It rattles me, consumes me, then comes to a stop.

There's silence as I look out at the full house, then applause breaks out as people stand from their chairs. I can't help but smile every time, and I'm relieved that I was able to connect with each and every one of them.

The other cast members flood the stage, and we stand hand in hand and bow before the curtain drops.

"A powerhouse as always!" Julie hugs me from the side.

I timidly smile, exhausted and exhilarated all at once. When I go to leave the stage, I spot Anya in the crowd right at the front. She offers me a nod with no smile as she walks toward the curtain as others make their way to leave. Matthew approaches Anya and escorts her backstage.

I'm surprised to see her but also thrilled and wanting to know what she thinks of the performance. I'm smiling when she comes into view.

"Anya, I didn't expect to see you here," I say honestly.

"Why are you smiling?" she asks, which makes me smile more. It was a very Anya thing to say.

"Did you like the show?" I ask.

"No," she says, and Matthew flinches at her direct honesty. "But your voice is quite magical, and I stayed for that alone."

"Wow, well, thank you," I reply, knowing that's probably as big of compliment as she can give. She turns to look at Matthew, as if shocked he's still standing there.

"Please walk away now." She shoos him off. He

stutters, then nods as he's quick to find himself elsewhere.

We both watch him hurry away, then I face her expectantly. Because Anya isn't the type of woman to simply drop by unless she has something she needs or wants.

"Look, out of the women my brother has come across in life, you are probably the one I least hate."

I don't have the heart to tell her that apparently her brother doesn't seem all that keen on me, since last time he all but ran out of the room after kissing me.

"You and your' brother aren't good at this compliment thing, are you?" I smile at her sweetly. She doesn't smile back.

"As I was saying. River suggested for our birthday we do a small, intimate dinner. Alek hates celebrating our birthday, but we're turning thirty, so why the hell not." She puts her hands on her hips, as if it pains her to celebrate a birthday. "So your answer?"

"My answer for what?"

"Will you come?" She huffs, as if I should have known what her question was.

I remind myself I can't outright laugh at how Anya asks for anything because it's still an order. But she and her brother are alike in that sense.

"Look, last time I saw Alek, he didn't seem too impressed about the house thing."

She seems shocked that I haven't said yes yet. "He loves it. I know because he hasn't changed a thing. Twice, I had movers take his furniture out and replace it without his knowing. When he returned, he had everything thrown out and then he purchased the *exact* items he had before. He hasn't done that this time."

How do you kindly tell someone they have weird family dynamics and way too much money?

"So you're coming," Anya says, and this time she hasn't tried for a question at all.

I throw my hands in the air, knowing there isn't really a way to say no to Anya. It's either that or I'm smuggled into the back of a car, which I feel is highly possible.

Besides, it's not like I dislike them. I think.

"I suppose so," I say, still not sure if it's the right answer.

"Good. It's tonight, so please get dressed." She waves a hand, and I look at her, stunned. Surely not. But she has her serious face on, which is really how she always looks, and is waiting for me like I'm a lost child.

"Dressed? Tonight?"

"Do you have plans?" Anya pops a perfect hip.

"Well, I did."

"Watching trashy TV and eating popcorn is not plans." Before I can lie and deny it, she looks around. "Do you have a nicer dress than this?" She waves her hand up and down my body.

"You are really subtle with what you don't like," I say sarcastically.

"Oh no, not subtle. What you have on is trashy, and, frankly, it's something I would have been forced to wear as a teenager who had no money. So, please, move along and get dressed. The restaurant is a five star."

"I don't have anything for a five-star restaurant. I literally just got off the stage from a performance."

"Lucky that your hair and makeup are already done," she says, glancing around. Just then, Julie walks out in a tight pink dress.

"You," Anya says. Julie stops automatically, knowing who she is, and her eyes go wide. "Remove that dress now, and I will give you one hundred dollars." Anya pulls out a hundred-dollar bill from her black clutch.

"It's good to see you, Miss Ivanov," Julie says rather formally as she begins to remove her dress.

"Not here, Julie." I gasp, and Julie looks up at me, then at Anya. She really isn't fazed as she continues to undress and then holds out the dress to Anya. Anya refuses to grab it, shaking her head.

"I'm not touching that. It's for Lena," she says as if it's obvious.

I take it from Julie's hand and apologize.

"Do you have other clothes?" I ask her.

"Yeah, I always carry two dresses with me, just in case. You never know what type of night it'll be." Julie winks as she riffles through her oversized bag and pulls out a loose dress and quickly puts it on.

I look at the dress she's given me. Fuck, this is going to be tight on me, considering Julie is half my size. I tug on the material. Thank fuck it stretches.

"Good. Get dressed, put your hair up, and throw on some heels. I'll be waiting in the car," Anya says, then turns on her heel and leaves.

As quickly as Anya comes in like a fireball, she vanishes.

"Gosh, she's bossy, isn't she?" Julie says as she finishes getting dressed.

"That she is," I agree, heading to the dressing room.

Julie should be used to it now since she's worked for her a few times at the auctions, which I still don't entirely understand. Had I been smarter, I should've asked about them, but instinct tells me I shouldn't ask too many questions.

Another part reminds me I probably shouldn't be involving myself further with the Ivanov siblings, yet here I am.

"Lena." I look back over my shoulder at Julie. "I know you're a smart girl, but be careful, will you?"

"Of course I will be," I tell her, smiling. She nods and walks off without a second glance. What was that about?

Quickly changing—I'm always cautious about not leaving Anya waiting for too long—I pull the brush through my hair and tie it up so it's out of the way, but not so grand in height and volume as it is from the performance. I inhale as I shift the dress down inch by inch, satisfied when it's over my hips and ass. I rest a hand on the wall for a moment, feeling as if I achieved something monumental by getting this dress on. I find a nicer pair of heels and slip my feet into them.

I open the back door, and her sleek black car is one of the few that remain in the lot. Vance—I finally learned his name the day Anya and I went shopping—holds the door open for me. Clay's waiting in the driver's seat. Anya's speaking on the phone in the back seat.

"Hello, boys," I say cheerfully as I dip into the car.

They both offer me a smile, and Vance says, "Good evening, Miss Love."

It always feels strange with how formal they speak. When Vance gets into the car, I say to them, "I don't care what everyone else says about you two, I think you're both all right." They understand the joke, and I can tell they're smiling as Anya finishes up her call.

When she hangs up and the car is moving, she turns to me.

"You don't scrub up half bad."

"Thanks, I think." She tries to hide her smile and amusement at my response.

Is it a rule in this family not to show happiness or humor in something?

"Does Alek know I'm coming?" I ask.

"No, it's best he doesn't. It was a pain to get him to agree to attend in the first place, but as they say, you only turn thirty once," she says, furiously typing away on her phone.

Great. Well, this is going to be awkward. I look down at my dress. I had to remove my bra because the dress wouldn't fit otherwise. It's fine now, but if it gets too cold, my nipples are definitely going to show through.

I watch her as she busily moves from one task to the next on her phone.

"You and Alek are so much alike," I note, and her gaze swings to me.

"You say that like it's an insult."

"No, just a fact."

"It's an honor to be anything like Alek. He is the best man I know."

"What about your husband?" I ask.

"Replaceable," she's quick to say, and I'm shocked. But then the corner of her mouth tilts up, and I realize she's joking. "But River also knows that nothing will come between Alek and me. Our foster mother tried in the past, and let's just say we had a family rift because of it."

My eyebrows furrow as I recall Alek mentioning something about foster care. "What happened to your parents?" I ask, but I'm not entirely sure if she'll answer. The siblings have being human vaults in common.

After a moment, she cautiously says, "If Alek wishes to tell you, then he will in his own time."

I highly doubt that but don't push any further. It's not my place. Hell, I'm not even a family friend at this point. But I doubt the twins have such things anyway.

She nods as the car comes to a stop. "We're here."

I open the door and get out of the car before Vance can help me. Anya walks ahead and into the restaurant.

I've learned not to be insulted when Anya does that. She's just constantly on the go, and either I keep up or I meet her at the finish line.

The hostess greets us eagerly and leads us to the back of the restaurant, where I see him, sitting with his back to me. He's hard to miss.

My heart starts pounding as heated thoughts from when I last saw him flood into my mind. That kiss. Grinding on his cock. Whimpering for more. His hand around my throat.

Even from behind, it's evident in every way that it's Alek. Anya walks straight up the few stairs, ignoring her brother, and to the man sitting across from him. She leans down and kisses him. And not in the friendly peck on the cheek. In the way someone wants to be fucking in a supply closet sometime soon.

I look away, feeling as if I'm intruding. I recognize him, however. He's the man who was kissing her when I had to sign the papers for the gig at the auction.

When I step closer, Alek turns his head toward me. His eyes narrow, and he looks back at his sister.

"You said just us."

Great.

"Yes, but it's my birthday too. And I like her." Anya takes her seat as the man next to her smiles at me.

"I'm River, pleased to meet you. Anyone who

Anya likes, sure as shit is a winner in my book," he adds. I pull out the chair next to Alek, careful not to touch him as I do, and take a seat.

"I'm Lena," I say with a warm smile. "Happy birthday," I say more so to Alek. He doesn't look my way again. Just sits there, his gloved hands flat on the table, one finger tapping.

"Pleasure. Shall we eat?" River suggests.

"Sounds fabulous," I say, trying to push through the awkwardness. "Is there a menu?"

"No, I asked the chefs to bring one of everything. The menu is small but fantastic. I'm sure you'll find something," River says. "Or do you have food restrictions?"

I'm quick to put my hands up. "No restrictions. That sounds delicious."

I wring my hands under the table. I know Anya wanted me to be here, but it's kind of awkward with Alek brooding like... well, like Alek.

I turn to him. "Is there anything you want for your birthday?"

"Want?" he asks with brows raised.

"Apart from Cinita. Sorry, I can't get her for you," I say with a shrug, and I have no idea why I even said it. Am I... nervous? Since when? The table falls silent, and when I look at him, I see his jaw is clenched.

Fuck.

The servers approach then, carrying plates of food and placing them on the table. The thunk of each weighted dish is the only thing to cut through the tension. One of them pours me a glass of wine, and I'm quick to thank them as I lift it to taste it. Damn, I need a whole bottle of this. The wine is sweet and crisp on my tongue. I lift my glass in the air to try to lighten the mood.

"Happy birthday. I hope this year is amazing for both of you," I say cheerfully.

"Hear, hear," River says, lifting his glass and clinking it with mine. Anya looks at Alek, who is still watching me, before she smiles and lifts a glass of water.

"Thank you, Lena," she says, and I turn to give Alek my full attention.

"Mr. Aleksandr, are you not going to say thank you?" Anya reprimands.

"Why would I?" he asks, his mouth set in a hard line.

"That's okay, there's no need," I say, forcing a smile. This was a mistake.

Fuck this guy and thinking he was capable of any type of human emotion.

I finish the rest of my wine and turn my attention

to the food. My stomach growls, but I need to go. The tension from him and how much he hates me is off the charts. I read way too much into what happened between us in his living room. The last thing he probably wants to hear is birthday wishes from me since he clearly despises me. I push my chair back and stand. "I have to go, but thanks for inviting me."

"Where do you have to go?" Alek asks.

I throw a thumb over my shoulder. "That way, out the door."

His eyes are on my legs as he speaks. "No, you don't. Sit back down."

He can shove his demanding ways up his ass, because I'm not in the mood to try to figure out the mystery of Aleksandr Ivanov.

"Thanks again, wine was great, happy birthday. I hope you get lots of sex." I smile at Anya, and that makes River smile. Anya's looking between me and Alek, clearly furious with him.

With a final wave, I leave. And don't look back.

CHAPTER 19
Aleksandr

"Where are you going? We haven't even eaten yet," Anya says as I stand. "I thought you might enjoy the company instead of all but shooing her out."

"When have I ever enjoyed anyone's company?" I grit.

"That's the point." She gives me a scornful glare, and I know when to choose my battles with my sister. Once she starts, she doesn't stop until she has her way.

I walk away from the table. Anya stands up, her chair screeching along the floor, but River pulls her back down. I don't bother to look back as I stride quickly through the restaurant and to the front. Lena's waiting on the sidewalk in that pink, form-fitting dress. She should not be wearing that dress. Fuck me, some women let the dress wear them, but not her. She owns that dress. It's a fucking crime how uncomfortable it makes me. I tug on my self-discipline in order not to rip it off her where she stands.

Stepping up behind her quietly, I lean in close to her ear.

"That's not really in the birthday spirit for you to just run off," I tell her. She whips her head around, and as she does, our heads collide, her nose and my nose hit each other, and she cries out as she steps back.

"Fuck! Is it your mission to leave me with injuries everywhere?" she asks, holding her nose and tapping her foot. "Shit, that hurt." Her phone dings, and she looks down at it while still cupping her nose. "I have to go. Thanks for another wound."

"Come back inside."

I wasn't expecting her tonight. But I don't want her to leave. I've done everything I can to stay away from her these past two weeks, then Anya had to go and basically plop her in my lap tonight.

Fuck, I wish she were on my lap again, grinding against me as those sinister little moans escape her perfect fucking mouth.

She swings her head around to glare at me.

"Did you not hear the part where I'm leaving?" she bites back.

"I did, I just didn't care. Now, come back inside." I hesitate before I add, "Please." Because I don't ever say please. Don't beg for someone to do anything. They just do what I want.

An Uber driver waves her down from a car a few feet away. When she goes to step forward, I grab her wrist and push through the onslaught of nauseating and chilling curses. Taking her phone from her hand, I release her, cancel the Uber, and start walking back inside with her phone.

"Give it back!" She tries to jump over my shoulder, but it's futile considering our height difference. Her breasts brush against my back, and my nostrils flare.

Disgust. Need. Hunger. Her.

"You made it really fucking clear I'm not welcome in there," she grumbles to my back.

I turn to her and drink her in as she adjusts her tits in that tight dress after jumping around.

That fucking dress.

"I don't want you to leave, sunshine. I just wasn't expecting you tonight."

She looks at me expectantly and crosses her arms over her chest.

My eyebrows furrow in confusion. I don't know what else she expects from me, so I hand her the phone as I say, "Come eat. You got dressed up, and there's a noodle dish in there I know you'll like. You don't want it to go cold."

"You're forgetting something," she says angrily. What could I be forgetting?

"Do you want me to kiss you?" I ask.

Her eyes bulge, and a red flush streaks across her cheeks. "No. When you're an asshole, you say sorry."

Oh. That's what she meant.

My jaw tics. Apologizing isn't something I'm too familiar with.

But with the way she's defiantly staring me down, I know she won't come in otherwise. And I want her to come in.

"I'm sorry for making you feel unwelcome. I was just caught off guard by that tight fucking dress."

She glances down, and a devilish smirk comes across her face. *Fuck me.* If I wasn't already going to hell, I'm certainly going now. "You like what I'm wearing?"

"I'd prefer if you weren't wearing anything at all."

Her eyebrows shoot up, and I internally curse myself. No. I tried to stay away so I wouldn't be tempted.

I open the door for her, unable to avert my gaze from her as she walks past me. When we return to the table, Anya is now sitting on River's lap as they make out, unfazed by the few staff who stand at attention in the private area. I pull Lena's chair out, and she sits as Anya finally notices us.

"You took long enough. Now, hurry up before it goes cold," Anya says, moving off River's lap and taking her seat. I sit beside Lena and notice she's looking at the noodles I'd mentioned earlier.

"Eat," I tell her. She glances around at the food and then starts grabbing items to add to her plate.

Anya watches us as she takes a sip of her water. One of the waitstaff refills Lena's glass of wine, and we sit in comfortable silence while we begin eating.

"So, Lena, I never asked how you got into singing," Anya says, and I know my sister well enough to know she isn't one for small talk, especially considering neither of us has ever been good at it.

Lena has a mouthful and seems caught off guard as she covers her mouth and tries to swallow quickly. A part of me is intrigued by what her answer will be.

Hopes and dreams are something I've always found fascinating. Especially those of the artists of this world who always chase something they're not entirely sure they can grasp. Whereas I'm used to taking things by brute force. But her singing was elegant in the same way I consider myself when using knives or escorting the living to the afterlife.

We all have our own calling, I suppose.

"'I started singing when I was a little kid. And I couldn't stop. My parents thought it was cute at the time. Not so much when I became a teenager and wanted to continue it into adulthood and make a living from it. My brother's a doctor, so, you know... saves lives and all," she says with a hint of attitude.

Anya watches her carefully. "They disapprove of your career?"

Lena offers a weak smile as she considers her words. "They don't understand it. A doctor... well, you know, they're making good money and helping society. But a singer? I think they envision me at some karaoke bar or something. And don't get me wrong, I've done that. I just don't think they'll understand it or accept it until I hit it big."

Silence falls over the table, and Anya shrugs. "You could always just make them disappear."

"What do you mean by that?" Lena asks innocently.

River interjects with a charismatic smile. "Cut them out of your life, is what my wife is trying to say. Apply healthy boundaries."

Lena eyes me from the side, and I try to hide my smirk. Sure, healthy boundaries.

"I still love them, and they're my parents. And

moving to the city is probably as far away as I get from them right now. What about your pare—" She cuts herself off immediately. "Oh shit. I'm sorry, I forgot."

"It doesn't bother us. Does it, Alek?" Anya says, shooting me a meaningful look.

About our parents? I don't even know how to explain the death of our parents or our foster mother, who pulled us into this world.

"No, it doesn't," I say.

"Alek and I always had one another. No matter what foster home we went to or mischief we found ourselves in," Anya elaborates.

Lena offers a curt smile and holds her glass high. "Well, cheers to family and turning thirty."

CHAPTER 20
Lena

"Thank you for a lovely evening and for inviting me for dinner," I say as I stand, surprising myself because I actually did enjoy their company.

"I'll take you home." Alek springs from his chair, and I'm caught off guard by his eagerness. Well, as eager as someone like Alek can be.

I say my goodbyes to Anya and River and say to him as I begin to walk away, "I can just call an Uber." But he continues escorting me out of the restaurant. I know he heard me, but me leaving on my own is clearly not an option. I know I should call an Uber, but a part of me wants to spend just a few more minutes alone with him. Something about Alek naturally pulls me in. And I'm trying to figure out if this is another one of those "bad boys" I shouldn't be falling for.

I silently follow him to his car, which looks different from the other two I've been in.

"How many cars do you have?" I ask as he holds open the passenger door.

"A few."

I slide into the seat, and he shuts the door behind me. And for once, I don't cringe thinking about his car. Instead, I'm trying not to laugh. Maybe it's the wine or the ridiculousness of the situation.

I watch him through the windshield as he walks around the hood. Men don't typically intimidate me, but there's something about him that holds so much power. You can tell just by looking at him that he is lethal in more ways than one.

He doesn't like to be touched, though I'm not really sure why. But I hope one day he'll tell me. I shake my head. Why the fuck am I even curious about Alek? He's not the type of man a normal girl like me falls for. Alek is bad, that much is obvious. And I'm smarter than this, aren't I? Yet I'm still in his car.

I also wonder what his obsession with Cinita is. I feel like he's just waiting until she gets in touch with me or something. Like I'm a placeholder.

As he slips into the driver's seat, I ask, "Have you stopped looking for her?"

He starts the engine, and I instantly reach to buckle myself in. I'm pretty sure the seat belt saved my life last time, so I'm definitely opting to wear it again. I notice his hands tighten around the steering wheel, and at first, I think he won't answer me. I mean, he doesn't have to, and he's certainly selective as to when he wants to speak.

"No."

My stomach drops, and I don't like the way it feels. I can't seriously like this guy, right?

"What is your fascination with her?" His eyes are dark in the moonlight as they lock on mine before he looks away and continues driving. He doesn't answer me right away. I'm used to him not responding, so we sit in the car in silence.

What is it about Cinita that has this man in such a chokehold? It can't be just about beauty. Though, yes, she's a stunning woman. She moves as if the air was her dance partner. I had never seen anyone dance as expressively as her, and it surprised me that she wasn't dancing for bigger shows. Cinita can dance, but she's also a wraith. One moment, she's there, and the next, she's vanished.

"I don't have a fascination with her," he finally says

after about five minutes of silence. "She was at the same orphanage as Anya and me."

I bite my lip because he makes it sound like that's explanation enough. But it certainly doesn't clarify as to what their relationship is now.

"Were you all close growing up?" I ask. Trying to pry information from Alek is like getting into a heavily guarded vault.

"No," he answers.

Right. So still no real explanation as to what type of relationship they have. One thing I'm pretty sure of is that Anya doesn't like her. But why should I care what their relationship is like? It's not like Alek and I are a thing. Sure, we kissed—and it was a hot fucking kiss—but that was it, wasn't it?

He pulls over to the curb, and I realize we're in front of my apartment building. As strange as things have been since Alek stepped into my life, I'm also grateful for his generosity and kindness.

I turn to give him my full attention. "Do you want to come up?"

"Do you want to fuck?" he asks boldly.

My jaw drops. "I..."

"I would fuck you, Lena, if you want to," he adds. I'm pretty sure my eyes bulge from my head at his words.

"I-I meant to see the f-furniture," I stutter. "Since you bought everything, I thought you might want to see it." I feel stupid now, realizing it probably did sound like I was propositioning him.

He's staring at me so intently I can't look away before he finally says, "Okay."

I climb out of the car, the awkwardness heavy in the air, more so coming from me than him. Then again, I couldn't imagine Alek ever being nervous, but now that he's brought up fucking, it's all I can think about as we walk up the five flights of stairs.

He waits patiently as I fish my keys out of my bag. My heart is pounding in my chest. I can smell him right next to me, and his words sink further into my head. It's been over a year since I've had a man in my bed. Do I want *him* in my bed? I've thought about it, but he rejected me so epically last time that surely he's made it clear he's not interested. I squash the hope of his words from the car. He says he would, but can he really? How does that even work for someone who hates touching people?

"Stop shaking. I didn't tell you I was going to skin you alive and fuck your corpse."

"Fucking hell," I mumble, managing to get the key close to the door. "You do that?"

He smiles, and I can't help but be mesmerized by it. In a horrific way.

"Skin people? Sure, I've done it once or twice. But fucked a corpse? No. I like my women to scream, and dead women can't scream." The keys drop from my hand, and he bends down to pick them up. "You dropped these," he says with a smile, and, fuck me, my panties just melted.

"Go in," I say with a wave. He steps in first, scanning everything before his gaze lands back on me.

Alek is a very good-looking man, but I never noticed this the first time I met him. It's hard not to notice that, but he also gives off don't-fucking-talk-to-me vibes, and he does it very, very well, so I really have no fucking idea where I stand with him.

"I see my card bought a lot of new things," he says.

"Yes, thank you. Though, it was your sister, not me. I had no idea what half of this stuff is," I reply, pointing at something on the cabinet that I'm pretty sure doesn't have any functional use other than looking pretty. "You should test the mattress, though. That is beautiful and ridiculously comfortable."

"You want me to get in your bed?"

"No. Oh no, I didn't mean it like that," I splutter, shaking my head. Fuck, why is everything I'm saying sounding like I'm trying to lead him on? Am I?

He steps closer to me, inches himself so close that I suck in a breath, and when I do, all the air I breathe is his.

"Are you sure?" he asks, then licks his lips.

Fuck.

He hates to be touched, but he seemed pretty into it last time, didn't he?

No, stop thinking like that.

This cannot happen.

Again.

"Lena."

"Hmmm?"

"Say my name." I look up at him, confused. What does he mean? Then it clicks.

"Aleksandr." I say his name, and his lips twitch before he moves on me as if snapping his restraint. His gloved hands reach for me, wrap around my waist, and pull me even closer to him.

Shit.

Our bodies are flush against one another, and unlike last time, I can't sense him lock up. His movements fluid, my need a pounding demand for more.

I want more of this man.

"Last chance to run," he says, a warning in his tone. I say nothing, just stare at his lips, remembering how he tasted last time. I swallow. "That's my answer," he says before his lips press softly to mine. Who knew this man could be soft in any way? His kisses are perfect. The way his mouth feels against mine before I part my lips and his tongue slides inside.

Perfection.

I don't want to end this kiss. I'm too afraid if I move my hands on his body in any way, the kiss will stop.

So I surrender to him, because I would like this man to kiss me even on my sickest days because I have a feeling it would make me feel better. That's the type of kisses this man gives. They're reviving and life giving. An inferno of pure fucking need.

He's taller than me, but I have on a pair of heels, so I only have to angle my head up slightly to kiss him more deeply. His tongue tangles with mine, and his hands on my waist pull me even closer, if that were possible, and I feel his hardness.

My breaths are shallow, and I'm not sure if it's because of the tightness of my dress or if it's just him.

"This fucking dress is a crime, Lena," he murmurs, and his slight accent curls my toes. My own discipline snaps as I pull him in, feathering my hands through his hair. He shoves me against the kitchen counter, something falling to the floor in the process.

His lips trail to my neck, and I arch into him, so

fucking starved. It's not because I haven't been touched in a year.

It's because I haven't been touched by this man my entire life.

"Alek." My breaths are shaky. "Off. I want this dress off," I say desperately. Because it's too tight, too limiting to give myself to him.

He cocks a smile as he leans back and pulls out a pocketknife. My breath hitches as I stare at him.

"Do you trust me, Lena?" he asks, and it feels like I'm making a deal with the devil.

It's not normal. But it's Alek, and I can see it then, the monster barely hidden under the mask that everyone's afraid of. But in his gaze, he's burning for me.

I nod and watch his hand as he traces it between my legs, cutting the bottom of the dress. The material is so close to my skin, I think he might cut into my flesh because it's so tightly wound around my body, until he puts the knife to the side and rips the dress from the bottom.

The dress is shredded in seconds, and he steps back, appraising me. He looks like a starved man as he stares at me. "Fucking perfect."

And a flood of relief and warmth fills me.

He grabs my ass and lifts me, lips back on mine, his kisses more intense, which, when you think about it, suits him. But his touch is gentle as he traces my body, as if he's afraid he'll break me.

His gloved hands rest on my lower back, not moving, just holding me to him so I can't escape. But then a phone rings, and I pull back. It's not mine that's ringing.

"Do you need to get that?" I ask. He shakes his head and pulls me back to him. This time, I move my hands to his chest. He moans into my mouth, and I move them lower, testing his boundaries.

Here I am, with a man who is infinitely dangerous, and I'm letting him kiss me. Take hold of me as I slide my hands down his chest. I go lower until I get to his belt. My hands start to work the buckle, but he doesn't slow the kiss, his hands still plastered on my back. When I get the belt undone, I slide my hand inside his pants and feel his hard cock. Fuck, it's big.

I push against him so I can wriggle out of his arms and land on my feet between him and the counter. He seems confused as I pull back and smile at him. As I drop to my knees, he watches me with hooded eyes.

I set his cock free, and as I study it, I notice his pubic hair is perfectly manicured. Why would he do that? Is it for someone else? I let those thoughts leave my head as I lean in and slide my tongue out to tease his tip.

He moans, and his hand grips my hair, not enough for him to take control, but as if he needs it to ground himself. His phone starts ringing again. He doesn't make a sound, so I take him in my mouth, my tongue darting lazy circles around him. He groans, not with pleasure this time, as my phone rings too.

We both freeze. I pull my head back and wipe my mouth.

"Ignore it," he instructs.

Disappointment and unease fall from my lips as I whisper, "That ringtone is Cinita's."

I regret it immediately. I wish I never mentioned her name. Because the moment I do, he tucks himself back in and reaches into his jacket for *his* phone. When he checks the screen, I see Cinita's name appear as his previous missed calls.

He rushes out of my apartment, leaving me on my knees, a sick stirring flooding my core, which was fueled by an insufferable hunger only seconds ago.

Now I just fucking ache like I swallowed something bitter.

CHAPTER 21
Aleksandr

I call Cinita back, and it goes straight to voicemail.

Fuck.

Now she decides to call.

She's ignored me from the moment I knew she'd returned, so why is she calling now?

She only calls when she's in trouble.

Last time I saw her, she told me to stay away. And now she's calling me again.

Something bad has happened.

Getting in my car, I glance back at Lena's apartment. Her lights are on, and I can just see her silhouette as she paces in front of the window.

Fuck.

I had her on her knees, and I walked out on her.

It's so ingrained in me to follow Cinita that it's only now I realize how fucked-up that is for Lena.

What the fuck am I doing anyway? Didn't I swear myself to stay away from her?

As I bang my hands on the wheel, my phone rings, and without even looking at it, I answer.

"Cinita."

"Oh fuck no. Again?" my sister says. "Alek, why are you still on her? What the fuck?"

I don't even have an answer anymore. Cinita was the first woman besides my sister I ever felt anything for in my life. I wouldn't say it was love, but a need to protect her was evident. And she loved it, played on it even.

But if I don't protect her, then who will?

"Where is Lena? You better not have pissed her off. I like that woman."

Her words take me aback.

And an odd lump forms in my stomach.

My sister doesn't like anyone.

We don't like anyone. Right?

"You like Lena?"

"Yes, I do."

"You don't like anyone."

"I like you," she says, as if she won the argument.

"No, there's a difference. We are one, Anya. We shared a uterus."

"Tomato, tomahto," she says dismissively. "I know you like her too, so get over whatever it is you have for this other woman. And start seeing what is in front of you."

Anya always has some kind of otherworldly sense of when to call me out on my shit. If she knew what I'd just done, she'd be mad, right? What I did was an asshole thing to do, wasn't it?

I've never thought of a woman's feelings before. But I know I've fucked up.

"Are you still listening to me?" Anya asks.

I hang up on her and get back out of the car. I run up the stairs two at a time, and bang on Lena's door.

Silence.

I bang again.

"Who is it?" Her voice rings through door.

I lick my lips. She most likely knows who it is.

"Me."

"Me? Well, you can leave," she snaps, and I can see her shadow under the door.

"Open the door, Lena." I knock on it again. She doesn't answer this time, though I can hear her breathing on the other side. "Now," I grit. "Or I'll break down this door."

At those words, the door flies open, and she stands there, now dressed in a robe, eyes as fiery as the sun. My gaze immediately dips to her pursed lips, lips that fit perfectly around my cock, as she seethes at me.

"You!" she screams. "Fuck you *and* her." She tips her chin up and goes to slam the door in my face. I stop it before she does and capture her wrist. Her eyes fly to my hand as my foot holds the door open. "Let go, Alek," she growls, and I drop her hand but don't move my foot.

"Are you mad at me?"

"Am I mad?" she yells. "I was on my knees for you, you fuckhead, and you still thought about her."

She attempts to push the door shut, but my foot doesn't move.

"Lena."

"Go away." She pushes against the door.

"I'd really like to taste you now."

She pauses, and her face scrunches in a fit of bewilderment, confusion, and rage.

"Now?" She throws her head back and laughs. "How about... no." She smiles. "How does that sound?" She kicks my ankle, and I pull my foot back, allowing her to slam the door in my face. "Go and fuck your precious Cinita, you dickhead." I hear her walk away, and think about breaking her door down.

But something stops me.

Right now, I don't even think saying sorry will help.

I take a step back. No, I need to let her calm down.

Why do I care what she thinks of me?

I don't know, but I do.

I know I fucked up, though.

And I have no idea how to make up for something like this.

CHAPTER 22
Lena

How dare he?

He really has some nerve. Who the hell does he think he is? My mouth was literally around his cock and he pulled back all because *she* tried calling. Maybe I shouldn't have played into the idea of how fun it would be to have one night with him. Let's just rack it up to not having sex for a long time. Not having sex for eternity is far less humiliating than how he made me feel.

I mean, that has to be the answer, right? Because I haven't had sex for so long?

Surely, I don't see him as anything other than a good lay. I mean, I'm assuming he is. He could be a two-pump chump, for all I know.

DERANGED VOWS

And I fucking know that's not the truth, but it makes me feel better.

I'm not going back down that road ever again.

I stare at the excessive bouquet that was delivered to me at the theater. No name, just a blank card. Well, at least he tried to send a card for once.

I trash them.

The delivery woman seems horrified as she hands me another bag. Almost hesitantly, like I'm going to trash that as well.

"More gifts?" I ask in disbelief.

She swallows and nods. I take the bag. So what is this, his form of groveling? Saying sorry without actually saying sorry?

I open the small white bag and pull out a white box with a red ribbon. When I open it, my eyebrows shoot up.

Long diamond earrings shine up at me, and my jaw tightens.

The woman is looking at me expectantly.

"These I'll keep," I say sheepishly. I'm pissed with the asshole, but these are fucking stunning. And now the nicest pair of earrings I own. It doesn't mean I'm forgiving him, though.

No fucking way.

I should've known better than to get involved with

a man who is pining over another woman. It's one of the reasons I called off my last relationship years ago. He was pining over one of his work colleagues, and I was never going to be anyone's second best. I am worthy of being someone's first choice, and I have to start picking men who see that. Not a man who is unavailable and clearly not interested in me.

But then, why did he kiss me like that?

Why were his hands so gentle and his mouth so fucking perfect? If there's one thing I'm going to take away from this it's that I need to find another man who can kiss me the same way.

But I have a feeling I'll never find anyone who can kiss better than him. But if I can get a kiss like that again, I'll be one very fucking happy girl. I can only imagine what those lips and tongue would do if they went just a little bit lower.

Shaking my head, I pocket my new earrings and sit back down in front of the makeup mirror. Matthew has been working on a new script for an upcoming show, and I wanted to come in early to look over it. But I've only read over the first line... ten times already. I look back at the flowers in the trashcan.

This asshole has really gotten under my skin.

Julie silently walks in behind me, and it's strange

for her to be so quiet. She smiles at me when she sees me, but I can tell by her side-eye that she's been crying.

"Julie?" I twist to face her immediately.

"I'm fine, it's okay," she says quickly. But she's anything but fine.

"What happened?" I hurry to her side.

"It's Cinita. She's in the hospital."

"Oh," I say, stepping back. Guilt grips me as my stomach sinks. Is that why she called last night? It has to be, right? "Is she okay?" I do care that she's okay, but I don't know how she became such a large part of my life without my knowledge.

"I don't know, but she's there, and it's scary. I'm already on two strikes with our dance coach, so I had to come in."

I bite my bottom lip. Cinita might be the bane of my existence right now, but I don't wish ill on her. And I hate seeing Julie like this. "What if I ask if I go see her? I'm sure I can twist Matthew's arm to let me leave for an hour or so."

Julie sucks in a shaky breath. "Are you sure?"

I sigh. "Well, we were roommates. It's the least I can do." A month was hardly enough time to grow any kind of bond with her, but I feel bad for Julie. "It's fine. Besides, it's not like it's a show day. I'm sure he'll let me off for one practice."

Julie throws her arms around me, and I'm startled by her affection. Then another lump of guilt forms in the pit of my stomach.

"Julie, I need to repay you for the dress I borrowed last night. It ripped, and I'd rather buy you a new one."

Julie wipes away her happy tears as she begins to chuckle. "Honestly, I don't care. I've owned that dress for years, and it looked better on you than me anyway."

"Oh, shut up," I say on a laugh. Her eyes go wide at the bouquet in the trash. I cringe as I look back at her. "A gift from an admirer that I don't particularly want."

She rushes over to them and plucks them up. Luckily, it was empty other than the flowers. "Fuck that. Your trash is my treasure." And just like that, she snaps out of her misery. "Is this from Alek Ivanov?"

I go to deny it, but she starts laughing. "You've really caught his attention, huh? I know I've already said it before, but be careful around him, okay? It's men like him that have Cinita in the hospital."

"Someone did something to her?"

She shrugs. "I don't know, but she always follows trouble, and men like him. That kind of life has its highs, but when it has its lows, it can be bad. Just be careful, okay?"

"Do you know much about Alek?" I ask quietly. I don't want to be asking about him, but, fuck me, he's all I can think about right now.

"Mostly rumors. The Ivanov twins are legendary," she says as she happily inhales the flowers.

"How?"

"They run auctions; a lot of them." She looks around to make sure no one else has yet arrived and could be listening. "Like the one we danced at. They are very dangerous and could make anyone disappear. I hear Alek is a wild card."

Disappear?

I got the impression of power from them. But make people disappear?

Yet I know in my heart it's the truth. This somehow makes it more terrifying because I've also seen their kindness. Was that just for me, or was I being played for a fool?

It shouldn't matter either way.

I should stay away.

"Cinita has always had a thing for Alek. She plays on his need to protect her. But things between them never really went further. As far as I'm aware, she never got what she wanted from him. But, damn, did she use him as a way to protect herself when she got into situations she couldn't get out of." She whistles.

"We were out one night, and a guy touched her inappropriately, and wouldn't stop. The following day, the news reported he was found dead.

"She and I weren't close, and she didn't like doing things with us outside of work. But on the occasions we did go out together, and she hit a buzz, all she spoke about was the men, the power, the toxicity. She thrived on it. And when times got tough for her, Alek was supposedly her knight in shining armor."

My jaw tightens at the thought.

He said they'd been at the same orphanage, so maybe he felt like a protective big brother?

Even I can't convince myself of that.

I need to put it behind me.

I shouldn't delve any deeper into their world.

I'm not Cinita, looking for my next hit. I want to focus on my career and living my life. Thriving. I won't be second best again.

But I will make sure she's okay. If she's what Alek wants, then I'll stop stepping between them.

CHAPTER 23

Lena

At first, I'm denied seeing Cinita. Only family is allowed in, but when they check her records, they realize she doesn't have a next of kin. One of the nurses has seen me in a show and is a fan. When I tell her Cinita was a former dancer in the show and I'm also her roommate, she leads me back to see her.

I hate hospitals. My brother may thrive in them, but they've always given me a sense of death.

The nurse explains that Cinita was found on the street in her current condition and brought in. She hasn't woken up since. Which means she must've called Alek and me before she lost consciousness. Could we have helped prevent this? Hearing about someone being in a coma and actually seeing it are two different things.

When I step into the room, my breath falters. She's lying in her bed, unmoving. Her eyes are closed, and the machines hooked up to her are beeping. Her cheeks are sunken in, and she looks nothing like the bright starry-eyed dancer I'd seen perform so many times on stage.

It's sad. I might not know her well, but she clearly needs help.

Should I call Alek?

I should, right?

She never mentioned family, and if on her records she doesn't have a next of kin, that means she has no one, doesn't it? When we lived together, she mentioned she didn't have anyone, but I didn't take that in the literal sense. I always thought everyone had at least one person.

Even if she had stayed in the apartment longer, I doubt she would've depended on me either. I would never have been enough for someone like Cinita, who is clearly looking for escapism in all the wrong places.

I suppose because Alek has been hunting her down this whole time, he truly might be the lesser of two evils.

All my anger at him evaporates. This isn't about

me. Cinita needs help, and I'm above my own pettiness.

I find his number under "Mr. Happy" and press call. After I shooed him out last night, maybe he won't answer. Or maybe he's waiting for me to call regarding the gifts. On the second ring, he says my name, and a shiver racks through me. I like the way he says my name. It does something to me, which only brings the humiliation and anger toward him back to the surface, but I swallow it down. He shouldn't hold any power over me. It was only a kiss... and an interrupted blow job.

"I'm at the hospital," I tell him.

"What? Are you okay?" His voice lashes out quickly, and I'm shocked. It doesn't even sound like Alek. "Lena, fucking hell, tell me which hospital."

I bite my lip as I look at Cinita. She has no family, yet she has this man who has been searching for her. Even though I don't really know why.

I'm sure if I were in her place, I would want someone here with me who really wants to be here. Despite how much I dislike the idea of him being here for her.

Whatever this pull he has over me, I need to untangle myself from this dangerous web.

"It's not me. I'm here with Cinita." He goes silent.

Finally, he says, "Is she alive?"

"Yes."

"And you're fine?" he asks.

"Yes. She's hooked up to a bunch of machines. They found her on some street in a coma. They won't let anyone in who's not family. But the nurse likes my singing, so she made an exception."

"Who doesn't like your singing," he mumbles. "No, she has no family."

Why does he care so much for what happens to her? Is he in love with her? And if he is, then why the fuck is he kissing me?

You don't kiss someone the way he kissed me if you're in love with someone else. Surely, I'm right in that regard?

I close my eyes, frustrated that my mind immediately spirals into these thoughts. I need to step away from Alek Ivanov and not lean into these questions.

"What hospital?" he asks again.

I tell him which one and add, "I'll wait until you arrive so I can bring you to the room, then I have to go back to rehearsal."

He hangs up, and I know he won't be long.

I sit across from Cinita, exhausted and chilled to the bone as I stare at her. She looks like a corpse.

Her long black hair is fanned around her face and over her shoulders. That eerie beeping fills the silence.

I never want to end up in this situation. It's terrifying.

But, also, I've never known what it's like to be truly alone. My parents might be harsh regarding my career, but at least I have them.

My brother loves me deeply and has always supported my endeavors.

I wasn't like Alek and Cinita, so who am I to criticize their relationship?

I fight against irrational thoughts, trying to be levelheaded, but it's not enough to bring the humiliation or anger down. No. No matter what, you don't leave a woman on her knees for someone else.

I sit with her and wait until the door finally opens thirty minutes later. I thought he'd need me in order to get in, but I should've known better, reminding myself that what Alek wanted he would find. He's dressed in all black, immaculate as usual, and it's just fucking unfair. Those green eyes find mine immediately.

He looks me up and down, as if making sure I'm okay, and then his gaze drifts to Cinita. He walks around the bed and grabs her arm. I'm startled by the lack of gentleness and then I realize what he's looking for. Track marks.

I thought he'd be gentle with her. Tender even.

But then, I realize he is *able* to touch her.

"Why does she mean so much to you?" I ask.

Now that Alek has who he's been after this whole time, I know I'll probably never see him again, and I just want to know why. What happened between these two?

"She has no one," he replies, and his jaw clenches. "I'm her someone."

"Not once did she mention you when she lived with me."

"No, she wouldn't have. Cinita loves trouble. I defuse her troubles," he explains, and it's the most he has ever told me about her.

Usually, it's nothing but silence when it comes to her. It's like she holds some type of key that's only made for her.

Silence falls over us for a moment.

He looks at me now. "Did you receive my gifts?"

I want to laugh at the way he looks so vulnerable as he asks in this fucked-up situation.

"Yes, and I threw them out," I say as I uncross my legs and stand. "Flowers and jewelry do not make up for leaving a woman on her knees, Alek."

"Then what will?" he asks, and it sounds almost desperate.

A small piece of my heart tugs on that, and I remind myself that this asshole is all sorts of fucked-up, and I don't have time to teach him how to act like a healthy adult when I'm focusing on my career.

"Nothing, Alek. It was a mistake. Now that you have Cinita, you don't need me for anything else, right?" He goes to speak, but I continue. "I should go. Will you let me know if she wakes?"

"She'll be mad when she wakes." He touches her arm, and I see all the track marks there. She's been using. He's telling me she will be trying to find her next hit.

"Do you love her?" I ask, hoping that he'll answer me.

I just need to know. Need that confirmation in order to truly be able to put this to rest.

Because for some reason, I'm struggling to walk away from him. I gravitate toward him, and it's a dangerous slope.

He stares at me, and I wait for him to speak. To say something. Instead, he looks back down at her. Her face is bruised and puffy, and her arms are all black and blue. You can really tell she's taken a beating.

"I killed her foster father. And the last man who hurt her," he says, and I gasp. His eyes find mine. "And

I will kill the one who did this." I have no doubt he will. "But no, I do not love her."

Hearing the warnings about Alek are one thing, but the outright confession that he's killed, is terrifying. It runs a chill down my spine. I'd deluded myself into thinking of him as something else. A knight in shining armor, perhaps. But I need to view him as the predator he is.

Love or sex or anything else aside, Alek Ivanov is dangerous.

Now that he has his prize, he won't fixate on me any longer.

Right?

I turn and walk out of the room.

CHAPTER 24
Aleksandr

"She needs protection."

"Fine, then send some of our men. You don't need to be there," Anya says to me a week later. Cinita woke up from her coma two days ago and is coming down from the drugs. She's promising anyone and everyone anything they want in hopes to get her next fix. She's a fucking mess, just like the last time I saw her in Russia.

"You don't love her," Anya says. "You have a savior complex when it comes to her. Write her off, Alek. You owe her nothing."

I know she's right, but I don't say anything else. I don't love her. That much I know now.

But when I first met her, and she would talk to me —Cinita loves to talk—she would tell me stories about how she was sad. How she had no one. How the foster care system failed her. And how the men who were sworn to protect her did the opposite.

Anya had the same experience with our second foster father, and we returned to his home when we were teenagers to put him in the grave for what he'd done to her when we were children.

Cinita didn't have anyone; she was alone in the world. She was in the orphanage at the same time as us, and was forgotten. Whereas our foster mother, Meredith Forks, took us in and taught us how to defend ourselves. She was a ruthless old bitch who brought us into her fucked-up world.

Cinita simply dragged herself into it and hasn't been able to escape since.

We're alike in that way. Neither of us can resist the urge, but where she struggles against her demons, I've become mine.

It's why she keeps running back to a world that she never should have been a part of.

I later found out it was her foster father who first introduced her to drugs when she was sixteen.

I hated the fact that, as a young man, I couldn't always protect my sister. But Anya is the only person I know of who doesn't need protection. She took back what was taken from her, and made herself a lethal woman. She cut men down for sport, used them for sex whenever she felt the need, and lived how she wanted to.

But Cinita has never truly escaped.

I killed her foster father last year, after I saw her dancing for the first time, hoping in some way it would set her free. It didn't.

Now she sells herself to men who will only use her.

She's still not willing to give me the name of the man who did this to her, choosing to protect him rather than herself. Is it fear or stupidity? I don't entirely understand.

"Send my men if it makes you feel better," Anya says gently after my long silence.

Dark brunette hair catches my eye, and I lick my lips in anticipation. I haven't seen her for a whole fucking week, and it's killed me not to touch her or even stand in the same room as her.

"I'll deal with it," I say as I hang up on Anya and pocket my phone.

Lena Love.

Fuck.

Her.

And the ballet dancer she works with, what was her name... Julie?

I step into the hallway in front of her, and she

stops. Julie looks back and forth between us and then says, "I'm going to check on Cinita. I'll give you two some time."

Lena watches her friend as she leaves, then tucks her hair behind her ear and looks down at the floor. She has on a blue sweater, jeans that hug her ass, and a pair of cowboy boots.

I wait for her to say something since she's ignored all of my calls and texts. Instead, she goes to step around me, but I sidestep into her path.

She glares up at me, agitated.

"We could play this all day," I tell her.

"You don't seem to take a hint well," she fires back, rubbing her hands over her arms, and I wish it was me touching her. This little ray of sunshine somehow has me *wanting* to touch her. Something I've denied myself for most of my life, and for her I want to embrace and feel every inch. I refuse to look into it any further. I know I'm fucked-up. But I can't deny the yearning I have for her any more than I could stop breathing.

"Not when it comes to you. You might think we're done, but we're not."

She looks at me in disbelief. "Do you really kill people?"

That's what she wants to ask me after ignoring my calls for a week?

"Sure, why not? Got someone you need dead?"

Her eyes widen in surprise before they narrow. Fuck, I love when they narrow at me.

"No, I'm being serious. Did you really kill Cinita's foster father?"

I lean in close so I can whisper into her ear. She sucks in a breath, and I savor the hit I get of her floral scent.

"I sliced him from his cock"—I reach out and touch her chin with my gloved hands—

"to here." I trail my hand to her stomach.

Her gaze doesn't leave mine, and as I touch her, I notice how the voices and immediate revolt from touching isn't as bad. It doesn't cripple me, and I think it's because I'm so fucking hungry for her. She's the only thing that's ever amounted to any bit of peace I've had, and it's terrifying as much as it is unyielding. I *need* her.

"No. You wouldn't have," she says, shaking her head in denial.

She's mistaken if she thinks I'm a good man.

I want this ray of sunshine to myself. I tried to stay away far too many times.

But I won't lie or delude her into thinking I'm anything other than what I am.

A killer.

"Whose cock did you think you were sucking?" I ask. Surely, she'd heard enough to know that I'm not a kind man.

She immediately steps away from my touch, and I feel her absence heavier than I'd like to admit.

"Lena, can we talk about this?" I follow her as she heads in the opposite direction of Cinita's room. She's walking into a dead-end exit. I know because I made it my business to know every exit in this hospital.

"Funny, talking isn't really your thing," she retorts.

"Lena, *please*."

It's the please that has Lena spinning around with her finger pointed in my face, seething rage in my direction.

"Will you just let me leave? You run off on me, and now you try to block me from leaving? Talk about back and forth."

Before I can stop myself, I step forward, palm the back of her head, and slam my lips to hers. At first, she tries to push me away, then her lips melt against mine.

She tastes like all the right decisions and everything I shouldn't be drawn to.

She's the light to my darkness, something I want to keep drinking in for days.

It's selfish for someone like me to want her. But I can't get her out of my thoughts or my system.

I might not be good with words, but I can express that much this way.

Her nails dig into my chest as she opens up to me, and a small whimper escapes her.

She's the calm to my raging mind. The thoughts are silent. My hands only want to trace every line of her body.

I need her like my next meal, and I've been starved this last week.

Pulling back, I stare at her, and she takes a deep, startled breath.

There are so many emotions in her eyes, none of which I understand. But one thing I do know is she wants me just as much as I want her.

"Come home with me."

"No," she answers with swollen lips. "Cinita is waiting for you." She pushes past me.

My jaw tightens as she's quick to stride by a nurse and toward Cinita's room.

It's not Cinita I want.

CHAPTER 25
Lena

I was really hoping when I visited her that I wouldn't see him. It's been over a week since he left my apartment, and he's been sending a multitude of gifts ever since. At this point, I'm just stockpiling them in the corner so I can hock them at a pawn shop when I have the time. Some of the jewelry, though, I like. I'll keep those pieces.

As I walk into Cinita's hospital room, I lick my lips. His kiss is imbedded on them. It's all I can feel, like a stain I can't wipe off. It brands me in ways I don't like to admit.

"Oh my gosh! Lena!" Cinita perks up in her bed, a bowl of Jell-O in her hand. It's night and day to how I last saw her. Her bruises are a bluish-yellow now. She's healing, but I can't shake the visual of how dead she looked before.

Julie gives me a kind smile as she sits on a chair next to the bed.

"Julie told me you were the first person to come. You know, when I was brought here and stuff. Thank you. Oh, and I'm sorry about the rent situation. Things got kind of crazy, but you can sell my stuff to make up for it and all."

I remind myself that punching a woman who's recovering in the hospital is not acceptable. She's not at all apologetic. She's also kind of off, in a jittery way, and I can see she's only had one mouthful of her Jell-O.

"It was an inconvenience," I agree, "but I'm glad to see you're doing better."

She's most likely going through withdrawals. I haven't been around someone who's dealing with substance abuse, but I was prewarned that she could have "moments."

"Oh yeah, I'm totally being waited on hand and foot." She rolls her eyes sarcastically.

Alek lingers near the door, and I see the way Cinita lights up around him. She's like a moth to a flame, and I'm almost certain one that wants to perish in the fire. It makes me uncomfortable.

"The doctors said if I wasn't brought in, I'd probably be dead. Which is super dramatic. I always knew he'd come, though." She points her spoon at Alek, who doesn't say anything. "Although, you didn't answer my call the first time, so maybe I might've died." Her tone has taken on an edge.

Silence fills the room.

He didn't answer because he was with me.

"Doctor is cute, though," she adds flippantly.

My phone rings in my pocket, and I couldn't have asked for a better time to excuse myself. Because as sorry as I feel for Cinita, I'm not her friend. I'm not her anything. And I just don't want this energy in my life.

When I pull out my phone, I realize I've missed a call from my mother. Seems like the lesser of two evils.

"I just need to duck out for a bit to call my mom back," I say as I make haste out of the room. I push past Alek, and when he goes to say something, I put my finger up to him because I don't want him to follow me.

"Alek?" Cinita calls out to him, clearly disgruntled by his momentary shift of attention.

I head out of the hospital, constantly touching my lips, unable to help myself. Despite the fact that I'm mad at him, I really do like the way he kisses me.

Looking over my shoulder to make sure he stayed with Cinita, I don't see any sign of him. A part of me expected him to follow me. If everything he said is true, I should want nothing to do with him. He's a killer. Imagine if I brought him home to my parents and introduced him. *Hi, what do you do for work? Well, parents, I kill people for a living. Oh, and I have auctions where I sell sex and other illegal things.*

No, thank you.

I call my mother back, grateful for the fresh air when I step outside.

Work has been a great distraction, but Alek just sucks me straight back in.

She answers and immediately reprimands me. "Lena, you haven't called or texted since you paid us back. Is there a reason for that?"

Maybe dealing with Cinita was a better idea.

"I've been busy with work," I reply.

"Well, your brother is a doctor, and he still manages to call. So tell me, Lena, who has more time?"

Of course she would compare us. That's what she's good at, and it's what she's always done my whole life. I'm pretty sure my brother could do no wrong in her eyes—not that I think ill of my brother. I actually think he's amazing. Every time she would try to pit us against each other, he would always tell her how lucky she was to have a daughter like me.

"How is he?" I ask, changing the subject, knowing full well she enjoys the topic of anything associated with my brother. I'm pretty sure every person from our hometown knows exactly who my brother is, even if they haven't met him, based on my mother's mouth alone.

"He's good. Actually, that's why I am calling."

"Oh?"

"He's in New York now. He just called and said he thought he saw you at the hospital. Are you there? At the hospital?"

My jaw drops, and I look back at the hospital entrance.

"Archer is here?"

"Yes. Why are you at the hospital anyway?" she asks skeptically.

"I was visiting a friend," I explain. Why didn't anyone tell me sooner he was in town?

"Mom, I'm going to go and find him," I say excitedly. My brother's timing couldn't be more perfect. He's exactly what I need right now—something familiar.

"Oh, he's working, Lena. You know better than to interrupt him at work."

"Okay, Mother," I say and hang up. When I step back into the lobby, I go to the reception desk and ask where I might find Archer Love. They direct me to the same floor I came from.

I offer a timid smile of appreciation because... fuck me, really? Why must I continue bumping into Alek when I'm trying to avoid him? Because now all I can think about is how many more of his toxic kisses I want.

Stepping out of the elevator, I turn right toward the nurse's station instead of left in the direction of Cinita's room. I spot Archer right away, standing behind the desk and talking to a nurse. He's instructing her on what to do with his patient. He signs something, then he looks up, and recognition blooms immediately. Archer's dazzling smile grows bright. He hands her the clipboard and beelines it straight for me. As soon as he reaches me, he picks me up and swings me around.

"Little. You're here." He's called me little since we were kids. He puts me down but grabs my hand and holds it in his.

"How come you didn't tell me you were in town?" I ask, surprised.

"I wanted to see your next show and surprise you. Are you here visiting someone?"

"One of my old roommates is here. I just popped in to see how she's doing."

"Oh, who is it?"

"Her name is Cinita. She's at the end of the hall." He drops my hand, and I see a look of worry cross his face.

"Archer?"

He reaches for me again and pulls me in to whisper in my ear.

"You aren't using like she is, right?"

I hit his chest with a shocked laugh.

"Never. You should know that," I say. "I would never do anything to hurt my pipes." I touch my neck.

"Good. That's good. She's had some questionable people come looking for her," he tells me. "Especially that one. Just don't look right away." I nod and step back. Turning my head slightly, I see Alek watching us. Tensing, I look back at Archer.

That man pops up from thin fucking air.

"Are you free for dinner later?" he asks.

I'm still shocked he's here, and I'm trying to will away Alek's stare that I can feel drilling into my back.

"That sounds good," I say with a grin.

He gives me another smile, and I know he wants to rough up my hair but won't while he's working. "I have to go, but I'll text you," he says as he pulls me in for another hug.

It's nice. And familiar. A bit of home.

I watch him as he walks into another room, trying my hardest to ignore Alek's presence. I head for the elevator. I don't want to deal with Cinita or Alek, and I'm sure Julie will understand if I send her a text to apologize.

I step into the elevator, grateful it opened immediately. I grab my phone to text Julie, but I'm startled as Alek invades my space before the doors shut.

The doors close before I can get off, and I silently curse under my breath.

"You've kissed a lot of men today, it seems," he says, standing way too close to me.

"Seems you want too many people," I shoot back, not looking his way, instead staring at my phone to type out the message.

"No, I only want one. Who was that, Lena?" His tone has a deadly edge, and I can't help but raise my head and meet his eyes. He's only a breath away from me. It's impossible to ignore this man.

"Why do you care?" I bite out. Because he doesn't get to have a say about anything that pertains to me.

"I have to decide whether I think he'll be good enough to keep treating Cinita or if I should kill him."

"Oh my god! Don't you dare threaten to kill my brother again," I growl, and shove him. He just smirks down at me.

"Your brother?"

The elevator doors open, and as I step off, I spin around and say, "Go and kiss your other woman, you pig."

The person waiting seems too nervous to step into the elevator with him.

Before I can take another step, he grabs me and pulls me back toward him. Our bodies collide, and he grabs my face with both hands and slams his lips against mine. I feel the elevator start to move, but I'm helpless to stop it. He pushes me up against the wall and runs his hands down my body. My hips are traitorous, as they grind against him, wanting and needing more than this panty-dropping kiss.

When he manages to pull away, he stares at me. "Just you. You're the only one I want to kiss." He takes my breath away as he traces the back of his finger along my cheekbone.

I can't look away as I try to catch my breath. I'm fighting against myself. I know I shouldn't want more. But every part of me comes alive when he touches me like that.

The doors open again, and I shove him away from me, wiping my mouth as an older couple walks in.

I step off and don't look back.

Even though I can sense his smile.

Asshole.

CHAPTER 26
Aleksandr

"Looks like your trouble has found you," River says through the phone. The moment Cinita ended up in the hospital, I called on River for a favor. She wouldn't give me the names of those who put her there, so I'll use my own resources to find out.

His tracker's name is Will, an Englishman who has a knack for finding people in hiding. He'd once found me in Russia. He was the only person to come close, and when he did, I put a bullet in his shoulder.

Now I'm paying double the price to have him discover the names of the people who hurt Cinita. I'd originally had him looking for her, but when she ended up in coma, I changed my focus to uncovering those who'd done it to her.

She was used as a toy for their amusement, and I won't let that slide.

I look at my phone screen and see live footage of three men sitting in a car outside the hospital. "This is them?" I ask.

"Yes," River says. "You better deal with this quickly. If Anya finds out you're not yet done with the dancer, she's going to gut both of us alive."

"I didn't take you for the type to be scared of my sister," I say as I take in the mess that is Cinita's hospital room. She's sleeping at the moment after trying to destroy the room an hour before because she couldn't get her next hit.

"If I wasn't scared of your sister, she wouldn't like me so much," River replies, and I agree with him. Anya thrives off the power.

"Have Anya send Clay and Vance to look after Cinita while I'm gone," I tell him, kicking off the wall. "I'm going to deal with these fuckers since they so kindly brought themselves to me."

I hang up on River as I make my way downstairs. It's late in the evening, and it makes sense that they'd come at this time. They most likely thought she'd be alone and jonesing for her next high, which means she'd go with them willingly.

Had I known I'd just have to wait it out, I

wouldn't have spent this past week fixated on trying to find them instead of being where I really wanted. And that was with Lena.

The mistake they made was bringing Cinita back to New York and stepping into Ivanov territory.

I didn't need a deal to go wrong or any other excuse to execute them.

It's just what I do.

And I do it very well.

CHAPTER 27
Lena

I twirl the pasta around my fork. My brother's spoken about his latest research and potentially moving to the UK. He's excited, and I'm happy for him but selfishly not for myself.

The server offers us more wine, but my brother hovers his hand over his glass, satisfied with only one. I do the same.

"Are you still working the bar job?" Archer asks.

I shake my head. "No, I quit a few weeks back, actually."

"Oh. Did something happen, or did you just want to focus on singing?"

I swallow. As if I could possibly tell my brother about the incident. He'd drag me out of this city himself.

"I'm earning enough from singing now."

"And living by yourself as well. That's impressive, Lena. I'm proud of you."

I offer a small smile because he genuinely means it. He's four years older than me, but he's always had this air about him that he's capable and knows what he's doing in life. It's exactly why I've looked up to him.

"What do you think about the move to the UK?" he queries. "It wouldn't be for another six months, but we always spoke about it when we were kids. Remember how we used to watch that British show and wish we lived in London?"

I snort a laugh, remembering how we'd try our best British accents. It was horrible then, and it'd be bad even now. "I think it's great for you. Not so much for me since Mom and Dad will be stuck with their least favorite child."

His expression twists. "You're not their least favorite. They just don't understand your singing yet, that's all, but they will one day. You know I'm proud of you, right? The first thing I did when I came to town was purchase a ticket for tomorrow night's performance."

"I could've just got you tickets," I say with a smile. My brother calms me, and I'm so happy to hear about his progress, but for me, as much as I love my current show and crew, I know I don't want to settle. "I'm still trying to hit Broadway in Manhattan. It's just tricky getting there, but having the off-Broadway shows as experience, I'm confident enough to pursue it. I want to keep moving forward too. Make Mom and Dad proud."

He puts his hand on mine, comforting me. "You know you should only be doing it for you." That's easy for him to say. "I don't know what the opportunity is like in London, Lena, but would you consider coming with me?"

It takes me a moment to register what he's asking. "I couldn't just leave everything here," I say, a little stunned. I hadn't thought about opportunities in the UK because I'd only ever aspired for New York.

"I know, but aren't you kind of lonely?" he asks, and the question catches me off guard. Is that how he sees me? "You don't really have anyone here. I don't know, it scares me that your old housemate is super unstable and an addict. And I'm not saying all of your friends here are like that. I just worry about you. We used to be thick as thieves before I went to college. It's just an offer."

"I appreciate that, but I don't think I'm done here yet," I say adamantly, but it plants the seed of doubt. *Am I lonely?*

He raises his hands in the air. "Fair enough. Is there a particular something you're staying for besides your career? Or *someone*?"

I choke on my next bite. "Oh gosh, please don't tell me you're doing the big brother thing again. You tried to run off all my boyfriends when we were younger."

"That's because they were idiots," he says, as if letting me in on a secret. I laugh. "So there is someone?"

I pick at the garlic bread thoughtfully. No. Yes. Maybe.

I certainly know Alek wouldn't be the type my brother could chase off. In fact, I never want them sitting in a room together.

I smirk at that thought. It's the same as Anya is with Alek, I suppose, in the way my brother is with me. Protective.

We might come from different worlds, but I understand that.

"No. Just focusing on my career at the moment," I say, but I don't think he entirely believes me. I don't even believe myself.

Alek is not my boyfriend.

But he's not nothing either.

No matter how hard I fight it.

CHAPTER 28
Lena

Dinner with my brother went well. I didn't tell him about Alek because there's nothing to tell. And even though I love and trust Archer, I know he'll tell our parents. The last thing they need is fuel to add to the idea that I'm already making reckless decisions in my life.

Which I'm not entirely sure I disagree with.

I can't stop thinking about my conversation with my brother about London. I never thought about going elsewhere, and I love living in New York, but it bugs me that he thinks I'm lonely. But maybe that's just the big brother in him coming out.

I've been tossing and turning all night in my bed, unable to stop thinking about what I want in my future. I came here to go as far as possible in my career, but I became stagnant in my current position at some point. Now that I'm not working at the bar, I should start networking and auditioning elsewhere like I'd promised myself.

It took me two years to get this spot in the theater company, so how much longer would it take for me to obtain anything else?

Rapid banging on my door has me shooting up in bed. *What the fuck?* It's two in the morning.

I'm scared for my fucking life until *his* voice comes through the door.

"Lena!" Alek calls my name.

I flop back to the bed, contemplating getting up.

"Lena, I know you can hear me."

I roll my eyes. My brother mentioned the bad-boy types he had to shoo off, so I bet he'd be beside himself that I'm letting someone like Alek into my home. Then again, he did purchase every furnishing in it.

Pushing off my blankets, I climb out of bed and make my way to the door. When I open it, there is Alek with a busted eye and blood dripping from his hand.

"Oh my god, what happened?" I ask, pulling him inside. I notice the cut on his shoulder. It doesn't look deep, but I'm not a fucking doctor. Blood is usually a bad thing.

Panic tightens its hold on me. He's going to be okay, right?

I usher him onto one of my kitchen stools and quickly go through my shelves to find the first aid kit.

"Take off your shirt so I can see how bad it is. Why didn't you go to the hospital, you idiot?" I lecture. Alek's patched me up before, so I know for certain he'd be able to help himself or find someone far more capable than me. He doesn't say anything and just watches me. "Does it hurt?"

"Yes."

"Where?" The only injury I can see is his shoulder, but what if there's a cut somewhere else? Or worse, a gunshot?

He leans in and kisses me, soft and tender. My thoughts short-circuit as I'm taken in by him. He pulls back, and I'm still stunned.

"Feels better now," he says with a slow smirk. I want to hit his chest and talk some sense into him.

"This isn't a joke, Aleksandr. You're bleeding," I scold, and I'm taken aback by how much my voice trembles.

"I wasn't joking. But if I were... at least I'd die a happy man."

I choke on a laugh. "That's not funny."

But he smiles like he's been holding out just to see

me laugh.

"Anyone can fix this for you Alek, why are you here?" I boldly ask.

"I thought if I was bleeding, surely, you'd let me in," he confesses. His hand cups my cheek, and my breath falters. "I had to see you. You were the first person who came to mind, and I wound up here."

I want to clutch his words to my heart. Hold them as truth. But I find myself fighting the tension instead. I shake my head and undo his shirt, pulling it off him. He has a cut on his upper arm, and blood is dribbling down to his gloves.

"Can I take them off?" I ask, nodding to the gloves. He looks at them and slowly nods. I reach for his gloves and take them off one by one, careful with each movement as I do so. "How did this happen?"

"Men came for Cinita at the hospital." I freeze at his words. "I showed them the way out." His gaze falls to my hands, which are now touching his bare one where I took the gloves off.

It's scary how easily he can say things like this. Yet I'm mesmerized by his immaculate, beautiful hands.

"Does it hurt to touch others?" I whisper. "Is that why you wear these?" I put the glove to the side.

"No, I just don't want to touch people. Why would I? Have you seen what people do? How easy it is for them to bleed?" he says with disgust, as if they're filthy. I feel like it's true but that he also uses it to cover up something far more wounded than his arm.

"It doesn't look deep, but you need to see someone who can handle this, Alek. I'm not a doctor," I say, still surprised that he came here in the first place.

"I wanted to see you," he says sincerely. "Even on death's door."

I hit his other arm, and he chuckles. "Stop pretending you're dying if you're not, Alek. You're going to give me a heart attack."

I search for a bandage in the kit, and I can feel him staring at me.

"Why are you really here, Alek?" I ask, wrapping the bandage around his shoulder. I learned a thing or two from Archer, but he still needs to have it checked out.

"I didn't know where else to go," he says, his gaze locked on me intently.

"Liar."

"I wanted to come here, Lena. I really wanted to see you. Had to." His arm raises, and he looks at me, his hand suspended as if he wants to touch my cheek. "Can I touch you?" I look at his hand, which is immaculately clean despite the rest of his arm.

"I may be dirty," I whisper.

"You aren't. You are anything but," he says as his hands land on my bare stomach just below the hem of my short tank top. His hands wrap around my waist, warm and surprisingly gentle.

For a killer, he sure knows how to touch.

Something is oddly intimate about his bare hands, as if more than the physical barrier has lessened.

"Aleksandr." At the sound of his name, his grip tightens on me.

"Say it again," he demands quietly. I look at him and touch his chest, careful not to hurt him.

"Aleksandr," I say just as he stands so quickly, I can't even prepare myself. His arms are under my ass, and my legs go around his waist, as he walks me backward until we hit the wall.

"Your arm," I breathe out, but his mouth is on mine, taking away any concern. I feel his hands all over me, sliding up and down while they hold me to him. Like glue.

Inseparable.

Undeniable.

Fucking painful if we don't see it through.

He walks into my bedroom and gently lays me on my back as he comes down on top of me. I can feel all of him against me, his warmth and touch, as if he's memorizing every part of me.

I'm being consumed entirely.

It's more than a kiss.

So far, only touch alone.

Touch—the thing he feared most but is making an exception for me.

"You're touching me," I whisper. He nods and locks eyes with me, those forest-green orbs taking my breath away. "How does it feel?"

"Fucking incredible," he says before he moves down, and his lips touch mine. His body presses me into the mattress, and before I can stop myself, my hands start moving, trying to tear off the remainder of his clothes. I want them off, and I want *him*.

He complies and moves with me so I can undo his pants and pull them down. I reach for my own shirt and break away from the kiss as he helps me pull it off so my breasts are bare in front of him. I shove at my shorts and shimmy them down. I don't sleep with underwear on, so now I'm naked, and so is he.

I notice his injury is still bleeding, and start to have second thoughts. He notices it because he moves quickly, taking me as if I'm his God-given right. His mouth assaults my nipple, and he sucks and bites before moving on to the other one. I drag my hands up and down his back, scraping my nails as I go, before he moves even lower. His mouth leaves kisses over my stomach as he trails downward before he reaches where I ache for him most.

"You are such a good girl," he croons, looking up at me. He touches me between my legs, and I spread them a little wider. "See, you know how to behave," he says as he inserts a finger, and I arch into his touch.

He moves his head lower until he kisses me just above where I want him. I look down at him and watch, enthralled, as his tongue darts out and makes its way down to my slit. He makes sure to taste all of me before he gets there. When he does, my hips buck, and he moves one of his strong, veiny hands—fuck, they're nice hands—and pushes my pelvis down, holding me in place, then slides his tongue up and down.

"Fuck," I gasp as he continues the slow and torturous pleasure. He slides another finger in. "Fuuuuck," I say again, unable to help myself.

"I think that mouth needs to be washed out with my cock," he murmurs against my pussy. A smile tugs at my lips as he continues finger fucking and licking me. He keeps going until my knees start to shake, my hips strain against his hold, and a scream rips from my throat.

"My good girl," he says as I come all over his hand and mouth.

CHAPTER 29
Aleksandr

If I could get her to scream my name all the time, I fucking would. She sits up with a look on her face that is pure bliss. Pure fucking glowing sunshine.

She licks her lips as I stand, and I shake my head as her gaze goes to my cock.

"No, not now. Right now, I want to fuck you," I tell her as she gets up on her knees and reaches for me. I let her grab my hand, and wonder why I like her touching me when I hate it when anyone else does.

The voices are finally gone. She is the only woman I feel liberated with.

Free from the shackles that have chained me since that day.

She's my serene silence and sunshine.

"Wait!" she's quick to say. "Safety first." She licks her lips, and I quirk a smile as she leans over to her side table and opens the top drawer to grab an unopened box of condoms.

"You won't be using those with anyone else," I grit out as I stare at her ass and cunt from behind. Divine perfection.

"Shut up. Actually, it says they're expired. Do you think they're still okay to use?"

"Give me the fucking condom," I growl, and she gives me a knowing smile.

I pull her back to me by the leg, and she squeals as I rip the packet open with my teeth and roll it over my cock.

It's fuckin tight, too small. But it's satisfying to know my little ray of sunshine has only ever dealt with average dicks.

Because this is the only dick she'll ever touch again.

I slap her ass, and she squeals again. "This fucking ass drives me insane." I curse and flip her over.

She seems satisfied by that, and I drink her in, admiring her on her back.

How can I savor this moment, savor her?

"Now, Aleksandr. You are the injured one. Maybe you should lie down for a bit," she says promiscuously. I want to fuck her in every way and from every angle, but I'm at her mercy. I lie on my back, and before I can move to properly rest my head on a pillow, she lifts one of her legs and swings it over me, straddling me. Her hands play on my chest as my cock stands tall and hard between us, right near her clit. She moves her body a little closer and starts to rub herself on it as she leans down to kiss me.

Fuck, I love kissing those lips.

Soft, full, and fucking luscious.

Her hips start moving, and I reach down to guide them. Fuck, she's so warm and wet, teasing me.

"Lena." She leans down farther, pressing soft kisses up my chest until she reaches my neck. I grab her hips and lift them so I'm at her entrance. She tries to keep rocking in my hand, but I can't stop. Fuck, I won't stop. Before I can push her down, she lowers, taking me all in. My hands freeze on her hips, and we both stay still until she lifts a little, and her mouth finds mine.

Lena's hips start rocking, and she takes control. Breaking our kiss, she sits up and lifts her hands from my chest. Cupping her tits, she pinches her nipples as she rides my cock.

Pure fucking perfection.

"Lena."

"Aleksandr," she whispers, her eyes closed in bliss.

"Look at me," I command. She opens them, and as she does, I sit up and slam my lips to hers. "Don't ever close your eyes on me again when I'm inside you. You will know who is fucking you." I flip her in one movement so her back hits the bed and I'm hovering over her. "Do you understand?" I growl, then lean down to take her nipple in my mouth.

She nods and watches me, fixated, as I pop her nipple out and start fucking her. First, I go slow and steady, even though I want to fuck her into the bed, but I want to savor this more.

Savor *her*.

She clings to me, her nails digging into my back, as she leans up and bites my ear.

Feisty little bird, isn't she?

I move my hips faster, and her breathing becomes quicker. I can feel her tighten around my cock as she chokes the fucking life out of it with her pussy.

Fuck, it feels good.

I have sex, and I have it regularly.

But not like this, not being so bare.

I don't touch the woman without gloves on. I fuck them from behind, or they suck my cock.

And I've always had to fight against the avalanche of nauseating disgust and despair.

But with Lena... it's only her. An anchor. *My* anchor.

I want to see. I want to watch as she comes. Fuck, I want to know what she feels like beneath my hands as she does.

"Oh my—" she screams, and I keep up my rhythm. I can't stop. Fuck, she feels so good. Her body relaxes, and I fuck her a little harder before I come not long after. She pulls me down, so my face rests against her neck, as we try to catch our breath.

Then her phone rings.

And it's the same ringtone as last time. Fucking Cinita. She freezes and pulls her hands away from me, but I pin her wrists down and stare at her, my cock still buried inside her.

"Don't pull away from me," I say. Because right now, I can't handle her absence.

I need her in every way she needs me.

"But it's Cinita's ringtone. Don't you—"

"I'm where I want to be, Lena," I insist, and I see something shift in her.

I'm exactly where I *need* to be.

It's the first time in my life I've ever felt this way.

And it's all because of her.

CHAPTER 30
Lena

He is wrapped all around me, his body against mine, as we lie here, my head on his chest. His hands on my back hold me tightly, as if I might up and leave at any moment.

It's strange in the way that it feels so right.

We haven't spoken, not uttered a word since my phone went off, and I'm sure I heard his phone buzzing somewhere on the floor.

Some might say that's weird, but who knows? I take comfort in his silence.

He's bled through his bandage, and I'm certain I'll need to buy new sheets, but right now, I don't care. I'm too scared to ruin this moment.

But I feel like this is the *only* moment.

"What's on your mind, Lena?" he asks, not even

opening his eyes. He just knows I'm watching him. And how could I not? He's so beautiful. Not that I'd ever tell him that, because it'd inflate his ego too much.

"Tell me about the gloves, Alek." I need something from him. Anything to show me that this is deeper than some one-night stand, because right now, I'm terrified of the way we gravitate toward each other.

I know he's bad news.

But can something so bad truly feel so right?

"Why do you want to know?" he asks, and it surprises me that he's opened up, if even a little. His eyes open now, and he's watching me in the same way that I am him.

I lick my lips, wanting to kiss him all over again because I sense the tenderness beneath. Or maybe I just want there to be *something* underneath. Something I can use to justify his actions. No matter what it is, it doesn't justify killing another. Yet here I am, being ignorant of those sins.

"Because I want to know *you*, Aleksandr. I need something if you expect me to give you anything."

I hold my breath, so certain that he'll deny me.

But to my surprise, he licks his lips, and I see the swallow of his throat before he replies, "You won't like a lot of the answers I have to your questions, Lena."

"Will they be the truth?"

"If you want it, then yes."

"Then tonight, we'll start with one."

He licks his lips again. "Not even Anya knows."

"And it'll remain that way." My heart breaks at the way he says it. Whatever burden he's carried has not even been shared with the one person he shares everything with.

He looks up at the ceiling, as if thinking as to where he even should start. "When we were four, our parents moved from Russia back to America. We were born here. We don't remember much from that time. We were just thrown into an orphanage and foster carers when our parents disappeared."

Oh shit, I didn't know they were abandoned. My heart twists.

"Our first foster parents were able to finally conceive their first child after we'd been with them for two months, and they took us back to the orphanage. Our second foster father..." His jaw grinds.

"I walked in on him with Anya when we were six. We were small then, but I was filled with so much rage and desire to protect her that I attacked him. I hated being touched even then, but I tried to dig his eyes from his head. I shoved him back hard enough that he cut his hand on the corner of the side table. Not enough to do any serious damage but it provided just enough time for Anya to run. But I froze.

"The blood... I don't know how to express it. Something that was suppressed in me was triggered by the blood. I just remember crying in a pool of it. Screaming for my mother to wake up. That swirl of terror and abandonment all over me, filth clinging to me. On my hands. My skin. Every part of me. I'm certain as distant as it feels, it might be the memory I have of finding my mother dead. But it's so foggy, that I don't know if it's something my mind made up. It's why I've never told Anya of it. It's only recently that my suspicions were confirmed that they were murdered. But I'd never been sure, especially after having this... *defect* from such a young age."

"Oh my gosh, Alek," I say as tears leak from my eyes. He seems almost surprised by them as he wipes them away, fascinated.

"I can stop," he says, as if the hardship is on me rather than him. I shake my head because I want him to keep going. I'm happy to carry this burden with him if I'm the only one who can share the weight. But my heart breaks, especially for his inability to connect emotion with it. For him to understand. Or perhaps he's outright denying the trauma of his childhood.

"Don't look at me as if I'm a broken man, Lena. Or I won't tell you anymore."

I offer a small smile and graze my hand along his jaw. "No, I was thinking about how incredibly strong you are."

His eyebrows furrow, but he doesn't look away. The intensity in his gaze is as unsettling as it is sincere.

"After that, I started wearing gloves, because if I touched anyone..." His body trembles of its own accord. "It's just like going back to that moment, being dirtied, sullied. I don't mind killing or bleeding, but touching someone is like my personal hell. Until you," he confesses.

My heart breaks a little more as he focuses on where he's stroking his thumb over my cheekbone.

"It wasn't until our third foster mother, a woman named Meredith Forks, took us in that I learned the power in killing. The art of detachment and intimidation. She was a woman with tremendous money, power, and ambition. She trained us from a young age to become who we are now. She ran her own illegal businesses and auctions, and was cutthroat in her ambition. Our empire and the beginning of the auctions started because of her.

"It was, however, just this year that Anya discovered the old bitch had been the one to kill our parents so she could adopt us. Driven by the notion that having children would make her look more 'approachable' to new clients in town. So Anya buried her while I was off chasing Cinita in Russia.

"I failed her."

The admission catches me off guard.

"That's a lot of fucked-up shit to happen to a person," I breathe out, because I can't even comprehend half of it. His gaze is locked on mine as he traces my cheek, jaw, and lips.

"Perhaps. But I don't look at it that way. I'm a killer, no matter what way I was forged. Don't think of me as a broken man or a good man, Lena, because I am neither."

"I don't think you're all that bad when you don't want to be."

"You'd be the first to say so," he says.

"Yes, but I was also the first to tell you the truth that you look like an old man." I laugh as his expression goes solemn.

"You think you're hilarious, don't you, sunshine?" When I stop laughing and look at him, I see how he watches me tenderly. With the eyes of a killer that I know I'm falling for ever so slowly but undeniably.

And it's terrifying.

I shouldn't. I can't.

But I've already given part of myself away to him.

I don't even know how to process everything he's told me, but I put my hand on his jaw, stroking the stubble, telling him in the only way I can that I'm here for him. For now, if he'll have me.

He pulls me in closer, and I rest my head on his chest again. "For now, I'd like to rest, Lena."

"Do I need to put some porn on?" I ask, biting my bottom lip with a smile.

He squeezes me, but when I look up, I see the crooked smile on his lips. And it fills me with satisfaction to know that somehow I can make a man like this, who's been so haunted by his earliest memories, crack even the smallest of smiles. That I can give him one moment of peace.

It's not long until his breathing evens out, but his hold on me doesn't loosen. Soon, I hear a soft snore leave him, and I stay there wrapped in his arms and feel the most protected I have ever in my life.

How can that even be, to feel so protected by someone who is a killer?

That can't be real, right?

Yet, in my own way, I want to protect him as well.

I lift my head to look up at him. His eyes and mouth are closed. I gently touch his lips. I want to believe all of this is real. That our bubble won't burst, and I'll discover this isn't real.

His eyes open slightly, and he peers down at me.

"Lena." He says my name quietly, and his lashes flutter.

"Aleksandr," I whisper. "Is this even real?"

"It is, sunshine. Now, go to sleep." He reaches down and lifts one of my legs over his hip. Pulling it up, he holds it to him while the other stays locked around me.

I'm scared the moment my eyes close, he'll be gone, but it's not long until I fall asleep in his arms.

CHAPTER 31
Lena

I felt his kiss sometime early in the morning, but I didn't fully wake because I was too tired for that. Rolling over, I reach for him but come up empty.

When I open my eyes, I realize I'm alone.

He left.

The only sign that he was here is the blood on my bed sheets from his wound.

Grabbing my phone, I see the missed calls from Cinita and nothing else.

No text goodbye.

Nothing.

A pit forms in my stomach.

Was last night real? Or was it only me who felt that?

Did I fall for the exact thing I told myself I wouldn't?

Sitting up, I debate whether or not to call him.

Should I?

I don't know.

He left without a word, so why should I follow that up?

It was the best sex of my life. Maybe that's why I've become attached.

But the things we spoke about... there's no taking away from the intimacy of that moment.

Putting my phone back down, I crane my neck, trying to get a better view of the living room. But I can't see him, and I would've heard him if he was in the bathroom since it's directly behind my room.

I can see the medical kit and bits of blood on the counter have been cleaned up.

It's like he was never here.

Just as I get up to get dressed, my phone rings, and his number comes on my screen as "Mr. Happy."

"Hello?" My voice is shaky at best.

"Miss me?" Those are his first words. I want to tell him he shouldn't have left, but I can't. I don't have the right to say that to him. One night together does not equal me telling him what to do.

"You left." I state the obvious.

"I did," he replies. "I'm also at your door, so open up." I look at the door and then my phone, a flurry of butterflies erupting in my stomach.

I hate this hopeful pull that I have no control over.

I walk to the door and unlock it before I pull it open. He's standing there, no blood in sight, gloves back on, and dressed ready to kill. Literally.

He hands me a coffee, and I take it, looking at him in confusion.

"You locked my door?"

"I did," he says, walking in. "I also got you a bagel. It's in the bag." He places the bag on the counter and sits in the same seat he was in last night.

I realize he's most likely already gone back home to shower and change into clean clothes. I look down at the pj's I was quick to throw back on, and somehow, he makes me feel misplaced in my own apartment.

His jaw clenches, and I know something's happened. I brace myself, because whatever happened last night... well, just as I dreaded, the bubble is about to pop.

"Why are you here, Alek?" I ask. "Do you plan to watch *The Real Housewives* and eat popcorn with me all day?"

His gaze meets mine, and for a moment, he almost

looks sad. "I want to hold you all day. I know that much."

"But you can't because...?" I wait for it. The disappointment. The cracks that already begin to show before he's even said anything.

I don't know how this man got such a hold on me, but I feel like I'm already grieving his loss.

"Don't you dare say her name," I whisper angrily as I wrap my arms around my stomach. Because I know... a woman always knows.

"I know you get upset about her and how I help her."

A chill runs down my spine because I know it's about her.

I want to laugh at him and his absurdity, but I'm not entirely sure if I'm the one who's being out of line. I've had sex with him once, and perhaps I'm the only one feeling this so deeply. And that's my fault.

"That's your choice," I find myself saying, and I can't help but immediately feel second best.

"I don't help many people in this life. I want you to be well aware of that," he says. "In fact, my way of helping someone is usually putting a bullet in their head." His words send a shiver down my spine. "She needs to stay with someone since she's been discharged from the hospital, and she's asked if she can stay with me." Everything stops when he shares this bit information. The hot coffee in my hand just burns my skin through the cup as I stare him.

"You can't say no?" I ask.

"The blood from last night," he starts, and I wait to hear what he has to say. "Was because I killed three men who intended to harm her."

The coffee cup slips from my hand and explodes all over the floor. I manage to step back, but some still splatters on me.

I frantically reach for a cloth and drop down to my knees to start cleaning it up.

Why? Why am I feeling like this? Wasn't I trying to convince myself it was only attraction? Shouldn't I be satisfied now that we've scratched the itch?

He says my name, but I ignore him. He crouches down and puts his hand on mine. "Lena," he repeats, and I have no choice but to look up at him. "I want to be honest with you. I need to do this."

"Okay," I reply, averting my gaze and going back to wiping up the mess. I manage to get it all and then stand and throw the rag in the sink. "You can leave now."

"Lena, I want you," he says, and I'm certain it sounds like he's pleading.

"*Leave.*" My tone is a cutting edge. "Thanks for

the coffee," I mutter and then turn to head to the shower. "Lock the door on your way out."

I slam the bathroom door in his face and turn the shower on scalding hot. I steady my breathing before I burst into tears, hating that I let him in so deeply. *How? When?*

When I climb into the shower, the water burns my already red skin where the coffee splashed me. I hear the door open but don't even look; I know it's him.

"I don't want to be a part of that life, that world. You get that, right?" I blurt out with my back turned to him. "Enjoy your dancer, Alek. Because you'll most likely get yourself killed trying to chase her, and I won't watch that or be a part of it. You've already done enough damage here."

The tension ripples through the bathroom, and I close my eyes, wishing him away. I hear the click of the door, and when I turn to look, he's gone.

CHAPTER 32
Aleksandr

Cinita sits on the couch every fucking day, complaining about God knows what. I don't know because I block her out. It's been a week since I've taken her in. A whole fucking week that I've been starved for Lena.

She was right to kick me out. But, fuck, it doesn't mean I don't fight against myself every day, trying not to hunt her down and claim her as mine all over again. I've been branded by her in every way, and I can't get her off my fucking mind.

The only reason I even have Cinita here is because there was a fourth man who was toying with her—who is still on the loose—and Will is currently tracking him down. After I find him and kill him, I have every intention of kicking her out of my home.

"Alek," Cinita yells as I walk in. I was trying to sneak by her, but she heard me. Which is uncanny, considering I can be very fucking quiet. "Please come here."

Sighing, I walk into the living room, which only reminds me of Lena sitting there.

Her plump ass has filled the very same spot where Cinita is all but lounging and snapping her fingers at me.

I stop in the doorway, and she stands from the couch and turns to look at me. She has on a barely-there white cami that skims the top of her thighs, and I have a feeling she's wearing it for a reason. But I really couldn't give a shit. The only woman wearing particularly revealing things I care about is Lena. And that's because I want to be the only one to see her that way. My jaw clenches, thinking about what she's wearing now and who might be seeing her.

"You haven't touched me. Why haven't you touched me?" Cinita asks. "Do you not want me anymore?" She sounds a little deflated but hopeful as well. She pouts out her bottom lip. I knew her personality was rotten to a degree, and I thought I recognized something of myself in her. But things have shifted since Lena. I tolerate Cinita less.

"I'm not sure I ever wanted you in that way," I say

truthfully. Perhaps I mistook it for loving her as I let her consume me. I thought even someone as pitiful as her deserved saving since she was dealt a shitty hand just like me and my sister. But in reality, somehow she latched onto me, exploited what little good I had in me, and then used it to manipulate me into protecting her.

I don't regret protecting her. She would have been dead a long time ago if it weren't for me.

And I like the dead. The dead don't talk back.

But I had to try to save her.

Killing is the only thing I'm good at, and if I can at least get rid of one more monster for her, then I will. Before I turn my back on her forever.

"Why?" She moves closer to me. "You've always protected me. You wanted me to stay. Hell, you found me halfway across the world, Alek. You wouldn't do that for just anyone." She lifts her hand to place it on my chest, but I take a step back before she touches me.

It's not her hands I want on me.

Never will be.

"Touch me again, and I will throw you out of my fucking house," I threaten. Her eyes widen, and she takes a step back.

"You wouldn't. They would find me," she says and gives me her best fake cry.

"I would. I've killed for you and helped you more than I would help anyone, but that does not give you permission to touch me."

It's moments like these that she has clarity. Understands the mess that she's gotten herself into. But it's when her edginess kicks in and she needs more drugs flooding through her body that she sees them more as friends than enemies.

"I can be better for you," she pleads. "I've tried all these years. Remember how you liked to watch me dance? I want it to be like that again, Alek. I just don't know how to go back."

My jaw tics as tears trickle down her face. I don't think it's entirely a lie. But how much more could I give her? Lena's words from just before I left her in her apartment have bothered me. That I'd die protecting Cinita. But that isn't the case. And neither will I be her caretaker.

"Once he's dead, Cinita, I'm kicking you out of this house, and we're done. I owe you nothing. No more. You need to learn to stand on your own."

I go to walk away, but her hand clutches at my shirt. She drops it immediately with the glare I shoot her. "I'm sorry, Alek. I really have no one else. I know I fucked up, and I'm scared. I don't know what to do. Please help me."

My jaw tics again.

There's something in her that I recognize, and it's that part I've been trying to save for so long. But I realize now that it's time to let go. Or I'll sink with her.

I turn and leave, ignoring her crying as I walk to my room. It's felt empty ever since the night Lena slept in it with her concussion. I smirk at the thought of when she frantically tried to change from the porn channel.

The truth is, I'd only had that TV installed that day, and I'm certain my sister had something to do with the porn appearing right away, because she knew it would grate on my nerves. Instead, it brought me, dare I say, amusement.

When I look at the painting of the dancer on the wall, I realize immediately how wrong it feels. Lena and Anya had changed most of the things in my house, but this they left.

I remove it from my wall, knowing there's only one thing to do with it.

Burn it.

CHAPTER 33
Lena

Two weeks have gone by since I last saw Alek, and I still count every fucking day. I'm furious with him for putting her first, and pained at myself for falling for him when I shouldn't have. I'm also confused that he had such an impact on me, and if anything, it's put a fire under my ass. I've gone for two auditions for roles on Broadway in central Manhattan. I didn't get either part, but rejection is my thing right now, so I suck it up and get ready for the next one.

However, sitting at dinner with my parents, the mention of rejections does nothing to boost their confidence in my chosen career. I know they're only here in the city because Archer is still here. They've been oddly quiet and skeptical of my apartment and the new furniture in it.

I also notice Archer hasn't told them he plans on moving to the UK, and it's not my place to tell them. But it'd be nice if they could focus on that instead of my failings.

Archer hands me the bottle of wine, and I pour myself a glass. It's my third one to help get me through this dinner.

"I saw Lena sing the first week I arrived. It was truly a beautiful thing to witness," Archer says, and my heart fills with the compliment, but I cringe at his obviousness. "While you're in town, you should go see her," he says to my parents, and I sit there gripping my glass of wine as neither speaks.

It's hard to describe parents who were there for you but were never really emotionally supportive. It felt like I'd become a chore to them when they realized my aspirations in life didn't go past singing. I'm not my brother, and I will never be my brother. We are two completely different people. Yet he treats me better than my own parents do, when he's the one with all the shiny papers and accreditations. They own their own accounting firm and can't see past numbers. They see an income and judge worth purely on that.

"Maybe tomorrow night, we can all go," Archer offers. "Mother?" he asks as she looks up.

"Yes, sweetie," she agrees with a tight smile.

"Do you not want to witness Lena's talent?" he asks her. Her gaze shifts to me, and I see the disappointment in her eyes.

"Yes, sure, of course. I left my schedule at home, but I'm sure when I check it, I'll have availability," she answers, and my father continues to eat.

I have lived a pretty clean and normal life. The only risks that I've ever really taken have been with Aleksandr.

That man was a bad choice.

But a very good one at the same time.

Right now, I wish I'd made a million mistakes so they could fault me for those instead. At least then I'd have done something truly worth their disappointment.

Or maybe I should really not give a fuck at some point.

"How did you get the money to afford those things in your apartment?" my mother asks. I know it's been on the tip of her tongue since Archer made them come to my place for coffee before dinner.

"My job pays well."

My mother scoffs. "Singing pays well?"

My father glances in her direction.

"Yes, very well," I say. Thanks to my new contract, I'm earning double, and I haven't even had to do any of the side work since things between Alek and I... ended.

"Not as much as being a doctor, though, I suppose," my mother adds.

I nod and down the rest of my wine.

"Mom," Archer chastises, and she simply shrugs as if she didn't mean to offend me.

My father watches but says nothing.

They're about to be really disappointed when I order another bottle of wine just for myself in order to get through fucking dessert.

"Lena." The harshness of my name grabs my attention.

I look over my shoulder to find Anya behind me, River standing next her. She's perfectly popped her hip, hand resting on it, as her watchful gaze glances around the table. When it lands on Archer, her eyes narrow, and I'm terrified he's going to go up in flames just by the stare alone.

"Anya, great to see you. This is my brother and my parents." I wave a hand around, quick to dispel any tension or hatred she might have for them. I certainly didn't expect to see her at a middle-class Mexican restaurant, but it's recently become my favorite.

She turns her gaze to me, and she offers me her version of a smile, which is quite forced but generous, considering who it's coming from.

"I haven't seen you around lately." No hello. No "what's been happening in your life." Just pure Anya. But she does surprise me when she addresses my parents. "Your daughter truly knows how to sing, and I hate musicals," she adds.

"It is an interesting hobby," my mother says with a charming smile.

Anya's perfectly manicured eyebrow perks up. "Hobby? I think if one cannot see clearly that singing is Lena's calling and her purest form of joy, they're narrow-minded or dim-witted. Potentially both."

My mother's jaw drops, and River bites his bottom lip.

"What my wife means to say is she's very passionate about the arts and supportive of Lena's performance," River interjects.

My brother's holding in a smug expression, and my mother seems flabbergasted.

Anya simply waves him off.

"No, they seem intelligent enough for the insult if

they can so callously throw it at their own daughter. Pitiful, really."

"These are the type of friends you make in New York?" my mother asks, shocked, as she points at Anya. And I realize she can't even hold Anya's gaze. If I had an older sister, I would definitely want it to be Anya.

The family beside us looks at my mother, and she shrinks back into her chair, running a hand over her dress indignantly.

"Tough crowd," Anya says. "Lena, please call me when you're done here. We have much to discuss." And just like that, she walks off. River offers a polite smile and dips his head in goodbye.

"Who on earth was that?" my mother demands, and I can't help but notice my father hides a small smirk.

I try not to mirror it.

"Investors," I reply.

CHAPTER 34

Lena

My parents didn't come to my show once in the remaining week that they stayed in the city. And I also never met with Anya after seeing her in the Mexican restaurant, which is probably why she's sitting in the front row of the audience right now, staring at me as if she wants to kill me.

I give the performance of my life because it may very well be my last, but it's also a testament to how professional I am that I could actually get through the entire show.

Once I walk backstage, I know it'll only be a matter of minutes before she comes back here to find me. Everyone congratulates one another, as per usual, but the excitement of a good show has dulled over the months. We haven't yet started practicing the new routines, but I think when we do, it'll liven up the morale. I start pulling the bobby pins from my hair, letting my long brown locks fall around my face while I wait for her.

I turn when I hear the click of heels approaching, and offer her a kind smile when I see it's Anya.

"You stood me up," she accuses, her arms crossed over her chest.

"I was busy."

"Yes, I know." She looks at me. "I'm not used to people standing me up."

"I'm sure you aren't used to many people doing anything you don't ask them to do," I say politely, but she notices the hint of sarcasm. "What's up?" I walk into my dressing room, and she follows me and shuts the door behind her.

"I have connections, you know that, right?"

I look back at her with confusion. "Are you... threatening me right now?"

Her eyebrows furrow. "Of course not. What I meant was I have connections to get you a better gig. I know you've been auditioning elsewhere."

"Shhh." I put my finger to my lips, and she seems perplexed. I haven't told anyone here I'm looking elsewhere because I'd like to keep this job until I find something else. "How do you even know I've been auditioning elsewhere?"

She raises an eyebrow, and I put my hands up in the air. "I actually don't even want to know."

"Alek has been asking around for you," Anya says, giving me a moment to absorb that. "He didn't want me to say anything, but I don't have time to dance around whatever is happening between you two."

"Nothing's happening between us," I'm quick to say, and she gives me a knowing look. "Or whatever it was, it's done now. Anyway, what are you talking about?" I try to shift the conversation. Because I want to push any discussion of Alek as far away as possible.

"Your dream is to work on Broadway, isn't it?"

I swallow and nod. "Yes, but I can't just step into something because you give it to me."

She narrows her gaze. "That's the stupidest thing that's fallen from your mouth yet. I don't care for humble bullshit. This is the business, is it not? It's not *what* you know but *who* you know. And have you not worked hard? Are you not equipped to sing on those stages? Do you doubt your talent?"

"No. I just—" The rest dies on my lips. What? Think I still have to struggle? Think it shouldn't come so easily to me? But hadn't I been trying time and time again? Isn't that exactly how I got this job?

Or is it because of Alek?

"Well, Alek got you an audition for a lead role. This one is worldwide, and they sell out of every show. Apparently." She shrugs her shoulder. "I still can't stand it, but Alek is certain you'll see. But you have to be the best version of you."

My entire body vibrates with a nervous type of excitement and confusion. It doesn't mean I have the job, but isn't this a start? It's so hard to find auditions, let alone be shortlisted.

I take a seat, shocked. "How did you— How did he get it?" I ask.

"He was a client," she says. "Also, why are you avoiding my brother?"

"Avoiding? I... uh... I'm not."

"Whatever. Did you two have a fight?"

I turn back around and start wiping the makeup off. But Anya is certainly someone who does not just magically disappear. Especially if she expects an answer.

"I have a contract here. I don't know if I can go to another company," I tell her half assed. I've been auditioning for other roles but accepting Alek's help seems... wrong? Most likely my own stubbornness of not wanting his help. Was this his way of saying sorry? I internally stop myself from looking further into it.

"Of course you can." She huffs. "If you get the role, I will tear the contract up myself." She pauses and narrows her eyes at me. "Don't think I missed the change of subject."

"I haven't seen him in a month," I confess. "I'm not avoiding him or anything. There's just nothing to discuss."

"Hmm," she says and looks around the room as if disgusted by its tiny size. "Alek has been off lately. Cinita is wearing on him. And, well..." She eyes me. "Do I scare you?" she blurts.

"Scare me?" I ask. "Like, am I terrified of you?"

She nods expectantly.

"I would say you're an intimidating woman, sure. And I think if you wanted to scare me, you would be able to. But am I scared of you, right now? No. I like you."

"Good. I like you as well. I'm sure my brother's warned you already, Lena, but we're not good people. We're coming to learn, however, that we do make exceptions for certain people we encounter in our lives.

"I won't tell you what to do with your life. But I will confess that my brother is different around you. He's calmer, more settled, and that is something neither of us have felt since our childhood. I want to see him happy, and I think you make him happy.

"If you choose not to associate with him, I understand. But take his offer. I suppose in his own way it's an apology. Which we don't do very well."

I twist in my chair and look at her, but she's examining her nails.

"I'll send you the details. The audition's tomorrow. Good luck."

She grabs the doorhandle and goes to leave.

"Anya," I say, and she pauses.

"Thank you. Truly. I don't think you're all that bad." I wink.

She offers a barely-there smile. And again, it's forced, but she's trying. "Don't tell anyone and ruin my reputation, or I'll have to kill you."

She leaves, and I'm not entirely sure if she was joking.

CHAPTER 35
Lena

I'm nervous because this feels different. The theater is beautiful, and it's in the center of Manhattan. As I wait, I wonder how this might change my life. This is what I've always wanted, yet I'm hesitant because I've gotten it with the aid of the Ivanov siblings; more specifically, Alek.

But Anya's right. I need to stop thinking it would be just because of them if I get this role. I need to believe in myself. Not for my parents or for the Ivanov siblings. Simply because I know I can.

"Ah, Miss Love, it's lovely to finally meet you," Steven, the show producer, says as he walks toward me and offers his hand. I've been shown around backstage by his assistant for the past twenty minutes, and a thrill runs through me with its potential. I shake his hand.

"Likewise, I really appreciate you taking the time to let me audition."

His eyebrows furrow slightly. "Oh, I've already seen you perform. There won't be any need for an audition. Though, if anyone asks you, tell them you did. I don't want a lawsuit about not being fair." He offers a charismatic smile.

"You've seen me perform already?"

We both realize we seem to be having a miscommunication, and he chuckles. "Did Alek not mention to you that he brought me to your show two weeks ago? My lead performer's mother is ill, and she has to move back home. I only have a few weeks to replace her. I mentioned this to Alek at..." He clears his throat, and I realize he almost let slip mentioning one of their auctions. I wonder what type of auction he attends. "Dinner. He mentioned his woman is a phenomenal singer, so he took me to see your show."

My stomach swirls at the insinuation of me being Alek's woman. Because I'm anything but. Aren't I?

"Whether or not I discovered you because of Mr. Ivanov does not take away from your talent, Miss Love. Someone such as yourself was always going to rise to fame. As luck would have it, I found you first."

I bite my bottom lip in a haze of mixed emotions. How many times have I received rejections? *It's just not your time yet. You don't look the part. You're just not the right fit.*

And now... Is it really okay for me to take this? To have this?

A smile breaks across my face, and a nervous but excited energy crackles around me. "I have to let my boss know first, but I'd be honored to be a part of your show. Thank you so much for this opportunity."

He smiles in response. "I must confess I was surprised to hear Mr. Ivanov had a wife."

I choke. "Oh no, we're not married. It's not like that between us."

His eyebrows shoot up. "Apologies. A partner in crime, then?" His eyebrows furrow at that. "What I mean to say is, in your best interest, you might want to be careful. This role will bring you a great deal of fame. Just be careful not to be caught in a scandal, if you understand what I mean?"

I nod. Because I understand exactly what he means. He himself is involved in less-than-savory business dealings if he attends the Ivanov's auctions. Not that I'm dating Alek, but if it was discovered that he's a murderer, it'd wipe away my career in seconds.

"Steven! We need to make adjustments to this," Claire, his assistant, says, but then she looks up from her clipboard and realizes we're still talking. "Oh, I'm sorry, I didn't mean to interrupt."

"No, we're done here," Steven says to her with a satisfied smile. Then he turns back to me. "I'll send over the contract and script. You'll only have a few weeks to learn the part. Are you up for the challenge, Miss Love?"

A thrill runs through me, and I grin. "I love a challenge."

Because this isn't a challenge, getting here was.

Despite our differences, there is one person I have to thank for that.

CHAPTER 36
Aleksandr

I watch from the edge of the room as Anya showcases her recent submissive on stage. The woman's wrists are cuffed in leather, a bar between them. Anya clips the restraints to the end of the stage, demonstrating how the contraption works, seeming all too pleased with the flogger she's holding as she brushes it over the submissive's skin.

Anya detaches the bar and clips it between the cuffs around her ankles, widening the submissive's legs, and locks the bar in place so the audience can have a better view of the backside of the woman wearing leather lingerie.

The audience is watching intently, and I know it will bring in a good amount of money tonight.

"Mr. Ivanov," Clay, one of Anya's bodyguards, grabs my attention. "You have a guest."

My eyebrows furrow. It better not be Cinita. I left Vance with her in the house because she's driving me batshit crazy, but Will has assured me he'll find the last man who hurt her any day now.

I want to hunt him down myself, but I've already wasted too much time being consumed by Cinita and making sure I'll be the one to deliver the final blow to the men who put her in the hospital. I have other things I need to prioritize.

I stop short as I see the person who's been on my mind is standing outside of Anya's office door, waiting for me.

"Lena," I call out, grabbing her attention. She seems nervous.

"I'm not here to dance," she quickly blurts.

"Good, because I wouldn't let you dance for any other man," I reply.

Tension fills the space between us.

I hold my hand up toward the office door. "Let's have this discussion privately."

She swallows hard but says nothing as I push into her space and open the door. All I can smell is her fucking floral perfume, and I'm doing everything in my power not to take her here and now.

I close the door behind her, and she seems to idly look around.

"I had a not-audition this week. I've been offered a role in a Broadway show," she says, watching me, hovering close to the wooden desk. It's taking all my control not to take the two steps over to her.

Anya has chewed me out so many times, telling me I don't have "tact." Whatever the fuck that means, and I don't think she knows either.

"Is the role not to your liking?" I ask. Because I'll get her whatever she wants. I'll set the world on fucking fire to make it happen.

She chokes out a laugh. "It's an incredible offer, Alek. I just... I don't understand why you did that for me."

"Because I would do anything for you," I say sincerely. "Whatever you want, I will make happen for you. You were made to shine bright on the stage as much as I was made to haunt the shadows."

She sucks in a breath, and I can't help but reach for her, take those two steps to fill the distance between us, because this woman... This woman has fucking consumed me.

"Alek. We can't. I won't be your plaything."

"Who the fuck told you you're just my plaything?"

I demand, because I have every intention of killing them.

She seems confused. "Alek, I don't know what you want from me."

"You. I only want *you*," I say as I brush my gloved hand over her cheekbone, and she sucks in a breath, her breasts rising under the long yellow dress. Just like sunshine.

"You and I are not a good match, Alek."

"We're a fucking perfect match," I correct. "Everything about you was built just for me. I refuse to be in denial about it. Aren't you tired of lying to yourself, sweetheart?"

Her eyebrows scrunch, and tears spring to her eyes. "The things you do scare me."

"And that won't change. I won't apologize for who I am."

"I don't want you to change. I just—"

Too much talking. I lean down, and she sucks in another breath, her tongue darting out along her bottom lip.

"Just us," I tell her as I slowly trace her neck with my fingers and then wrap my hand around her throat. Her eyes go molten. "I'll give you everything."

"Aleksandr..." A tear slips down her cheek, and I fucking hate myself so much that I've made her cry.

That I've done this to her. I press my lips to hers, and she's already open for me, melting into me as I pull her to me. Her warmth, her softness. Like fucking sunshine, and the voices don't even put up a fight.

My sanctuary.

I lift her and wrap her legs around my hips as I devour her. This fucking woman who has somehow become my world. "Stop running away from me."

"Stop being a dick," she breathes.

I smile as I kiss her neck and place her on the desk. She grabs my gloves, ripping them off.

"I want you to touch me, Alek."

Fuck. This woman.

I slip my hand under her dress, noting every touch and how soft she feels under my hands. I can't stop kissing her, taking all that she'll give me. Fuck, this is all I've been thinking about these past few weeks.

I feather my fingers along the edge of her panties and then push them to the side as I insert one finger. She gasps as I push in a second and watch her. Every hitch of her breath, every arch of her back as she grinds into my hand desperately.

"Ride my hand like the good little girl you are."

"Fuck, Alek," she says as she opens her eyes and stares at me. I insert a third finger, and those eyes widen in complete bliss.

"No one else can make you feel like this," I remind her. "Only me."

"Yes," she breathes, riding my hand and the high.

"Come for me, sunshine."

She grabs my arm for dear life, a quiver beginning to shake her as I smugly smile. "I haven't even tasted you yet, and you're already coming undone for me."

"Shut u—" Her moan cuts off her words, and I kiss her, taking her cry and consuming it as her pussy clenches around my fingers.

I want all of it—day in and day out. I might not change, but I may have a reason to never leave the house if I have her there.

"Of course I'm going to buy more jewelry." Anya's voice breaks into the room as she opens the door.

"Oh my god!" Lena yells, pushing me away and wiping her lips. Her dress was covering everything already, but she's quick to stand, red streaking her cheeks.

"Looks like you two have made up. I'd rather it not be on my desk, though," she says, crossing her arms over her chest. Her gaze lands on my bare hands, surprised to see them ungloved. She doesn't know Lena is the only one I'll touch.

River is trying not to laugh behind her, and I have to shift myself uncomfortably.

"I need to go," Lena croaks as she beelines for the door. I grab for her, but she's already gone.

Anya stops me, and I try to push past her. "Before you go after her, you have a guest who has something you want."

She looks over her shoulder, and a tall, blond-haired, blue-eyed man who does not look happy to see me, waits in the hallway. I remember him because I put a bullet in his shoulder the only time we met. When he was tracking me in Russia.

"Will?" I say.

"Hello, dickhead," he replies in a proper British accent. "I have what you want if you're willing to pay the price."

I'm torn. I want to chase Lena, but once I get rid of Cinita's last man, I can get rid of her. Truly put her to rest for both me and Lena.

I look him up and down. "Last time, I thought you were taller."

He gives me an insincere smile. "Last time, I thought you talked less."

CHAPTER 37
Lena

The timing couldn't have been any better. The change from my current show to my new one has been a lot more fluid than I expected. Matthew was sad to see me go but not surprised. And it's bittersweet as I give my last performance tonight.

I'm on stage, gratefully embracing everything this role and cast have offered me. Nerves have no place as I get ready for my next endeavor.

So I sing to the audience.

To the cast.

And to the Ivanov siblings who sit in the front row. One more so than the other.

A brooding Aleksandr, who has never once sat in the front. Only in the back, in the shadows. His gaze consumes me, and for the first time, I feel truly seen. Much is shifting as I spread my wings.

I finish the song, my heart racing as my breasts rise and fall with my breathing. Everyone stands and claps, and I smile but also want to cry. It's bittersweet. I'd felt stagnant here, but now I feel sad to leave.

We join hands and bow, waiting for the curtains to fall. When they do, Julie jumps on me and explodes into tears. "That was your best yet! I don't want you to go!"

I laugh as others congratulate me, then say to Julie, "You know you can always visit."

She laughs too. "Give it a little bit, girl. I'll be aiming to hit it big like you as well. Just so you know, when I see you on the screens in Times Square, I'm totally bragging to everyone that I know you."

I laugh with mixed feelings. How strange this has all become.

Anya walks through to the backstage area. I expect Alek to be with her, but he's not. We haven't spoken since the other night when Anya walked in on us.

I needed to process what I want. I know I want Alek, but there are many other things to consider if we're to have any type of relationship. That, and I hadn't asked him about Cinita, which is a problem for me. I can't help how I feel and won't apologize for it.

"The show is still shit, but you shined," Anya says, trying her best at a compliment. Which she does not give freely.

Julie offers me a courteous smile and says goodbye. She's warned me against Anya, and to be honest, I kind of like to make my own opinions about someone. Anya, although prickly, has been amazing. She is turning out to be a very unlikely friend, and I feel like I'm benefiting more from our friendship than she is.

Matthew walks in, adjusting his belt as he holds a bouquet of red roses for me. "Before you run off, I want you to know that no matter what, you'll always have a job here."

I offer him a sweet smile. I don't know how exactly he'll give me my spot back since I've already been replaced, but I appreciate the sentiment.

"I'll just quickly get changed," I tell Anya. When she found out about my acceptance of the new role, I received a short text.

> Upgrade your wardrobe.

Compliments are hard for Anya. She might've meant "congratulations," so I invited her out for dinner to celebrate.

Before I step into my dressing room, I ask, "Will, ah... Will Alek be joining us?"

She looks up from her manicured nails. "Am I not enough?"

"No, that's not what I meant," I say as we walk into my dressing room. "I just noticed he was sitting with you, is all."

I change into a new dress that I bought just for this occasion. It hugs my body but also flows just below the hips. It's a dark blue silk. I pull my hair out of its bun and let the soft waves flow over my shoulders.

"He has business to attend to this evening. But he wanted to see your last performance first," she informs me. It fills me with butterflies, and I feel foolish that he can make me feel that way. But I can't control it.

"Oh," I mutter, realizing I sound far too disappointed. "That's okay. Girls' cocktail night."

"I don't drink alcohol," she reminds me, and I feel silly because I'd completely forgotten. Anya had explained to me she doesn't like her judgment being impaired.

"More for me." I offer a big smile. "I thought we could go to the Mexican restaurant where you met my parents. I was actually surprised to see you there that night. I didn't think that would be somewhere you would go."

"Trust me, it's not my usual choice. Unless River makes me. He owns restaurants. He is for sure the more social one of the two of us, and will drag me out to try new places. That Mexican restaurant was where I first met his mother. So we go from time to time."

My jaw drops. "You met River's mother?" If her meeting with my mother was any indicator, it must've gone disastrous. It's not so shocking that she's met his mother but I could never imagine Anya as the 'daughter-in-law' type.

"Yes of course. She likes me. Why, I'll never know."

I smile at her through the mirror as I touch up my makeup. "Does she know... you know, that you..." I don't even know how to ask.

"Kill people? Sell people and illegal things? Fuck her son like a dirty whore?"

I choke and grab the celebratory glass of champagne from beside me. "All of those things, I suppose."

"Of course not. And she still thinks her son is an angel and that he doesn't sell guns and drugs."

"Guns and drugs?" I repeat quietly. "Why do you tell me these things, Anya?" Because I have the distinct impression neither she nor Alek share this kind of thing with others.

"If required, you'd be an easy target to remove before you could expose us," she says matter-of-factly, and a chill runs down my spine. She's offering a hint of a smile, but I still don't know if she's joking. "But I like you. My brother does too. If I were to have any kind of... little sister, I imagine it would be someone like you. With no fashion sense or defenses."

I choke on a laugh, assuming she meant it as a compliment, which it is. It's nice to hear that she thinks of me as a little sister, because I consider her a friend and somewhat of a older sister.

I muster up the courage to ask something I've always been curious about.

"Why do you kill people?"

"It's one of the things I'm good at, just like you are at singing. Natural talent."

I swallow at the ease with which she compares my singing to her murdering.

"Okay, but, like, how many people are we talking?" I want to ask about Alek, too, but feel like that's something I should ask him.

Her eyebrows furrow. "Have you counted every one of your performances?"

"Well, no, but it would be well in the hundreds." She raises a brow at me pointedly. "You've killed hundreds of people?"

"In our world, consequences are harsh. If you

don't kill, you will *be* killed. What's the expression? Dog eat dog world?"

Hundreds of people. I let that sink in. I'm actually sitting in the room as a murderer discusses it like an intrigued woman sitting on her couch watching a crime documentary. Don't get me wrong, they're fascinating, but this... this is real and right beside me.

"And it doesn't bother you to kill someone?"

She shrugs. "Killing gives me power. Authority. And my favorite thing—money. It's only a crime if you're caught, Lena. And my brother and I never leave loose ends."

All of these things I have to take on board.

It should scare me. *They* should scare me.

I bite my bottom lip. "If Alek and I were a thing and we didn't work out... Would one or both of you kill me?"

She laughs, and the sound is as menacing as it is beautiful. "I don't think my brother has any intention of ever letting you go. If you were to bring another man home, he would most likely kill him. But you? No. My brother will never hurt you."

It goes without saying that when I'm with Alek, it's the safest I've ever felt. But it's a lot to absorb. I'm just a normal person. I'm not from their world. And I wonder how much I'll have to change if I decide to be by his side.

"Have you told your parents about the new role?" she asks as I stand and collect my handbag. I down the rest of the champagne, enjoying the little buzz it gives me, but I'll need it when it comes to any kind of conversation about my parents.

I haven't called to tell my parents. I'm not ready yet. I know Archer will be ecstatic for me and come back to the city to watch my first performance, but I still don't know if my parents will be impressed that I have a lead role in an actual Broadway show.

The pay increase is quite nice, and the opportunities that this new part will get me will be even more than I have right now. But I don't know if it's enough. If *I'm* enough.

"Not yet. I want to wait until I've performed a few times. As you saw, they're not the most supportive of my career."

Anya rolls her eyes, and her slight Russian accent comes out when she says, "You might be disappointed that we kill people, but at least we don't kill children's dreams."

I give her a side glance and can't help but smirk. "Are you trying to be poetic or supportive?"

The back door is opened for us by Clay, who has

been waiting there for us, and Vance stands beside the car.

"Oh, shut up, or I really will put you in the trunk of my car. I've become quite good at it," she says with a chilling smile.

I don't think I'll ever get past the shock factor of the things she says, but I think she enjoys teasing me because of it.

It's oddly... nice.

CHAPTER 38
Aleksandr

Will's an asshole but an effective one; he found everything I need in order to free Cinita of the people who hurt her. With the information on the final man who's been following her, I intend to get rid of him tonight.

But first I have to see Lena perform. It's her last performance, and although I'd already seen her sing in the same show countless times, I want to see her one more time before she moves on to her new gig.

Captivating is the only way to describe her.

Vance is once again babysitting Cinita. I advised her to pack her things because the next day, she's on her own again and she and I will be done. This is my parting gift to her. Anything after that is up to her.

Had it not been for Lena, I most likely wouldn't

have been able to free myself from the shackle I'd misguidedly attached myself to Cinita with.

Anya had called it a savior complex. I didn't think of myself as anyone's savior or hero, but perhaps that's what it was. I didn't care to think any deeper on the matter.

I adjust my gloves as I approach the old, worn-down bar on the outskirts of town. These men had been nobodies, only connected to the Bratva by their dealing of small amounts of drugs.

How had Cinita fallen into the hands of men like these? They weren't even powerful. But now it's obvious she's satisfied with wherever she can got her next fix.

"Would you consider this as a brother bonding experience?" River asks over my shoulder.

"I can't fucking stand this prick," Will says. The feeling is mutual.

"I told you, you didn't need to come," I remind them.

"Alright, Rocky, calm down. You think you're going to take on an entire bar by yourself?" Will asks.

It's somewhat rhetorical because, in many ways, I'm certain all of us are capable of it.

"Anya told me I needed to be here. And what Anya

says, goes," River confesses. "And besides, I wanted to try out a few of my guns."

"All of this for a woman you're not even fucking," Will says lazily as he places his hands on the back of his head.

I ignore his intentional digs.

What was about to transpire required my focus and, of course, my enjoyment.

I can free both of us after this.

CHAPTER 39
Aleksandr

I'm in the bathroom washing my hands since a little blood got inside my gloves. I look up in the mirror and notice some has also splattered across my face. I begin to wipe that away as well.

When I walk out, one of the hanging lights is still swinging. River and Will have a buzz about them as they casually sit on the bar chairs. The bartender—the only person we left alive—is shakily pouring them each a whisky.

Eleven men in total were here tonight. The guy chasing Cinita might've thought of himself as more important than what he was, and he apparently had no regard for his drug dealings on our turf.

Either we would've dealt with him or Crue Monti,

who runs the Italian Mafia here in New York, would have. I'd be sure to let him know he's lacking in his vigilante duties to have let this slip under the radar. But part of me is certain they weren't conducting business here until Cinita fled back to New York.

"Would you like a celebratory drink?" River asks. "Also, cleanup should be here in a few minutes."

"I thought you'd be more the drinking-the-blood-of-your enemies type of guy," Will says. "But I guess they say don't meet your heroes."

River sighs. "You really want to get shot in the other shoulder?"

"You'll be paying for it if I fucking do," Will retorts.

My phone buzzes in my pocket, and I pull it out. *Anya*.

I answer and am startled by the loud music that floods into my ear.

"Anya."

River's eyebrows perk up, and he almost looks like some kind of lost puppy because she called me instead of him.

"Umm, Lena's really drunk. And dancing on a table," she says. "Clay tried to get her down, but she threw her drink in his face."

"It's three a.m. Anya, speak fucking English."

Even though I hardly ever fucking sleep, I'm dead tired as I begin to come down from my adrenaline high.

Through the bar's filthy front window, I see a van pull up, and I know it's the cleanup crew, here to get rid of the bodies.

"Lena is dancing on a table. I think she'll regret it in the morning, but she won't listen to me."

The thought of that woman swaying her hips in front of anyone has my teeth grinding.

"Where are you?" I ask. She rattles off the address, and I hang up.

"Sounds like trouble," River says.

"My little bird has decided to dance in front of others," I grit.

Will laughs. "Oh yeah, I see it now. The blood-hungry monster. I doubt your singer has any idea what she's even signed up for."

River gives him a pointed look. "Coming from the man who's never had a relationship."

Will shrugs and downs the rest of his drink. "Not all of us get married and become pussy whipped."

The moment the cleaners step into the bar, I'm heading toward the door, the other two following me. It feels weird to have people around me, especially while killing. I usually do it on my own. I prefer it that way.

But considering River will most likely want to pick up Anya, I can't tell him not to join. And Will? Well, it's not appropriate to put a bullet in his brain since he led me here. But if he keeps chatting, I might think better of it.

"River, mate, you have blood on your shirt. I told you to wear black tonight," Will scolds.

River peers down at it, unfazed. "No one is going to notice in a dark club."

I unlock the car, and before Will's properly closed the back door, I hit the gas. He curses when he hits his elbow on the door, and I feel a slight sense of satisfaction.

* * *

When we arrive at what Anya described as a bar but looks more like a fucking club to me, my temple pulses. I *was* in a reasonably good mood.

When I arrive at the door, the bouncer lets us straight through. I find Lena leaning over to take a drink from a guy as she gives him her sweetest smile.

Fuck, that smile makes my cock hard. And it's about to get the other guy's teeth broken.

I pull the guy's shoulder back and, before he's aware of what's coming, hit him. He's knocked down to the floor.

Anya whistles from behind Lena but says nothing. She's dead sober, and Lena is as messy as a beautiful fucking dream. She's staring at me, her mouth open in shock.

"Alek! He was just giving me a drink!"

"I did warn her," Anya says, and I have the sense that she didn't intervene because she saw me walking through the crowd.

People stand around us, stunned by what just happened, and the bouncer comes to remove the guy because none of them would be daring enough to touch me.

"You don't accept drinks from other men," I growl at Lena.

Her eyebrows furrow, and she pouts. "You don't get to tell me what to do."

"When you're not behaving, I do."

She crosses her arms over her chest, and those fucking tits drive me berserk. "You don't own me."

A ruthless chuckle escapes me. "Oh, but I do, sunshine. You don't accept drinks from other men. Do we have a clear understanding?"

River's hands snake around Anya's waist. "I didn't expect to see you in a place like this," he says to her.

"It smells, and the patrons are filthy," she says, apparently disgusted with the place. "But she insisted. Now, take me home."

"Aren't you two a bore, leaving as soon as you arrive," Will interjects.

I ignore him, only focused on my very drunk singer. "Did you have fun celebrating?"

She pouts again as she wobbly steps forward and grabs my shirt. "Well, it's better now that you finally showed up, Aleksandr."

I reach up for her, and my hands go to her waist. Even drunk, she calls me by my given name. Not Alek.

I like it.

She's so drunk that I expected her to be more upset about me hitting the guy, but it's as if she's already forgotten.

"What the fuck has she been drinking tonight?" I ask Anya as they walk past.

"It went along the lines of the song she kept singing as each one went down. One margarita. Two margarita—"

Lena cuts her off with her hands in the air excitedly. "Three margaritas."

Anya gives me a scathing look. "I prefer when she's

on stage and sings. I *cannot* unhear that awful song now."

I try to hide the smirk at Anya's disapproval.

Lena looks up at me, and I smell the alcohol on her breath as she gazes at me with a smile. "Do you like my new dress?" she asks.

"I prefer how you look with it off," I grit. She chuckles. "Yes, you look beautiful, sunshine. We're leaving now." I grab her hand and begin to lead her through the crowd as she complains.

"I was having fun," she whines as I walk her out the back door, where there are fewer people. She leans on me as we go, and she clutches to the back of my shirt. I hope I don't have too much blood on me.

"You smell good." I look down to see her grinning up at me. I don't know if I should tell her or not, but I think it's best to leave it. Surely, it's my cologne she can smell.

I spot my car up ahead, but before we make it, she comes to a halt. I turn and face her, noticing she looks pale.

"I feel sick."

I manage to move back in time and pull her hair back just as she bends over in that fucking dress and throws up near a dumpster.

"How did that song go, sunshine? One margarita, two margarita?"

"Shut u—" She hurls again, and I can't help but smirk.

It's strange. I never thought I'd be in a place like this. Or Anya either, for that matter. But I suppose we were both making exceptions in how we might cater to Lena in our world. I'm willing to bend backward for her if she'd so much as ask for it.

"Hey, man, get her out of here," a bouncer calls out from the back entrance. Clearly, he's not familiar with who the fuck I am. When I don't reply, he comes closer.

Lena throws up again, her hands going to her stomach.

"Man, fuck off with her. Fucking women never know how to handle their shit," he sneers.

I hold her with one hand as I reach beneath my jacket with the other and pull out my gun. I aim it at his head, and his hands instantly go up.

"How about you give me that towel in your pocket and keep your fucking opinions to yourself?" I say, tilting my head to the side as I hold her hair, the sound of her hurling echoing through the back alleyway.

"Of course. Fuck, man, calm down." He steps

forward with one hand still up and hands me the towel hanging from his pocket with the other.

I wave the gun from him to the door.

"Now, fuck off." He nods and runs inside the club.

I lean over Lena. "Feeling better?" I ask. I wipe around her mouth with the towel.

"Oh my g-god, is that a g-gun?" she stutters in a whisper. I put it back in my pants and nod my head.

"It is. Now, if you would be a champ and get in the car, I need to take you home."

"Who were you going to use a gun on?" she asks, clearly having missed the past few minutes due to hurling.

"You're going to feel this tomorrow, sweetheart."

She groans but looks up at me through thick eyelashes. "Have you missed me?" she asks. Her hands go to my chest, and she leans into me. Her head rests over my heart.

I'm not at all fazed by the vomit because, frankly, I currently have someone else's blood on me. I wonder how she'd handle that knowledge.

I can't deny enjoying this side of Lena; all her resistance pushed to the side. Pure vulnerability with flushed cheeks. And it's exactly why I don't want anyone else seeing her in this state.

"Yes, now get in the car." She smiles as I lead her to

the car and open the passenger door. I notice River and Anya getting into the back seat of her car. Clay is their driver. Will most likely stayed in the club. Besides when he takes payment for the job, hopefully this will be the last time I'll see him.

"Can we drive through McDonald's?" Lena begs.

"McDonald's?"

"Yeah. I want a cheeseburger meal and chicken nuggets," she says as she pushes out her bottom lip.

"Sweetheart, that surely can't be good for you."

She looks at me, stunned, as if I'd just offended her entire existence. "But if it'll soak up some of those margaritas, we can make an exception."

Then she beams with excitement, and she proceeds to sing. "One margarita, two margarita. Six chicken nuggets and a burger in my belly."

I'm certain that's not how the song goes, but I don't tell her otherwise.

It's shocking how much she begged for the food but only had one bite of the burger and two nuggets before passing out on the drive to my house. When we get there, I lift her from her seat, the McDonald's paper bag in hand, and carry her inside.

The only light comes from the lamp in the living room, and the moment I arrive, Vance excuses himself.

Lena stirs but doesn't wake as I put her in my bed.

Where she belongs. As soon as I remove her heels and pull the covers over her, she curls herself into a ball and lets out a contented sigh. I'm not entirely sure what to do with the bag of food, so I put it on the bedside table, then watch her as she sleeps. I remove my gloves and brush my fingers through her hair.

She is breathtaking, even passed out drunk.

CHAPTER 40
Lena

I wake surrounded by warmth. And something solid next to me in the bed. *Shit, is that a person? Did I go home with someone last night?*

Oh my god.

I can't remember much past the happy hour margaritas. I vaguely recall forcing Anya into what I told her was barhopping, but she didn't seem impressed.

I'm afraid to open my eyes and see who it is. And why they're still holding me.

My stomach turns, and I go to roll away, but his grip is unrelenting. I try again, and he speaks.

"Lena."

I know that voice.

"I'm gonna be sick," I manage to say. His arm lifts

away from me, and before I can move, my stomach churns. I throw up right where he was lying. I don't know how the fuck he moved so fast, but he's already off the bed, watching as I lose whatever was left in my stomach.

"Oh my god, I'm so sorry." I wipe at my mouth as I stare at the pink mess on the sheet beside me. I'm never drinking anything pink again.

I cover my mouth as I feel the urge to throw up again, and manage to get up and run to the bathroom this time. I make it to the toilet and hurl again, but hardly anything comes up.

Dropping down to my ass, I sit next to the toilet and look up to find Alek leaning against the doorjamb, naked. His cock is semi-hard, no gloves in sight, and he's watching me.

"How did I get here? And did we...?" I glance down and see I still have on my dress and panties.

"You spewed on me, and you spewed on my bed. So no, we did not," he says.

"So then why are you naked?" I ask, too shameless to look away.

"I figured, what was the point? You know, with you vomiting all over me throughout the night. If you look on the floor next to your side of the bed, you might even find a half-eaten chicken nugget." I cringe at his words. "Though you did try to rub my cock several times in your sleep."

I gasp

"You should shower; you stink. And now I need a new mattress."

"I'll buy you a new mattress," I tell him breathlessly. Oh my god. The horror and shame.

"Why did you drink so much last night?" he asks as he steps past me to the shower, and his toned ass comes into view as he turns the water on. I stare at it because it's a damn good-looking ass. Fuck, I feel horrible, yet my pussy still throbs at the thought of him inside me.

I'm seriously messed up. Maybe I'm still drunk.

"I was celebrating my last night and got carried away at happy hour. I saw you at the show," I say quietly.

"You were phenomenal, as you always are. I'm sorry I couldn't partake in 'one margarita, two margarita' with you."

"Oh my god," I say on a groan, putting my head in my hands, remembering bits of the night.

He smirks as he bends down and starts tugging at my dress. "But I very much would like to take you out to celebrate. Whatever you like."

"I never want to drink again."

He chuckles. "We don't have to drink to celebrate, Lena."

I let him pull the dress off, lifting my arms to help as I remain on the floor. When it's off, I'm left in just my G-string. He looks down at me, fucking me with just a stare.

"I don't know if I can have sex with you right now," I say as I look at his very hard cock, which is right in front of my face.

He chuckles. "Sweetheart, you're the only one suggesting it. I'm trying to get you to shower."

But, damn, it's hard not to want to fuck this man.

"Shower," I say, nodding. I manage to stand, and as I do, my hand hits his cock. "Cock!" I scream, and pull my hand away. He fights a smirk.

"Didn't know you were into slapping," he says. Then he glances down at his cock. "He likes it, if you want to do it again." His cock twitches at his words.

"I'm sorry," I quickly say. I can only act like a quarter of a person right now.

"I'm not," he replies, then turns and steps into the shower. I follow him. His shower is big enough for the two of us, and I can smell myself now. I do stink.

He hands me a toothbrush with toothpaste already on it, and I instantly put it in my mouth, start brushing, then spit the foam onto the shower floor. He raises a brow.

"Spitting too. Damn, what else have you been hiding from me?" I know he's joking. And I get a warm feeling in my chest because he doesn't usually joke. Always so serious. I hand him the toothbrush, and he puts it in his mouth. My own mouth opens in surprise.

"What?" he mumbles around the toothbrush.

I say nothing and reach for the body wash.

He just watches me with those come-fuck-me green eyes, and I can't help but watch him too.

He didn't touch me last night. Not even as I was supposedly touching him in my sleep. I wouldn't go so far as to call him a gentleman, but to me, he is that and more. He is such an unusual man, and I get confused every time I'm around him. Because when I'm with him, my world drops away, and I only see him. It's like he creates some type of bubble and wraps it around us, but sooner or later, we both know it's going to pop. Something this intoxicating can't hold out forever, can it?

"Wash my back?" he asks, and turns around. "You drooled all over it."

"I did not," I scoff, then take his loofah and start washing his back. I take my time, scrubbing the hard planes of muscle, and he just stands there, letting me touch him. I don't take for granted the fact that he lets me touch him. I understand that he doesn't give that away willingly. I don't even know if he has before, so I take full advantage of it, and I let my other hand roam down his side until I reach his waist. My fingers rest at the start of his V, and I can feel him sucking a breath at my touch, but again, he makes no move to reach for my hand and pull it even lower.

A small part of me wants him to take control, but the bigger part knows I don't want him to, even though I'll enjoy every second of his authority.

My circles are slow on his back. *Fuck, fuck, fuck.* I'm a good girl, remember? A smart girl.

He slowly turns, the water trailing over his face and down his chest. His hands wrap around my waist, and I can't help but look down at his well-groomed, beautiful fucking cock.

"Lena," he says, voice gravelly, and before I can even stop, I throw myself at him.

I just can't resist this man, and all I can see or want to see is him.

Just him.

All of him.

He catches me. Of course he does.

I feel like I could jump from a cliff and he would

catch me. He lifts me up, and I wrap my legs around his waist. I feel him between my thighs, and he lifts me slightly higher before he pulls me back down and slides straight into me.

Heaven.

Hello, God, are you there?

I find his mouth. He tastes like peppermint, and I bet I do too. He kisses me back, neither of us moving at first. I feel so full with him inside me, like I've been starved from the last time he stayed with me for the night.

"Fuck, you're perfect for me. You were made for me, weren't you, sweetheart," he says against my lips. He gives a small thrust, and it strokes everything inside me in the right places. Leaning in, I bite his shoulder and dig in until I break the skin. "Use me," he breathes, encouraging me to keep on fucking him up.

He pulls me down even harder so he is seated fully in me, filling me.

Fuck, it feels good.

"Use me," he says again, and I bite my way up his neck until I get to his chin, where I nibble before I find his lips and bite the bottom one. He kisses me back and takes everything. Perfectly.

"Harder," I demand, and his hands on my hips move me up and down on his cock with more force.

"Harder," I say again, pulling away from his lips. "Fuck, I want you to come inside me," I breathe, deprived of any thought that isn't about pure, carnal bliss.

"You going to milk my cock, sweetheart?"

Fuck, his filthy mouth. I bite down on his bottom lip again and grunt, my nails digging into his flesh. "Yes, I want it all."

"So fucking greedy." He encourages me as I move my mouth to his shoulder and sink my teeth in, muffling my cry, riding the wave and realizing that hot water is still raining over us.

He leans back to stare into my eyes as he grabs my throat and pounds into me. "So fucking perfect."

I can't help but smile because I know he means it. Alek may be many things. Some of which I haven't yet been able to come to terms with, but a liar he is not. "Do you like my pussy, Aleksandr?"

His eyes go hooded. I know he loves how I say his name.

"Alek." His name is spoken from outside the shower, and I freeze. He pushes me against the wall and slams into me again. Gripping my ass with his hands, he moves me as someone says his name again. I realize then it's a woman. I pull back a little to look at him.

"Who is that?" I ask with a heavy breath. But he keeps thrusting, and my orgasm hits me hard. It rocks me, and I scream his name. I can't help it; it falls from my lips effortlessly.

"Who are you in there with?" the voice asks.

"Get the fuck out of my room," he says against my neck. He bites down, and I feel him suck on my skin before I pull away, because I know exactly who that is, and I feel like I'm going to break apart. Every-fucking-time, she's there.

"Put me down," I command.

Within seconds, our bubble is shattered. He does as I ask, putting me down. I step out of the shower, and I'm not at all surprised to find Cinita in his bedroom.

"You've got to be fucking kidding me," I say under my breath, not even embarrassed by the fact that I'm naked.

Cinita seems startled, her eyes wide when she sees me. "Lena?" Her expression twists. "Wow, I didn't take you as someone to go after what's mine."

What's hers?

I bite my tongue, too fucking hungover for this kind of shit.

Alek walks out then, putting a towel around

himself and then one over my shoulder to try to cover me up.

"Why the fuck are you in my room?" he asks her.

I shrug off his hold and grip the towel. Wrapping it around me, I look back at her and see her staring at his bare hand that was just touching me.

"I didn't hear you come in last night," she says and pouts her bottom lip. I want to laugh, as it's so clear how she manipulates him.

"I told you last night you were to leave by this morning. Now, get the fuck out of my house."

"But I thought—" She stops and looks at me with a fiery rage. "Is she the reason you don't want to touch me, or are you just collecting broken women now?"

"You're a piece of work, you know that," I shoot back angrily. I've fucking had enough.

"I thought you knew we were living together. Where else would I go?" she says with a casual shrug. "Sorry he's been two-timing you, love."

I scoff. "I know for a fact he wouldn't touch you. And, I don't know, maybe you can move in with one of the men you're actually fucking." My tone is venomous.

"Out," Alek yells from behind me.

She's shocked, and even I flinch under the harshness of his tone. I stay frozen as tears well in her eyes and then she runs out of the room. I step away from him, but he moves in front of me so quickly, I almost get whiplash.

I realize he's blocking me from running. "Your dress has vomit on it. You can wait till Anya brings you clothes, and we can talk calmly about this. Cinita won't be staying here anymore. She was supposed to be gone as of this morning."

"Is that where you were last night?" I scoff in disbelief. "After I sang, you went to be a hero for her and kill the bad men for her? Then, what, felt sorry for my drunk ass and picked me up?"

He seems shocked. "No. It's not like that, Lena, I swear to you. I've done this so I can move forward with you. There is nothing between Cinita and me."

I sneer. "Just because you haven't put your cock in her, Alek, doesn't mean you're not susceptible to her charm. She's been playing you like a fiddle all these years. You don't have room for someone like me in your life. And I don't have room for you in mine."

"Lena, I did this for us," he insists, grabbing my hand, his expression twisting in ways I don't think it even was aware it could.

"Give me some clothes. I don't care if they're yours. I just need to get the fuck out of this house."

His jaw tightens, and he walks to the closet and

pulls out a shirt. I take it from him, then drop the towel to the floor and slide it on. Then he hands me a pair of boxers, and thankfully, they fit once I roll the waistband a few times.

I don't know what I expect from him. To fight? To scream? We're not even a thing, and my jealousy is an unrelenting beast, and I'm the one it's hurting the most.

"I need to get the fuck out of here," I say as I grab my handbag from the side table. I then notice the nugget he'd mentioned earlier. Oh fuck, I really did vomit all over his room.

"Tell me what I need to do, Lena," he begs as I head out of his room.

"I don't know, Alek. You gloat about how good you are at killing people. Why don't you put a bullet in her head?"

Cinita gasps from where she's standing at the end of the hallway.

"Fuck. I didn't mean to say that. I—" I look at him, those forest-green eyes that suck me in too often meeting mine. "I don't like this part of me. This isn't who I am."

I push past him and then Cinita, who's glaring at me as I walk out the door.

Clay holds the car door open as Anya steps out of

the back seat, removing her designer sunglasses. "Oh, Lena, good to see you're part of the living still. I brought you clothes."

"I want to leave," I say, storming toward her. Finally, she seems to really look at me and then notices everything going on behind me.

Her gaze narrows, and she places a hand on my shoulder as she pushes me toward the car and steps in front of me as Alek tries to grab me.

"Why is Cinita still here, Alek?" Anya spits, her slight accent thicker and tone furious.

Alek pauses. "She was supposed to be gone by this morning. I just need to talk to Lena. To explain."

"No," Anya says, pointing at him and staring him down. "Not today. You don't get to hurt her twice. Clean up your mess, Alek."

My heart fills with the way she stands up for me.

It's like having a protective sister.

She leans toward him and says something else, but I can't hear what she says.

She gets in the car and slams the door, furious. But she's quick to brush her hand over her hair to make sure not one piece is out of place.

"I swear if he weren't my brother, I'd kill him for making you cry."

I burst into tears, and she seems taken aback,

unsure as to what to do. Hesitantly, she pats my shoulder. I know it's because I'm hungover and tired, but is it really supposed to be this hard?

And why would I say those ugly things?

"Even I can't remove my brother's shackles for him," Anya admits. "But I know he loves you, Lena. As best as what people like us can."

I sob and say, "What if it's not enough for me?"

She's silent for a moment until she says, "Then that's all right."

CHAPTER 41
Aleksandr

"You really are fucking this one up, aren't you?" Anya whispers furiously and looks over my shoulder, where I know Cinita is standing behind me. "Trailer trash fucking ho."

My sister and I are always frank with one another, but right now, she's scolding me.

I watch as the car pulls away, taking Lena with it, and want to implode. I've fucked up again.

No matter how hard I try, Lena continues to slip through my grasp.

I know I fucking deserve it. But I can't live without her.

I turn on Cinita, furious at putting myself in this situation. I should've cut her off a long time ago. She begins crying and falls into a heap. I know she's trying to manipulate me. Once, those tears had a pull over me, but not anymore. Not when my weakness toward them made Lena cry instead.

"You don't really want me to go, do you, Alek? You're all I have!" she wails.

"I want you out of my fucking house. I never want to see you or hear from you again. Are we clear?"

She sniffles, startled that I haven't played into her theatrics. I step over and past her.

"What?" she says behind me, shocked. Then she's furious. "Then what the fuck has all of this been about?"

I turn to face her. There it is, the ugly little beast beneath.

"You always do as I say." She stomps her foot. "We were always going to be together! You think because some fucking singer steps into the picture that's going to change things?"

I step into her space and grab her chin painfully hard. Her eyes go wide.

If we're both showing our unmasked version, it's best she sees who she's raising her voice at.

Disgust. Revolt. Blood.

Touching her makes me want to vomit.

It hurts.

A cold shiver runs through me at the nauseating

swirl of all the voices and the memory of crouching in that room, blood pooling under my hands and knees.

I can embrace the blood now. But never enough to push away that moment. The coldness of when I touched my mother's dead arm.

"You don't ever speak about Lena like that again. Do you understand me? You are not to ever breathe her name because of how filthy it is when it leaves your mouth. You disgust me."

Tears spring to her eyes, and her bottom lip trembles, but I tighten my grip, and she grits her teeth, immediately stopping the crocodile tears. "No more of your games. We're done. I want you out of the city and to never see you again."

"You can't tell me where—"

"I'm not in a good mood today, Cinita. And I'm ready to kill someone. So you best make sure you're gone within ten minutes."

Her eyes go wide, and I know she can see my murderous intent. I release her, and she stumbles back and makes haste to pack her few things.

I walk to my bedroom that looks like a bomb went off in it. It smells like vomit but also the slight remains of Lena's perfume.

My hands bunch into fists, this situation tearing me up from the inside.

I'd been too late to realize, too slow to prioritize Lena.

I'm fucking livid, and the only way I know how to release this rage is to kill. I throw on my pants and black shirt, then grab my knives.

Lucky for me, I know a handful of people whose debts need to be collected.

I want to kill. *Need* to. If only to prove to both Lena and myself what I really am.

How could someone so beautiful love something as monstrous as me?

When I walk out the front door, the house is empty, and I don't see any sign of Cinita.

CHAPTER 42
Lena

I haven't left my apartment for an entire day now. Not only did I have to nurse that nasty hangover but emotions were running high when I least expected it. I've done nothing but DoorDash food and binge watch *The Real Housewives*, yet not even that can put me in a better mood.

I didn't get any sleep either, my mind too busy replaying the argument we had. I can't believe I told him to put a bullet in Cinita's head. I cringe at the horrible things I said. Jealousy is an ugly, spiteful thing.

When my brother called, I let it go to voicemail.

The only call I answered was one having to do with my new job.

It's the only thing I have to look forward to, right?

So why am I still so fucking sad? Why does it pain me to know he has her there?

We're not even anything official, yet I act like I can tell him what to do. But he's clearly hung up on her. It's like having an ex, isn't it? Or am I just thinking that to justify my outburst?

I don't dislike Cinita, but I know she's using him. I can see that despite him being a cold asshole, and a deadly one at that, he's a good man. At least to those he gives his trust to. He may be scary as fuck, but he's good at his core.

A knock sounds on my door, and I ignore it.

"Lena." Alek's voice sounds from the other side.

I ignore him.

Another knock. "Lena, I know you're in there."

"She's not home right now," I call out.

The front door opens, and I whip my head around to see him in the entryway, my jaw unhinging. "How did you get in?"

"I have a key."

My eyes bulge. I never gave him a fucking key. He's holding a brown bag in one gloved hand, and what looks like a bag from my favorite Thai restaurant in the other. He's wearing a black suit, his head freshly shaven. He looks like a killer, which I suppose is fitting.

I look away from him and back to the TV. "I

already ate."

"That's okay. I'm not hungry either," he says.

I try to ignore him, unable to avoid suffering under these painful emotions.

"Are you on birth control?" Alek asks, and that grabs my attention.

"You can't be serious, Alek. Did you come all this way to make sure you didn't accidentally impregnate me?"

His eyebrows furrow. "I just thought... I—"

"Yes, I am," I answer. "And don't worry, even if I did fall pregnant, it's not like I'd want to have your kids anyway." And I know the minute it leaves my mouth it's wrong. And mean.

I want to say I'm sorry, but I don't.

He licks his lips, and I'm certain my words are enough to push him out the door, but he doesn't go. He places the brown bag on the counter. "Yes, well, I got you the morning-after pill."

"Such a gift giver," I say with a sharp tongue.

I watch him wearily as he drops to his knees in front of me. I don't know what to do, so I shift uncomfortably, as if to get farther away from him, because as mad as I am with Alek, I'm always victim to this relentless connection we share.

"I'm sorry, sunshine," he says earnestly. "I'm not

good at things like this. But I'm trying."

"What are you even trying at, Alek?" I ask, exasperated.

"To be a better man for you. To be someone who is good enough for you."

It tugs at my heart, and I hate the way his sincerity rips me apart. "It's not enough, Alek. Cinita—"

"Is gone," he's quick to say. "I never expected to have someone like you in my life. I hadn't made it clear enough to you that you're the only woman I've ever *wanted* in my life. Cinita reminded me of us as kids, and I wanted to protect her. I didn't realize doing that made you feel less than. I literally could buy you anything in the world, Lena, and I'm still stumped as to what to give you."

"I don't want your money, Alek."

"I know. But it's the only thing I've focused on my entire life. That and protecting my sister. This is all I have been, and if it's not enough for you, I want to find more, become more so I can give you what you need."

He seems confused, and I hate how young he looks. How lost, even.

"I will spend the rest of my life making it up to you. To give you everything you want, just so I can stay by your side, Lena."

My heart swells, and I hate him so much right now because it's so unfair to us both. We come from different worlds.

I slip onto the floor beside him, tucking my feet under my ass as I do.

"Alek, I was emotional because you brought me to your house and still had her there. I won't come second to anyone. I can't keep playing this game." I shake my head.

"She has nothing on you, don't you get that? She is beneath you in every way," he says, the sincerity of his words rocking me.

I bite my bottom lip, trying my hardest not to cry.

"Lena, Cinita was an old wound, but she's gone now. I've never felt this way about anyone, and I sure as fuck don't know how to navigate it, but I'm trying. For all the hell she caused me, the one and only good thing she's done is lead me to you. You are the only thing I need in my life. Tell me what you need from me, what else I can give you, and I'll give you everything."

His words hit my like an avalanche. I don't want to be fool enough to believe them, but I can't deny the truth when it's right in front of me. Because Alek might be many things, but a liar he is not. And for someone who has never known love, I can't deny that he is trying his best. But even I don't know what that might look like in the future.

"What would we ever be, Aleksandr?"

"What do you mean?"

"You and me. What would we ever be?"

"Us. We would be *us*."

"I get that, Alek, I do. But while I'm focusing on my career right now, eventually, I want more. Have you thought of that?" I say. "Cinita may have been the better choice for you. I know she doesn't want kids, and I doubt you do either."

And I hate myself for comparing myself to her, but if I already feel so strongly for him now, how could I possibly walk away in a few years' time?

"You never even asked me if I want kids."

"Well, do you?"

His eyes search mine, and for the first time he seems lost for words. "I've never thought about having children because I've never loved anyone before. It was something I didn't even think was a possibility for me."

"I know that's what I want. To be married one day. I want to be pregnant and work in my garden, growing my own vegetables. I want to go on vacation once a year to a fancy destination and have sex in every city with my husband." I take in a shaky breath. Because as much as I believe him that Cinita is finally gone, can I really believe that we'll want the same thing in five, ten, fifteen years' time? I'm sure that's a risk in any relationship, but with Alek it's more intense. "I want all of that, Alek. So while this is fun, what you and I have, it's never going to last.

"I know what I want, and you don't. That's not a bad thing, it just means we need to end it before it gets out of hand."

"And what if I would never accept you with someone else?"

"Would you kill them simply because you couldn't have me?" He just gives me a pointed look. "That's crazy, Alek."

"Aleksandr," he says, correcting me on his name.

"It's crazy," I say again.

"Is it crazy to want someone so badly you would kill for them?" he asks. He leans closer. "I want you, so fucking much." My breathing gets heavier at his touch, and I close my eyes because this is everything I want to hear, but I know I should run. It won't last. Better it hurt now than destroy me in the future. He shouldn't be able to do this to me.

But he is.

"No other relationship could ever compare to what we have. You get that, right? One day when you're married and fucking your shit of a husband, you'll think back and wish it was me who was fucking you."

I gasp as my eyes fly open, surprised by the desperate plea in his voice.

"I might not be sure about kids now, and I know I'm fucked up..." My stomach twists as I wait for him to continue. "But I could be a husband. *Your* husband. I'll be your biggest fan. If children are something you really want..." He swallows. "I wouldn't be a good father."

I brush my hand over his cheek. "Have you ever thought of the possibility?"

He stares at me longingly, and it breaks me. "I never thought I'd be capable of loving someone as much as I do you. So maybe, if you can teach me."

My heart stops, and I can't breathe. Butterflies flitter throughout my stomach. "Did you just say you love me, Alek?"

"Is it so wrong?" he asks. "I just can't let you go. I refuse. I will make every promise, take every vow, and tell you I love you every day, just to remind you how right it is for me to stand by your side. We're made for each other, Lena. I always thought killing was my only purpose in this life, until I met you."

My bottom lip trembles. "Alek, you've put me through hell."

"I know I'm not easy, but I will give you everything you ask of me, Lena. I'll even send you cards."

I can't help but laugh at that, stupid tears springing to my eyes.

"I can't be second best, Alek. You can't make me feel second to anyone again. My heart just can't take it anymore."

"I'll fucking worship the ground you walk on. I never meant to hurt you, Lena, I swear it."

I hate how easily his words lift me up. But they can so quickly destroy me too. "I can't do another roller coaster, Alek."

His body goes rigid, like his entire world has just come to a crashing end, and my heart breaks. Because this man has somehow become my everything. And it's terrifying, as much for me as it is for him.

"But we'll try. One more time," I say as I press my lips to his. I feel his breath against my lips as the tension drains out of him and he desperately consumes me.

"I need you," he growls as his hands skim up my outer thighs, and a shiver runs down my spine because I know without a doubt that I fucking need him more.

CHAPTER 43
Lena

"And that's what you call a flush," I say, laying down my cards with a smirk. "Take it off."

Alek sighs as he throws his cards into the center of the mattress. So far, I've only lost one hand, and all that came off was my earrings.

Alek, however, is down to... well, after removing his loose pj pants... nothing. He sits comfortably naked at the end of my bed. All masculine muscle with a semi-hard cock.

I bite my bottom lip, realizing I really lost out on this game.

"Anya doesn't mind if you're not at the auctions as often?" I ask as I collect the cards.

"Please don't speak about my sister while I'm

sitting on your bed naked, sunshine."

I giggle. "I bought something for you yesterday," I say. "Give me two minutes."

I turn to get up from the bed, but he grabs my ankle as I hop on the other foot, trying to keep my balance. "Don't worry, I won't be gone long." I smile, and he slowly releases me, not satisfied.

I race out of the room rather giddily. It's been two weeks since Alek kicked Cinita out, and Alek's been staying here every night since. We've fallen into a comfortable routine. Orbiting each other around my rehearsals. It's only another week until I perform for the first time with the new theater company, and I'm filled with anticipation and excitement.

The black box I left unopened is in my spare room. I wanted to hide it from him so it would be a surprise. Some of the auctions he and Anya run are sex themed, and although Alek hasn't asked anything of me specifically, I'm certain I can try things with him.

I shuffle out of my pj's and strap only the leather cuffs on my wrists. Alek has bought me all sorts of lingerie he's wanted me to wear over the past few weeks while we've been in our bubble. Just us.

I'm certain I've lost a bit of weight between the rehearsals and all the sex. Because there is *a lot* of sex.

I come back to the room to find him holding up my pink vibrator with an arched eyebrow.

"Hey, I leave you for two minutes, and you snoop through my stuff?" I reprimand.

His gaze roams down my naked body, and his grip tightens on the vibrator. "And you come back like that."

I bite my bottom lip and step forward. The spreader bar I'm carrying can be hooked between my legs or arms. Whatever way he might like.

"Come here," he commands as I step forward. He grabs the bar and tugs me forward. I chuckle, my heart racing.

His gaze drifts to the hanging plant in the corner of my room, and I can see when an idea has sparked in his mind. His cock is rock hard as he leads me over to it. I'm confused at first, and maybe slightly concerned that the people in the building across the way can see us.

But Alek is unfazed as he removes the hanging plant from the hook.

"Okay, I have no idea what you're doing," I admit.

"Did I tell you to speak?" he growls.

I bite my bottom lip again as he pulls the bar over my head, and my eyebrows shoot up as it slips perfectly over the hook.

"Oh, I didn't even think of that."

Alek smirks as he grabs my throat, then he kisses me deeply, passionately, intoxicatingly. My arms begin to ache, and raise on my tippy-toes to try to relieve the pain.

He flips my pink vibrator in his hand. "When was the last time you used this?" he asks as he walks over to my bedside table, and I can't help but admire his ass as goes.

"I've been preoccupied with work for quite some time; no time for men," I confess.

"Really?" he asks as he saunters back to me, cracking his neck from side to side. He squirts lube along my vibrator and then on his other hand. I'm confused at first, but then he rubs the toy against my clit and switches it on.

"Have you been fucked in the ass, sunshine?" he asks.

My eyes widen and I swallow hard. "No, just a finger once," I admit.

His lubed hand snakes around to my ass, and I realize suddenly why he's asking. He flicks to the next level up on the vibrator, and I moan. *Oh fuck, it's hard to focus.*

"You know how much I love this ass, don't you?"

"Yes," I whimper as he shoves the vibrator in, little

by little, teasing and stretching my pussy bit by bit. But I'm confused as I try to focus on where his other hand is going.

"Can I have your ass, sweetheart?" Nerves shoot through me as look down at his hard cock. "Don't worry, I'll take it easy on you tonight."

"Thank fuck, because your cock's way too big," I blurt out, relieved.

A masculine smile passes over his lips. "Do you think this is too big?" he asks, pulling the vibrator out and raising it to my eye level. But as he does, his finger that's rimming my asshole pushes in.

It stretches me, and I'm both elated and unsure as the blood drains from my arms. I'm almost entirely suspended and at his mercy.

"I don't know," I whisper. "But I trust you."

"You tell me if it's too much, sweetheart," he says as he reinserts the vibrator, and I lean into it, moaning as he slowly but surely tortures me with it. His thumb slides into my ass gently. And I'm self-conscious but also in pure bliss. I feel full as he syncs the movement of the toy to that of his thumb.

He leans forward, kissing me. Taking me in. I want to touch him and pull him to me, but my bound position won't allow it. My ass and pussy are soaked from the lube, and it all feels so good.

"Do you want more, sweetheart?" he asks, and I'm shaking because it's too much but not enough.

"Yes," I'm quick to say, because this slow torture is killing me.

"Good girl," he says as he pulls out the vibrator, and I'm immediately frustrated until I realize he's lining himself up under me. I hold my breath as he pushes into me, stretching me farther than my toy ever could.

He props his foot on my reading chair, and I groan as he sinks in deeper, one of my legs loosely hung over his leg as he continues to thumb my asshole.

"Oh my god," I say, never realizing sex could feel *this* intense.

I'm frustrated when he pulls his thumb out, but my eyes burst open when I feel the nudge of the vibrator at my asshole.

"Do you want it?" he croons.

I do. I want it all.

I nod slowly, trusting him, knowing full well if it's too much, he'll...

Oh my god. My eyes roll into the back of my head as he slowly pushes it in. Little by little, he works it into me. I don't know where to focus—on him or the intrusion in my asshole.

All I know is I'm in pure bliss.

"Aleksandr," I whimper.

Does it always feel this good? My arms hurt from being suspended, but I don't care. Even though I've given him full control, I feel like he's worshipping me.

He thrusts deeply into me, and I moan, fighting my urges to grab onto him. The vibrator buzzes as he kicks it up a notch, and I feel like I'm going to come undone. I'm so fucking full.

Alek's fingers brush against my lips, and before I know it, they're slipping into my mouth, along my tongue, and pushing to the back of my throat. I suck on them, moaning and whimpering as he fucks me.

Fuck, has it always been like this?

Alek's pace picks up, and my legs begin to quiver as the pleasure climbs, and I realize I'm about to come. I can't tell him because my mouth's full of his fingers. When it breaks over me, I bite down on his fingers. Licking along them as I ride wave after wave.

He seems to slow down, letting me focus on the pure bliss washing over me. He removes his fingers from my mouth and then kisses me. With a glazed look, I murmur, "I love you, Alek."

He chuckles as he stretches up to unhook the bar, his cock still hard as he slides the toy out of my ass. "Now you tell me that, after I fuck you so good. But I'm not done with you yet, sweetheart," he says as he tugs the bar toward him again. I'm limp against him, but he shoves me onto the bed, and I bounce.

"I'm going to fill all of your holes with my cock tonight, sunshine. And you're going to swallow my cum like a good girl. Do you understand?"

I nod obediently as he lovingly brushes his fingers along my jaw, then grabs the hair at the back of my head and stuffs my mouth with his cock.

CHAPTER 44
Aleksandr

I watch her, amazed. It was only last night I was filling that beautiful mouth with my cock, and now I watch her in awe as she captivates the crowd. A crowd that is far larger than the previous theater where she performed could hold.

With or without me, she was always meant for this stage. I dip my gaze toward Anya, who's sitting in the box with me. Her arms are crossed, unimpressed by musicals in general, but her eyes light up when Lena comes on stage.

To think at any point I thought Cinita's dancing was captivating. I was so fucking wrong. That has nothing on Lena's singing.

Lena's voice dramatically cuts off. The air fills with

suspense, and right on cue, everyone stands, applauding. I can see the rise and fall of her chest, and I stand with them and clap.

Beautiful.

A masterpiece.

Everything.

We leave as everyone else does. This time, Lena told us we can't come backstage because she wants to celebrate her first show with her new colleagues. It works out well since Anya and I have a few things to clean up. It doesn't make me any less miserable that I have to share Lena, though.

"Stop pouting," Anya says with arms crossed over her chest as she sits in my passenger seat. I'd become so used to Lena sitting there that I'm sadly disappointed by my sister's company. Not that I'd ever tell her that.

I didn't understand these feelings when she'd found River.

Neither of us had been raised on love, and we were still doing a shitty job at it. But I understand why my sister got married. She's the same woman who tears men's balls off for sport, but there's an added something to her now.

"You're still doing it," she reprimands.

"I'm not doing anything," I grit out, my leather-covered hands gripping tightly around the wheel. "I want to make tonight quick, though."

She smirks and angles herself toward me. "Do you have a curfew now?"

"No. I just want to be there to pick her up."

"No hours of torture, then?"

I lick my lips, wanting to ask her but not at the same time. What if she despises what I say. Then again, my sister and I have only ever had each other. For the most part, we're honest with each other.

"Do you still enjoy killing as much?" I ask.

Her gaze lands on me. It almost feels like a taboo question to ask. It's all we've known. But knowing that Lena doesn't approve, I've found I don't take as much satisfaction in it anymore. I still do it unflinchingly for our money and empire. But it's not the same as before I met her.

"Do you mean since I met River?"

"Yes."

She's studying me now, awkward in her own honesty. Because this type of talk is dangerous. But not with my sister.

"No. I do it because it's necessary. I take pleasure if they've personally offended me, but I'd much rather have River massage my feet when I get home."

"He massages your feet?" I ask in surprise.

"You repeat it, and either River or I will kill you," she says ruthlessly, and I chuckle.

"We cannot change the role we play, Alek. We own this city," she reminds me, not that I need it.

"But it doesn't mean we can't grow ever slightly. Even for stunted orphans like us that's possible."

I eye her, taking in her words. Because for Lena, I want to grow. Shield her from this side of my work as she comes to terms with it. River and Anya are as crazy as each other. But Lena... If she saw the gore I often deal in, she'd hide from me, terrified.

"You really care for her, don't you? It'll be harder for you to keep a low profile as she rises further in her fame. Are you okay with that?"

"I'll do whatever is required of me to stay by her side."

A mischievous light flashes in Anya's eyes as she says, "You've become soft."

"And you haven't?"

She's smiling as I say it, and silently we know this is the only time we'll probably have this discussion. We're checking on one another to see if, in some small way, we've found happiness.

Something we were never entitled to but seems we both secretly wanted.

"Shall we use knives or guns this evening?" she asks, putting an end to the personal talk.

I look at the time. "Guns would be more efficient. But I think we always have time to use knives. Wouldn't want your blade going rusty, would we?"

She smiles at that, satisfied.

I mean, we aren't turning into fucking saints.

CHAPTER 45
Lena

I snuggle into bed, exhausted after my first week of performances. I'm waiting for Alek to get back from getting us breakfast. I don't expect him to cook me breakfast, because I'm certain the only thing he's touched in a kitchen is a knife, and not for the good reasons. It's just that my favorite bagel place down the street doesn't deliver. And when I told him I was going to walk down the street, wearing my short pj's, he was suddenly dressed and rushing out the door because he didn't want anyone else to see what's his.

I smile thinking about that. I yawn and am startled by a knock on the door. My eyebrows furrow. I doubt Alek would ever forget anything, let alone his keys.

I walk to the door and my heart sinks as hear my mother on the other side. *Fuck*.

"Maybe she's not here," she says.

"Archer said she should be home this weekend," my father replies.

I glance around my apartment, making sure Alek and I haven't left out any of our toys that I've recently come to love.

I open the door with fake enthusiasm. "Mom. Dad. What are you doing here?"

My mother looks me up and down. I'm wearing a crop top and booty shorts.

"Why are you dressed like that?" she asks disapprovingly.

"I was sleeping," I tell her.

"It's the middle of the day," my father says.

"I work nights, did you forget?" I leave the door open and turn to walk into the living room. "Why are you here? I didn't know you were in town. Archer isn't here anymore, is he?"

His contract at the hospital was only for a month, and he called me the day he was leaving.

"Well, you haven't been answering my calls lately," my mother says, rather disgruntled. "And your brother sent us something interesting, so we wanted to check it out ourselves."

She pulls out her phone and shows me a picture of

myself standing in front of the cast of the new show. "We were walking Times Square to find this. Honey, this is huge."

I freeze at the compliment. Waiting for the backhand to come. "You're famous," my mother adds, and when I look up from the phone, I see her smiling. An actual smile directed at me and not my brother.

At first I like it, but then I let it sink in and know it's as fake as our relationship.

I'd been hoping for this moment for so long, but now, it's not as satisfying or as fulfilling as I thought it would be.

"Lena." Behind my parents is Alek, standing there with his shaved head, wearing his gloves and a black suit. God, he looks like a killer.

"Who is that?" my mother asks in disgust, much like the first impression Archer had of him.

I cringe. Alek doesn't seem to care, though, as he pushes past them with a bag of bagels in hand.

"Lena, who is this man?" my father asks, eyeing him. If there was a poster boy for bad-boy-do-not-mess-with, Alek's it. Even if he does dress in Versace. He's a killer who oozes the predatory atmosphere of being exactly that.

Alek is unfazed by them as puts the bagels on the

counter, ignoring them. Most likely leaving me to my own decisions.

But fuck it. This whole time, the person driving me to rehearsals in the city was either Alek or Clay—Anya having offered up her bodyguard for the job. The commute was too long, and they refused to let me on public transport because I'd catch the plague, in their opinion.

They might be scary, and for good reason, but they care. And they helped me get this role. My parents did nothing but frown upon me. They'd never even come to any of my shows.

I walk toward Alek and grab his hand, tugging him toward my parents. I swallow hard. "This is my boyfriend, Alek." He hides his smirk as he casually throws his arm around my shoulders, looking all the more like a stereotypical bad boy.

I can feel my heart in my throat. Alek and I haven't put a label on ourselves, but he's not denying it, and in my way, I want Alek to know that I'd like him to stay.

My parents look affronted.

"You don't have a boyfriend. You would have told us. And don't you think you should go for someone more..." My mother clears her throat as Alek stares her. "Are you going through a rebellious stage?" she whispers quietly to me.

"In that I'm twenty-four and making my own decisions? Sure, call it what you will," I say.

"I think what your mother means is perhaps we should go out for breakfast and discuss the direction you're heading in life," my father says earnestly.

"I already have breakfast here," I say with a smile. "I want to clarify something. Did you come to congratulate me or remind me yet again how I haven't reached your standards?"

It feels freeing. Liberating in every sense to finally say what's been on my mind all this time. Alek's hand on my lower back anchors me and gives me strength.

I'm not ashamed of Alek. I don't necessarily agree with what he does, but he's a part of my life. More supportive than my parents have ever been.

My mother is flabbergasted. "We've only ever wanted the best for you."

I nod. "No, you've only ever compared me to Archer. You've never much liked who I've become as an adult, and I actually like myself a lot. So when you're ready to accept me and my life choices, then we can celebrate my success together," I say, confidence filling me. "Until then... I love you both and safe travels home."

My mother's jaw drops open before she snaps, "I can't believe how disrespectful you're being. Barry, we're leaving." Then steps into the hall outside my door.

I'm torn. I'm sad to see her go but also delighted. Had Alek not been with me, I most likely would have taken her condescending comments without a fight.

My father glances at her before he leans in. "Congrats, sweetheart," he says and presses a kiss to my cheek, and it fills me with a bittersweet feeling because I know he's not referring to Alek.

"Look after her or—" He gulps, not able to finish the half-hearted threat aimed at Alek.

"Barry!" my mother shouts from the top of the stairs.

"Thanks, Dad," I say, because I know deep down he's happy for me. It's never been him with the scathing tongue. He follows her down the stairs, and Alek's arms wrap around me, his hands on my bare stomach.

"Am I your boyfriend now?" he whispers into my ear while pressing kisses down my neck.

I chuckle. "Depends if you got my favorite bagel. We'll see how well trained you are," I say as I close the door.

I know I'm going to hear about this from Archer, but I think a part of him will also be proud that I stood up for myself.

I'm sick of apologizing that I'm not enough. And if I wasn't enough for them when I was doing my best to get to where I am now, then they don't deserve me at my best. Especially when they'd intended to bring me down again because of it.

CHAPTER 46
Aleksandr

I walk into Anya's office during one of the sex auctions. I realized after pulling up that I had three missed calls from her. But it made sense to just come in and see her since I was already here. I just dropped Lena off at her show and am feeling pretty proud of her for standing up to her parents.

She'd told me how much it'd hurt her before when they didn't believe in her or her singing. Had they not been her parents, I would've killed them without a second thought.

I interrupt as Anya and River are making out against her desk. "It's different on the receiving end," I say, remembering when she walked in on Lena and me. "Shouldn't you be managing the floor?"

"It's managed, and it's about fucking time you

arrived." She puts her hand on a white Styrofoam box on her desk. "A package arrived for you."

I stride across the room and peer into the box. There's a pinkie inside.

I shrug. Am I supposed to know something about it? I haven't cut off any fingers as of late.

"It's your little pet's finger." I freeze at that and lock eyes with her.

"Who?"

"Cinita, your little ballerina."

My jaw clenches. I told her to leave the city. "How?"

I told her I wouldn't chase or protect her anymore.

That old wound flares up. But then I think of Lena. I can't drag her through this again.

Won't make her second again.

"How the fuck would I know? I guess whoever she pissed off chopped it off, and with the finger, it asks that you bring cash. To collect her." She takes a deep breath. "She is trouble, that one. I've told you as much. I thought you said you dealt with this?"

"I have," I grit out. "Throw it in the trash for all I care."

Anya's eyebrows lift in surprise. "You're sure?"

"Weren't you the one telling me to stop protecting her because I had a savior complex?"

"Yeah, I did, but..." She hides her smile as she puts the lid back on and trashes it like it's spoiled cake. "I'm just really happy to hear it because I can't have you fuck this up with Lena any more. I'm shopping with her tomorrow, so I don't want you making it awkward."

"Who's dating her, me or you?"

She shrugs. "You and I come as a package deal, you know that."

I peer back at the white box in the trash, my jaw clenching.

I know I'm not the one to fight her battles any longer, but it doesn't make it any easier to ignore.

What have you done this time, Cinita?

I know when the money's not paid, it'll be worse for her. Because I would send the same type of ransom.

But I promised Lena whole-heartedly that I was done with Cinita. And there is nothing that I would do to risk fucking that up again. Cinita is an old wound that I refuse to continue reopening.

Lena's too kind, and if she knew what was going on with Cinita, despite not wanting me to be involved with her anymore, she'd tell me to go. But in this world, these types of situation will never stop if Cinita keeps dropping my name.

I have to be the one to cut this final tie, and I'm willing to do it to protect what I have with Lena.

I turn my back on the box.

I'm not a hero. I can focus only on Lena.

I promised her that much.

CHAPTER 47
Lena

"Do you want kids?" I ask Anya as we walk through the store. I have a red-carpet event tonight, and it wasn't so much as a suggestion but demand that Anya would take responsibility for my wardrobe.

"What type of question is that? Of course I don't want kids," she scoffs.

She runs her hand along an expensive dress and nods to the saleslady, who takes it to the dressing room. She's picked out four different dresses since we've been here, and the saleslady has grabbed every single one.

I'm still trying to wrap my head around how Alek and I might look in the future together or if I'm clinging to a fantasy. But every day I'm with him, the harder it will be to let him go.

She pauses, eyes another dress, then turns to look at me. "Are you pregnant?"

"No, absolutely not, I swear. I was just, you know, wondering whether it's common for..." I don't know how to say it, but Anya finishes the sentence for me as she appraises another dress.

"People like us to have families?"

I swallow at how prejudice it sounds.

She shrugs. "Of course, all that bravado shit of having heirs. It's even written into some contracts for arranged marriages. But it's a personal choice as well. Some wish for a family, and others not so much. It's no different than it is for anyone else, there's just more danger involved."

I know it's probably highly inappropriate to ask these questions, but she and Alek are twins. I want to gauge what kind of future I might have with Alek. He might say he's not ready now, but maybe in time... Or am I just deluding myself?

"Have you discussed this with Alek?" she asks.

"Only once, and just briefly," I admit. "He said he didn't want them, but I wonder if that will change in time."

She looks me up and down. "Don't get me wrong, I think I would be a fabulous auntie." I laugh at that because I agree. "But you have to understand, Alek and I were raised in a hostile environment. Before we found our last foster home, our living situation wasn't the best.

"To us, kids are an expense. Not something you can nurture and love. We don't come from a family like that, so we don't know any different." I think what she just told me explains a lot. Has he ever really had someone to truly love him apart from his sister? And I do believe that she loves him without a shadow of a doubt. The way they interact with each other, it's like they have their own secret club that no one else is to be a part of. But the way he is with me, it's like stepping out in the freezing cold air, and it feels really fucking good.

But am I just fooling myself, trying to encroach further by including myself in their family because I've at least partly rejected my own?

"He takes his gloves off for me," I tell her. I watch as she grips the dress and turns to me again, this time with a strange expression on her face.

"He touches you, regularly?" she asks in disbelief, and I nod. It's an odd question to ask, but Alek is the furthest thing from normal. I know Anya saw us once in her office, but perhaps she thought it was a one-off thing.

"A lot."

"Without the gloves," she confirms.

"Yes."

She continues to wander through the racks of dresses, seeming puzzled by what I just said. She scans a few more dresses before she follows the saleslady to the back, and I go with her, even though I picked absolutely nothing.

Alek's my date for the event, and I'm nervous about taking him. I know he doesn't like crowds, but he knows how to navigate a room, and he's used to interacting with wealthy people. It makes me feel more comfortable.

"Get in there." Anya waves to the dressing room. I look at her, confused. "The dresses are for you. Move it."

I try on dress after dress that she picked for me, until I step out in a black velvet one. It has a plunging neckline and one strap that crosses over the chest. The back is completely open and it has a slit up one side that goes almost all the way to the hip. It's very sexy but still has a formal, elegant edge. She claps her hands in delight and points at it. "That's the one. We will take it."

"I can get it," I tell her, looking at the price tag. Holy shit, maybe I can't. Who pays four thousand dollars for a dress? Has it got gold on it somewhere? I mean, my pay went up, but I'm still not comfortable enough to spend that much on a dress.

"No, it's my gift to you. Take it." She smiles and walks up to the counter and pays for it before I can stop her. When Alek or Anya make up their mind about anything, it's set in stone. And often, when it comes to money, it's not even a drop in the well of their fortune. To them, it's just things.

I look at my phone. I haven't received a text from Alek yet but know he'll pick me up for the event tonight.

"My brother's going to have a heart attack when he sees you in this. Finally, all our fortune will be mine," Anya says with a mischievous smile.

"I think he'll be happy because it matches everything in his closet, being that it's black."

She laughs as we walk out.

I guess I have a date.

With a killer.

CHAPTER 48
Lena

He knocks on my door ten minutes earlier than when he said he would be here. When I pull it open, I'm awestruck by his black suit. It's more upscale than his usual suits. Tonight, I realize, he's not wearing gloves.

"You look..." He trails off, and I glance down at my dress and black heels. My hair is half up, I have a nude lip with just a swipe of clear lip gloss, and I'm carrying a small black bag to match my dress. "Ravishing," he finishes.

"Thank you, you look good yourself," I reply. "You're not wearing your gloves tonight?"

He offers his hand to me. "The only one I'll be touching is you."

"You didn't have to change anything, Alek. I don't mind if you wear gloves," I say, suddenly insecure yet moved by his thoughtfulness.

"I'd rather not raise questions for you," he says.

I eye him. "Since when do you care what people think?"

"I don't, but I care about you. Deeply. This way, if I decide to take you to a supply closet, there will be less clothing to take off."

"We're not sneaking off anywhere." I chuckle as I take his hand. I lock my apartment door and then he leads me to his car.

Any butterflies I might've had about tonight evaporate as I look at my hand in his. I know that no matter what, we'll be okay.

As we drive to the event, I tell him about last night's show and some of the people I'm excited to meet at the event. A lot of other actors, performers, and singers will be there, and I'm elated to meet them. But I'm also nervous because some of them I've looked up to for years.

When we arrive, a well-dressed gentleman opens my door, and Alek hands him the keys as he walks around to grab my hand. I suck in a sharp breath, surprised by the red carpet and number of cameras that are flashing our way.

Alek leans in and whispers in my ear, "You are stunning, sweetheart. Now, do what you do best—shine."

I smile as someone takes a photo, and any tension I might've had floods away. Alek leads me onto the carpet, and it surprises me that he hates crowds and rowdiness yet the sophistication with which he holds himself seems so natural. But perhaps that's because he has a different air about him when we're together.

We pose for a few photos, with his hand on my lower back, and I find it just as shocking that this fucker knows how to pose. But with cheekbones and a jawline like that, how could he not?

As we step through the doors, I lean in and whisper, "I didn't think I could be any more attracted to you."

"Shall we find that supply closet?" he teases, and I smirk as I raise my head to take in the great chandeliers overhead.

A few acrobatic performers dangle from the ceiling, the room full of chatter as classical music plays in the background, and I realize someone is playing the piano.

"I need a drink first," I confess; just something to take the edge off.

Alek leads me toward the first bar as he quietly

begins to sing under his breath. "One margarita, two margarita..."

I slap him on the arm playfully. "Oh shut up, that is so not happening tonight."

He's smirking as he pulls out the barstool for me and then sits beside me. He orders himself a whisky and I order champagne.

"Ah, Miss Love and Mr. Ivanov," Steven, my director, says with great enthusiasm. Ever the showman. He goes to put his hands on our shoulders but thinks better of it as Alek gives him a warning look.

Steven clears his throat. "It's magnificent, isn't it."

"It's really something," I agree. "I'm just trying to take it all in at the moment."

"Well, you may only have a few minutes of peace, so enjoy it. I have no doubt you'll be surrounded in no time at all. There have been raving reviews about your performance."

It's still humbling to hear that, especially from someone who is so respected in the industry.

"I'll leave you two lovebirds for a little longer while I do a sweep of the room," he says, looking a little pale as he looks at Alek. Glancing at Alek, I realize Alek is giving him a death stare.

I slap him on the chest. "Hey, no territorial business. He's my boss."

"And if he touches you, he won't be alive to sing your praises."

I laugh. "Alek, I will be talking with a lot of men tonight. But I'll be going home with you."

That seems to lighten his gaze as the corner of his mouth cocks up. "Really?" he says as he yanks my stool closer to him.

My tongue is poking at my cheek because even in this roomful of people, I just want to tear his clothes off. "Behave," I warn.

"We shall see," he replies, and butterflies swoop in my stomach.

I sweep my gaze around the room and notice a few members with security personnel standing behind them. "I couldn't imagine being so famous that I have to take security with me everywhere."

Alek watches me carefully. "It's something I've been wanting to discuss with you for a while, actually."

I hover my drink at my lips as I say, "What do you mean?"

He glances around us. It's fairly private for the time being, as the bartender is distracted on the other end of the bar.

"I want to assign someone to you when I'm not around. Like Clay and Vance are to Anya."

I offer a disbelieving smile. "Alek, I don't need that."

His glare is penetrating as he grabs my hand and considers me. "I'm a selfish bastard for having you, but it's dangerous being with me. You could become a target purely because of our association."

I'm slightly baffled as to why he's bringing this up now. "I know that. I knew that when I decided to date you, Alek. I understand there are risks, but there are in any relationship. I don't need someone loitering over my every move."

He sighs, exasperated. "Just promise me you'll consider it. You are my priority. Your safety is everything to me." My heart twists at his words, at his earnest plea.

I notice one of my co-stars walking over, so I press a kiss to his cheek, not entirely sure where this has come from all of a sudden. "I'll think about it, but for now, do your best to smile and not scare anyone away."

"Lena!" She bursts with excitement as she approaches in her dazzling red dress and holds her arms wide for me. I stand and embrace her.

She's beautiful.

Everyone here is.

I'm still reeling by the fact that this is my new reality.

I look over my shoulder at Alek, who does his best to appear approachable, but he's failing miserably.

And it makes me love him all the more for trying and being here with me tonight.

CHAPTER 49
Aleksandr

"Are you sulking again?" Anya asks as I tap my gloved hand against the table. River has his arm around her shoulders as we sit at our table to overlook the engagement tonight at the auction.

I ignore her. Pissed that for some reason this fucker is still here even after I paid him for tracking down the men who were after Cinita.

Will puts his glass to his lips with a smirk that infuriates me. He really grates on my nerves. "Don't get shitty with me because your woman is having drinks without you," he says, and I feel the vein my temple throb.

How the fuck does he even know that? And it's not like I'm not allowed to join, but Lena "advised" how important it is she has a girls' night out. Now I feel like an asshole for placing a bodyguard on her to blend into the crowd. It's the only way I feel comfortable with her actually going anywhere without my personal protection.

"Don't you have other people to find? Or did your clients stop calling because of your shitty personality?" I ask.

Anya's eyebrows perk, obviously amused. I'm not one to usually bite back or play into someone's games, but something about him really irritates me.

"If I didn't know any better, I'd say you two are flirting," Anya chimes in, and I give her an unimpressed glare.

Will chuckles. "I wouldn't be against bedding you and your—"

"I'd be very careful with what you say next," Anya warns him on my behalf. Because I will fucking kill him if Lena's name leaves his lips.

Will looks at River. "Don't look at me. You're a big boy, picking your own fights," River says with a grin.

Will sighs and throws back his drink. "If you must know, I'm rather interested in River's new offerings, which is why I'm here to bid."

"Then shouldn't you be sitting elsewhere so you can bid?" I grit out.

He only smirks, and I feel my temple pulse again.

Fucker.

I open my phone to look at the tracking app to see where Lena is. She's still at the same restaurant.

The auctioneer announces the highest bidder on the current lot, and Anya's eyes light up, most likely because she's already spending that money on new jewels.

It's strange in a way. I thought buying Lena extravagant gifts would bring her as much excitement as it does Anya. But the only time she lights up like that is when I bring her a bagel and coffee from her favorite café down the street from her apartment.

I close my phone and look at the stage again. She said she'd text me when she's heading home, and I'm sure as shit leaving the moment I receive that text.

Fuck, is this what they call being whipped?

CHAPTER 50
Lena

I finish texting Alek that I'm on my way home. I should've messaged him when I was leaving the restaurant, but I was talking with my castmate as we waited for the cab we were sharing before dropping her off first.

Alek insisted Clay or Vance pick me up for the evening, but I reminded him I wanted to do normal things. Which, of course, he seemed confused about, but I've been insistent on keeping my independence.

When the cab pulls up to the curb at my apartment complex and I step out, my mood sours. Cinita is pacing back and forth at the front.

She spots me immediately and comes striding over in a long, lavish green coat. She looks gaunter than the last time I saw her. She might've cleaned up a little during her time with Alek but it's likely she's using again.

"Yo, girl, you changed the locks? My key doesn't work," she says.

I furrow my eyebrows. "Yeah, you haven't lived her for months now"

She licks her lips. "I need to grab some things."

I stare at her in disbelief. "You do realize that someone broke into the apartment shortly after you left. And in the hospital you said I could sell everything if I wanted to."

Her eyes widen. "You sold everything?"

"No. Well, except for the broken shit. There's only like a box left in your old room."

"Can I go through it?" she asks, wide-eyed.

I'm uncomfortable with her being here, especially knowing Alek is on his way. But at least this way, once she's taken her shit, it's done. I hadn't even remembered that box in her room until now, and I haven't had a need to get a new roommate.

"Sure, but try to make it quick," I say, and she lights up with a bright smile.

"Thank you. I know I kind of fucked you over a bit when I left, but thank you for being such a good friend."

I eye her incredulously. That's certainly not the

impression I had about the way we left things, But I'd rather her feel this way than remember the horrible things I'd last said to her.

"Were the stairs always like this?" she asks as we walk up them, she's breathing heavily.

"Yep, they've always been a killer," I reply, but I've gotten used to them now. I grab my keys and open the door, then switch on the light. I quickly scan the apartment to make sure none of Alek's belongings are in sight. He keeps a few article of clothing here now, but everything is in my wardrobe.

I take my coat off. "The box is just in your old room." I point toward the second room on the other side of the bathroom.

"Thanks," she says as she licks her lips. She doesn't look well, and it's unsettling. I consider messaging Alek that she's here, but a small part of me is hesitant. What if he comes rushing forward for her again? It brings insecure feelings to the forefront of my mind. Old hurts that haven't yet healed. But I trust Alek and where we are in our relationship right now.

So I pull my phone out of my pocket.

"I saw your photos in the paper from the red-carpet event," Cinita calls out. "Looked really nice."

I don't like the way she says it, because I know the photo she's referring to is the one with me and Alek.

My mother sent me a photo of it from a magazine. We haven't spoken since they showed up here, but I know in a small way she's trying to reach out again. I still have mixed feelings about her efforts considering she didn't deem me as 'successful' until now.

"You must feel pretty lucky," Cinita says, and before I finish my text, I look up at her, and my stomach drops. She has a gun pointed in my direction. "Put the phone down," she orders with a smile.

Oh fuck. Goose bumps erupt along my skin, and the temperature in the room feels like it drops. She licks her lips again as she yells. "Put down the phone, Lena!"

I do as she says, taking a shaky breath. "What do you want Cinita?" I ask cautiously.

She chuckles, as if I'm the deranged one. "I don't know, maybe a bullet to your head." I wince at the reminder of the comment I'd made about her only months ago. "It was *me* he was in love with."

"You never loved him," I accuse, and she makes a point to hold the gun higher, reminding me I really don't get an opinion here. It just fell from my lips. Adrenaline is pumping through my veins. *Fuck, is she going to kill me?*

"Maybe not. But at least he listened to what I said until you came along." She glances around the apartment. "You're dating a guy who could literally buy you anything, but you're still holed up in this shitty place?"

She looks at the photo I have beside the TV of me and Archer, and my jaw tics. *What if she goes after my family once she's done with me?*

"You know I sent Alek a ransom demand for myself a week or so ago. Buddied up with one of my friends and sent him another woman's finger, telling him it was mine. We asked for a lot of money, and would you believe how shocked I was when he never came?"

She has crazy eyes as she stares me down. I didn't know any of that.

"Why didn't he come, Lena? He always comes. My friend and I were going to share the money, but when Alek didn't arrive, he decided he didn't want to be my friend anymore. And now I'm at square one again. Fucking alone." She raises the gun again, a tear leaking from her eye. "Because you took him from me."

I raise my hands in the air. "I didn't mean to make you feel lonely." That's the only thing I manage to say. She's expecting some kind of response, but I don't know if I can give her the one she's looking for. One she won't shoot me for.

She begins laughing and crying and looking around, as if she's trying to remember where the fuck she is. My heart hammers in my chest, and I glance in the direction of my kitchen. Fuck, there's no knife or anything else on the counter I could use as a weapon.

"As if you didn't already have enough. Family. Rising to stardom. But you had to take him as well?" She bites her bottom lip, bewildered. "Maybe I should cut one of your fingers off and see if he's willing to pay a ransom for that?"

Another shiver runs down my body as I fight against crippling terror. No, if I panic, I'll make it worse. But can it get any worse? I'm literally stuck in my own apartment with a psychopath right now.

"Oooh, I know! Luckily I came prepared," she says, nodding with excitement as she puts her hand in the pocket of her green coat and pulls out a sheathed blade. She puts her gun down on the edge of the TV cabinet and unsheathes the knife. I swallow and take a step back.

"Ah, ah, ah," she scolds as she steps forward menacingly. "I mean, what's a finger to a singer? It would be worse if I slit your throat, right? Then how would you sing?"

A lump is caught in my throat as she steps toward me. Fuck. I can run around the counter and pull out a knife, but what if I don't make it in time? And what will I do? Stab her?

Protect yourself.

It's a distant voice in the back of my mind but one that takes precedence as it tries to take over my raging fear and shock.

What if I do die here? Who would be sad to see me go?

A pair of green eyes are the first thing to come to mind, and a tear slips down my cheek. Alek would be sad, right?

The front door bursts open, and I'm so shocked, all I can do is take a few steps back as Alek breaks into the room and rams into Cinita. The TV knocks off the cabinet as he slams her hard into the wall, and she screams.

A tall, blond man I don't recognize stands in front of me. He's covering me, but I'm angling myself to look over his shoulder, unable to move or speak, frozen in place.

Cinita's face twists into a soft, bewildered expression. "You came," she says, sounding relieved even though Alek holds a gun under her chin.

"Look away, Lena." Alek's voice is labored. But I can't. He looks like the light to her world, her eyes locked on him.

"You wouldn't hurt me, right, Alek?" she breathes.

"Look away, Lena," he says again.

Cinita smiles as she begins to cry. "Alek—"

Bang.

I jolt under the deafening sound of the gunshot and stare in shock at the blood that splatters against the wall. I can't breathe.

I immediately bend over and hurl as I hear the sound of Cinita's body slump to the floor.

"Lena," Alek rasps. I can't help but raise my head, shocked, as if in a daze. But when I look at him, my vision is laser focused as he takes a wobbly step forward. My eyes widen at the knife protruding from his stomach.

"Are you okay?" he breathes, struggling to take his next step.

"Alek!" I scream as I push the blond-haired man out of the way to catch Alek as he falls.

"Fuck, I'm calling your sister," the man says with an English accent. But I can only focus on Alek, my fear and terror gripping me for an entirely different reason now.

"Alek." My voice screeches as tears spill over my cheeks. It looks bad, there's a lot of blood, and I don't know what to do. I don't know how to stop it.

His hand reaches for my face as he slumps back, and I catch him in my arms. "I'm sorry," he breathes.

"Stop talking," I breathe out. *What do I do? What*

do I do? "Aleksandr, don't you leave me!" I cry, and it's the weakest I've seen him. But also the kindest as he stares at me lovingly.

He becomes blurry as tears continue to spill over. "Don't leave me!" I say defiantly. "It's going to be okay." I try to turn my head to locate the Englishman so he can help, but Alek's grip is surprisingly firm against my cheekbone.

"Sing for me, sunshine," he rasps.

"No! You're okay. You're going to be okay. You're invincible."

The door slams open, and I hear a flurry of Russian as Anya rushes into the room. She tries to tear me away from Alek, and River and the Englishman grab him, but I cling to him, staring into his forest-green eyes that seem to be dimming.

"No!" I scream as I elbow Anya in the face to pry myself from her grip. "No!" I trip on myself as they carry him out, and I'm on my knees, staring in horror as they take him away. "No, you're supposed to be invincible, Aleksandr Ivanov! Don't leave me!" I yell on a sob as they carry him down the hall.

I'm eye level with Cinita's body and feel another nauseating swirl of bile and hatred.

I'm furious I can't kill her myself for taking the one thing I've ever truly loved.

CHAPTER 51
Lena

I haven't slept for two days, not for any length of time anyway. I know I've probably dipped off for a few minutes here and there, but the moment my head drops, I'm awake again.

We're in one of Anya's spare rooms, and the doctor has been in and out nonstop. Anya has been in here almost just as much as me. Just like now, as she leans against the door and stares down at Alek as if she's fending off the Grim Reaper herself.

We haven't spoken since that night. I stroke over Alek's thumb as I sit beside his bed. The doctor said the blade hadn't hit anything vital, but he'd lost a lot of blood. He should make a full recovery, but it doesn't take away from the sense of impending doom.

"You need sleep, Lena," Anya finally says.

"I'm fine." But my voice is nothing but a rasp. "I want to be here when he wakes up."

"There won't be much left of you if you don't eat or sleep."

I look at her then. "I could say the same to you." She has bruising around the eye I elbowed, and I cringe that I can still see it through her makeup.

"I'm sorry about hitting you in the face."

She pins me with a lethal stare. "Just know if you'd broke this perfect nose, you would've left in a body bag."

I would usually laugh at that. But there's no humor in this room. It seems impossible for Alek to be in this state. He always seemed untouchable. Invincible. And it's because of me he's in this mess in the first place.

"I should've killed the little dancer the moment I realized she was using him," Anya says thoughtfully. "No one will know about this. None will learn that Alek Ivanov bleeds. Especially at the hands of a junkie bitch."

I flinch under her harshness. I still can't get the graphic image of Cinita out of my mind. I haven't gone back to the apartment, don't want to ever again.

Apparently, it'd been "dealt with," but I can't scrub the ordeal from my mind.

A tap sounds on the door. Anya steps forward to let in River and the English fellow, whose name I've learned is Will.

"We tracked down Cinita's associate who attempted the ransom demand with her. He denied being part of it," River says.

"So what did you do with him?" Anya asks, her arms crossed, not looking away from her brother.

"Dealt with him, of course."

I've discovered that "dealt with" meant they were dead.

"Good," she replies.

"You're quick," Anya tells Will, who gives her a charismatic smile. She then looks at me. "Will here was the one who realized Cinita was at your home that night. That's why he and Alek arrived when they did, and River and I shortly after."

A chill runs down my spine. Had they not gotten there at just that moment... Alek would've been too late. But was that so bad? Then he wouldn't be here like this.

"Even once I'm done with a target, I tend to watch their movements a few months after, especially if I think they're a wild card," Will explains, and offers me a gentlemanly bow. "I think your boyfriend's a dickhead, but I'm glad I stayed around. I would've hated to see him on a rampage in this city if anything happened to you."

My jaw tightens, and I try to hold in the tears as I quietly rasp, "Thank you," then look back at Alek.

Sing for me, sunshine. He'd said it as if it was the last and only thing he wanted before leaving this world.

Danger or not, I realized at that moment I have no other place I'd rather be than by his side. Alek is many things, including a killer. That fact once terrified me, but now I realize not having him in my life is worse.

A world without Alek would not be worth singing in.

CHAPTER 52
Aleksandr

Everything hurts.

My eyelids are too heavy to peel open as I brace myself at a sharp pain in my abdomen as I try to sit up. I realize then that I can't. It's dim in the room, but I make out the outline of Lena, thanks to the bedside lamp. As I gather my wits and thoughts, I see I'm in a spare room at one of Anya's mansions.

I'm tired and my mind is foggy, but I think back to the last thing I can remember. *Cinita*. I've never hated or despised anyone more in my entire life. I kill because I'm good at it, but I wanted her dead, destroyed in every way, so Lena is never at risk again.

Lena. I gaze down at her and brush a lock of her hair from her face as she snuggles beside me. And I recall her horror, the shock of seeing the monster that I am.

I'm a selfish bastard, and after seeing her like that, realizing how easy it is for someone to slip through the cracks, I know the better part of me should let her go. But I just fucking can't.

What if she hates me now? What if she wants nothing to do with me? Shouldn't I free her?

She twitches under my hand and murmurs sleepily, "Aleksandr."

"Yes, sweetheart," I reply, and my voice is raspy, most likely from sleeping.

Her eyes fly open, and she goes to move, but I keep my hand on her face to hold her in place. I wince at the movement.

"Don't move!" she says, almost hysterical. Her eyes dart back and forth as she looks at me, as if shocked that I'm really here with her. Then she bursts into tears. "I thought you were dead."

"Lena."

"Don't you 'Lena' me!" she snaps angrily as she clings to me tighter, and I'm abundantly aware of the burning in my stomach. I vaguely remember Cinita's knife stabbing into me, but I was on such a rampage to erase her from this world, that it was overshadowed by my rage.

"You... you..." She sobs, not able to finish.

"You're okay?" I ask, and her eyes widen as she springs up, propping her head on her hand.

"Are you fucking crazy? No, I'm not okay, Aleksandr. I saw you get stabbed and I thought you were going to die. You haven't woken up for three days," she spits as tears spill over her cheeks. I rub my thumb under eye, wiping them, willing them away.

"Well, I haven't been getting much sleep lately since you keep me awake at all hours," I say.

She stares at me in disbelief. "Alek, this isn't a time to joke!" She grabs her pillow as if to hit me but then remembers I'm wounded.

A small laugh escapes me, but I'm paying for it immediately as I try to sit up. "Don't move too much," she says but helps me.

I love her. Love waking up with her by my side. But it's not fair to her. I didn't want my world touching her like that. She was so pure in comparison.

"You know I love you," I say, and she nods slowly. "But I can never have you in that situation again."

"What are you saying?" she asks, confused. And I give her a pointed look. She knows exactly what I'm saying.

"No," she snaps defiantly. "So I get a bodyguard.

Or I learn self-defense. Or you teach me how to hold a gun. Or—"

"Lena," I say, cutting her off. "If it weren't for Will, I might've been too late."

"But you weren't," she's quick to say. "You're a selfish prick, so stop pretending to be selfless."

I laugh but quickly cut it off as searing-hot pain flares in my abdomen. Lena throws back the blanket and is in shock when she sees my bandages stained red. "Fuck, you've opened your wound. I'll call the doctor."

I grab her wrist. "No. I just want you, alone, for a few more minutes," I say as I pull her to me, and she awkwardly leans against my chest. I need her warmth. Need the soothing of her calm presence. Embracing the fact once again that the thoughts and vile, nauseating tension that once sat at the pit of my stomach is gone.

Only for her.

"Alek, it was really scary," she whispers, then begins to cry again, and I hate that I've done this to her.

"Don't worry, I'm not going anywhere anytime soon."

"You mean it?" She sobs. "No more talk of breaking up or dumb shit like that," she says, wiping her eyes.

"Who said anything about breaking up? I was just waiting for you to think that having a bodyguard in my stead was your own brilliant idea."

She startles at that. "You really are an asshole. Do you know that?" she says, then sobs harder.

I kiss the top of her head and realize my vision is beginning to fade in and out. Okay, maybe my wound is bleeding more than I thought. But holding her is worth it.

I lock on to her until the darkness sweeps me back under.

I'm not a good man.

And I am never letting go of the only light I have in my life.

CHAPTER 53
Aleksandr

"You have a lot to make up for since you haven't shown up to any auctions for two weeks," Anya says in way of greeting after inviting herself to my house. She's not entirely welcome, but she's already here, so I let her in.

"Lower your voice. Lena's sleeping upstairs," I tell her as I walk to the kitchen. She had a show last night, and Tyson, her now bodyguard, didn't drop her off until late. "And you were the one who told me not to show my face for a few weeks."

She points her nose higher in the air, but I know she's here because she's worried. "Will left town, said he had another job back over in the UK."

"You say that as if I'll care," I grit out.

I'm wearing loose pj pants, as my stomach's still

wrapped in bandages. The doctor hasn't had to visit for two days since Lena's insisted on changing them for me. I pour myself a glass of water.

"He's a good ally to have. If he ever needs anything, we owe him," she says. I don't like the guy, but I'll forever be in his debt. The what-ifs have consumed me these past days. Had I been too late... I hold Lena tightly every night with the very shattering thought.

"I thought you didn't take to people. You've become soft," I reply.

"Says the man who got stabbed by a deranged junkie bitch," she says with a sharp tongue. *True*.

"Don't ever do that to Lena or me again, Alek," she says quietly. "I don't mind if you choose a woman who is..." She tries to find the right word. "Softer. And if you want to avoid her being involved as much with our businesses, I'll allow it. But don't put yourself at risk like that again."

"Are you telling me you wouldn't do the same for River?"

She seems affronted. "No, I'd throw him in front of me like a human shield."

I try to hide a smirk and so does she.

"What I'm saying is, don't put yourself in that position again. Especially if you two choose to have a family one day."

Silence fills the air, and it's unsettling. I grip the water glass hard as I stare into it.

"Do you think it would be bad to bring children into this type of world?" I ask, so unlike the man I was only six months ago. I was so against even the thought of bringing a child into this life. But for Lena... I'm willing to give her everything and anything. If she needs me to be a husband, I will adapt to that role. If she needs a father for her children, then that will only be me.

"I know I won't have children, Alek. But I won't look down on you if you do. If she is okay with who you are, monster and all, and you choose to have children, then we make sure they're safeguarded and we raise those obnoxious little trust fund babies together. *If* that's what you choose."

I smirk, feeling a slight shift within me. "We'll probably fuck them up."

She scoffs. "No doubt. We were hardly able to raise ourselves, let alone innocent babies. But you will try. Lena will be nothing short of a great mother. Why, is she pregnant?"

"No," Lena says from across the room, and I'm startled to realize I hadn't even heard her approach.

Anya narrows her eyes at her, most likely surprised she didn't sense her sooner either.

"I'm not," Lena says and pokes out her tongue. "But if I were, we'd probably have to take a DNA test to make sure it's Aleksandr's," she adds as she walks toward the fridge.

I pull her into me and she squeals. "That's not funny, sweetheart," I growl into her ear, and she chuckles.

Anya rolls her eyes. "You two disgust me, and I'm losing money by being here. I expect you around for dinner at eight." She throws her hands in the air as a goodbye, then takes her leave.

"Why were you two talking about children?" Lena asks. Those big brown eyes look up at me through thick eyelashes. I stroke my knuckles along her cheekbones, memorizing every supple line.

"I just want to make sure when I promise you the world, I'm capable of giving it to you. That's all," I say honestly.

She smirks. "Alek, I said I want children one day. Right now, I'm living my best life on stage. There's no rush."

"But we can practice plenty, right?" I ask eagerly.

She chuckles and slaps my chest. "No, because you're still recovering." Her hands glide down my stomach, over my bandages, before she reaches for my semi-hard cock. "It doesn't mean I can't help relieve a sickly old man."

I grab her hair, yanking her neck back, as she smirks at me. "What did I say about you calling me old?" I ask, hissing as she begins to stroke my cock. The way she looks at me is sinister and deadly.

"Should I be punished for it?" she asks with a raised brow.

I cock a smile and kiss her, consume her as her wicked little tongue lazily keeps with my pace.

"Yes," I grit through the next breath. "Get on your knees like a good girl."

CHAPTER 54
Lena

"Bye, Lena, have a good evening!" Susan, one of my fellow singers, waves goodbye after final rehearsal before our new show goes live tomorrow. I'm nervous but excited. I walk out the back door and around to the front of the theater. The city bustles as the billboards glow bright. I look across the road, and red streaks my cheeks, but I'm also really proud. I'm in the photo advertising the show.

"You're late," Alek growls as he steps up beside me and slips his gloved hand into mine.

"Sorry, rehearsal took a little longer than expected," I admit. I look him up and down. He's in his usual attire, and I smirk. Even in the middle of Times Square, he stands out.

"It's busy here," he complains.

I offer him a smile. "Then why don't you take me somewhere quieter?" I ask as I slide my arms around his neck. Any sign of complaint leaves as he leans in and kisses me, unfazed by anyone else who might be standing around or watching.

He's picked me up every evening after rehearsals. The only nights he's had Tyson collect me instead are the ones when he has his gun auctions. It's taking me time to process exactly what he and Anya do during their auctions. And— as River so kindly explained to me a few nights ago—that the pair are known as gatekeepers to the underworld in New York.

They run this territory, and everything has to be passed by them. If someone tries to conduct business without their permission, then there's consequences. Bloody consequences.

It feels strange to have a man like that, holding me tenderly in the middle of Times Square.

"Where are we going?" I ask as I pull back to look up at him. I haven't returned to my apartment for over six weeks and have been staying with Alek, but it's definitely a commute to get to work every day since Alek's home is in a more peaceful area outside the city.

"It's a surprise." He grabs my hand and leads me through Times Square. It's strange to have an evening stroll with him because, for the most part, Alek always wants to leave the rowdiness of the city immediately.

He asks me about my rehearsal, and I happily tell him about the cast, the performance, when I sing, and the swirl and excitement for the first official performance tomorrow.

It's nice to tell him these things. That he listens and lets me rile myself with excitement about all the possibilities. He watches me adoringly, and I now feel genuinely supported in what I do, when I was chastised for so many years for following my dream.

We come to a stop in front of a tall building. It looks fancy, and I can't tell if it's a hotel or restaurant. I think it's both. The doorman greets us as we walk through.

"Are we having dinner here?" I ask. I'm still getting used to the restaurants that Anya and Alek take me to. But they never seem to really care about which fork is used first or what other people think. And more often than not, they book a private room or the whole restaurant, because they can't stand other people.

"Soon," he says as he leads me to the elevator. I'm confused as he pushes the button for the penthouse.

"Are we staying here for the night?"

The corner of his mouth lifts slightly, and I can tell he's trying to hide a smile. Which is sinful. I admire his profile, his shaved head and sharp jaw. There's not one angle on this man that isn't devilishly handsome.

The doors open to the penthouse, and I'm confused because it's completely empty. Large white pillars with golden frames flank the entryway, and there's an unobstructed view to the kitchen from here. But my jaw drops at the sight of Times Square beyond the floor-to-ceiling windows.

"Why is there no furniture in this place?" I laugh as I step toward the big bay windows to admire the view.

"You were complaining about the daily commute to work, weren't you?"

"Well, yeah, but—" My jaw snaps shut as realization dawns on me. "Aleksandr, what is this?"

He holds out a gold card. "Yours."

My eyes bulge. "Alek, I can't accept this. It's too much."

He steps into my space and raises my hands to his chest. "Then think of it as ours."

I stare at him in disbelief. "Alek, you hate the city. Hate the rowdiness."

"Yes, but I love *you*. Did you not say right now you want to focus on your career? Is this not the perfect place for this time in your life?"

I'm speechless. "You can't just buy girls apartments, Alek."

He smirks and squeezes my hand. "I don't do anything for anyone. But I'll do everything for my woman," he says as he leads me to a large balcony. I'm trying to figure out what's being built on it with wooden pillars.

"You said you wanted a vegetable garden, didn't you?" he says, almost shyly, as if I might not like it.

I cover my mouth with my hand, overwhelmed he remembered that.

Living with him was a brief solution until I found a new apartment, but I wanted to wait to move out until after he'd fully recovered.

But this...

"Alek, it's too much."

"It's not enough for the shit I put you through. But I'm trying. And I'll even let you fill it with furniture, but please have Anya restrain herself. Our taste in art is different." His jaw tics, and I laugh.

"Are you... serious about this? Wait, are you trying to ask me to move in with you?"

He casually shrugs. "I don't recall asking."

I laugh. "Alek, we don't have to live in the city if you hate it so much."

"I wasn't asking," he growls, and my heart fills when I look up at him.

This gloved monster.

This vault of a man who, little by little, is growing.

For me.

For *us*.

I look back at the vegetable garden.

"Should we get a dog too?"

"Let's see if you can keep the plants alive first."

I laugh as I wrap his hands around my waist from behind and admire the view.

He dips his chin to the crook of my neck, and I know, no matter what, we'll be okay.

No matter what obstacle or demons we have to face—no matter how gory.

We'll protect one another.

Also by T.L. Smith

Black (Black #1)

Red (Black #2)

White (Black #3)

Green (Black #4)

Kandiland

Pure Punishment (Standalone)

Antagonize Me (Standalone)

Degrade (Flawed #1)

Twisted (Flawed #2)

Distrust (Smirnov Bratva #1) FREE

Disbelief (Smirnov Bratva #2)

Defiance (Smirnov Bratva #3)

Dismissed (Smirnov Bratva #4)

Lovesick (Standalone)

Lotus (Standalone)

Savage Collision (A Savage Love Duet book 1)

Savage Reckoning (A Savage Love Duet book 2)

Buried in Lies

Distorted Love (Dark Intentions Duet 1)

Sinister Love (Dark Intentions Duet 2)

Cavalier (Crimson Elite #1)

Anguished (Crimson Elite #2)

Conceited (Crimson Elite #3)

Insolent (Crimson Elite #4)

Playette

Love Drunk

Hate Sober

Heartbreak Me (Duet #1)

Heartbreak You (Duet #2)

My Beautiful Poison

My Wicked Heart

My Cruel Lover

Chained Hands

Locked Hearts

Sinful Hands

Shackled Hearts

Reckless Hands

Arranged Hearts

Unlikely Queen

A Villain's Kiss

[A Villain's Lies](#)

[Moments of Malevolence](#)

[Moments of Madness](#)

[Moments of Mayhem](#)

Connect with T.L Smith by tlsmithauthor.com

Also by Kia Carrington Russell

Insidious Obsession

Mine for the Night, New York Nights Book 1

Us for the Night, New York Nights Book 2

Stranded for the Night, New York Nights Book 3

Token Huntress, Token Huntress Book 1

Token Vampire, Token Huntress Book 2

Token Wolf, Token Huntress Book 3

Token Phantom, Token Huntress Book 4

Token Darkness, Token Huntress Book 5

Token Kingdom, Token Huntress Book 6

The Shadow Minds Journal

T.L. Smith

USA Today Best Selling Author T.L. Smith loves to write her characters with flaws so beautiful and dark you can't turn away. Her books have been translated into several languages. If you don't catch up with her in her home state of Queensland, Australia you can usually find her travelling the world, either sitting on a beach in Bali or exploring Alcatraz in San Francisco or walking the streets of New York.

Connect with me tlsmithauthor.com

Kia Carrington-Russell

Australian Author, Kia Carrington-Russell is known for her recognizable style of kick a$$ heroines, fast-paced action, enemies to lovers and romance that dances from light to dark in multiple genres including Fantasy, Dark and Contemporary Romance.

Obsessed with all things coffee, food and travel, Kia is always seeking out her next adventure internationally. Now back in her home country of Australia, she takes her Cavoodle, Sia along morning walks on beautiful coastline beaches, building worlds in the sea breezes and contemplating which deliciously haunting story to write next.

Made in United States
Troutdale, OR
05/29/2025